Book VI of the Austen Gaskell Series

Economy & Ever After

A 'Pride & Prejudice' and 'North & South' Variation

NEY MITCH

ECONOMY & EVER AFTER

ISBN: 979-8-88653-447-4

Published by Satin Romance
An Imprint of Melange Books, LLC
White Bear Lake, MN 55110
www.satinromance.com

Published in the United States of America.

Cover Design by Caroline Andrus

Hello readers! Welcome to the official last entry of the Austen Gaskell series.

Readers, this time, I make good on my promise and that you have reached the conclusion of the series.

I know that conclusions are rarely satisfying for anyone, but hopefully you'll find some pleasure out of this.

Special thanks, once more, to the reviewers who left me comments and suggestions, on my first edition when publishing this series. Years ago, when I had read them, I took your advice, and you will still find some of the choices in the narrative!

I give much appreciation to my family, publisher and spectacular cover artist. Your artwork captured the spirit of the tale to the very end!

And for the last bit of appreciation, I wish to give all the credit to Helyn-Guy Roberts, Ms. Novo, A.K. Madison and all those who chose to pursue this tale to the very end.

Once last time, friends, one last time... Now here we go!

Chapter 1

Church Bells

With some, they say that a kiss is just a kiss, while a smile is merely a smile.

But with marriage, a kiss is the beginning of everything and anything. All is possible. All is both exhilarating and daunting. With marriage, so much is left to the wayside of the unknown, but that was not what I was frightened of.

When I was blessed with hearing that Darcy, Bingley, and Colonel Fitzwilliam would now be the blessed husbands to my sisters and I, the daunting emotion still hung there, and I could not wait to tell Mr. Darcy of it.

However, such talks of trepidation were not for the moment.

"Come," Jane said, truly exhilarated, as Mr. Bingley's arm was wrapped in hers. In her face was the glow of being in love, which made her beauty even more pronounced. "We have an arch to walk under."

"I am for it," Kitty said, laughing as she talked. "Now, who shall do it faster?"

"Jane is the eldest, beloved," Colonel Fitzwilliam said, pressing his cheek against hers, being wholly not serious.

"And I would hate to think that I married a man who cannot tell when I am talking in jest," Kitty responded. "What sort of man did I marry?"

"One who must always be reminded of his wife's lighter side, to compliment my darker element."

"You have a darker element?" Kitty asked. "When did you develop that side of yourself?"

"Between running to the church doors and now. I develop fast."

Amused, I looked at Mr. Darcy.

"Oh, aren't our siblings so adorable, Mr. Darcy?"

"Yes, they are, Mrs. Darcy. Yes, they are."

As we walked down the aisle, I passed Margaret Hale, reached out my arm, out of solidarity. She clasped hands with me, before she smiled, excused herself and ran out of the church to assist with the laurel arch.

"You called me Mrs. Darcy?" I uttered.

"Yes," Mr. Darcy replied, chuckling as he took my hand fondly, "I did. And I am about to do it again."

"Good. I was meaning for you to repeat yourself. I don't think that I would have forgiven you if you did not."

"Mrs. Darcy."

I chuckled.

"Again, sir."

"Mrs. Darcy."

"Once more."

"Mrs. Darcy."

"Now, I am satisfied."

"You take pleasure in taking up my name."

"Was there any doubt?"

Mr. Darcy's eyes twinkled.

"No, I am happy that there had not been."

When we exited the church, Margaret Hale and Georgiana held up the Laurel arch for us.

Being the eldest Bennet sister, Jane and Mr. Bingley stepped under it first.

Next, I passed under it with Mr. Darcy.

And Kitty, being the youngest, passed under it with Colonel Fitzwilliam. When she did so, she kissed Georgiana on the cheek. This sudden act of affection startled Georgiana, but it was not unwanted.

"Do not fear, Miss Darcy," Kitty said, "affection is just my way. I cannot adhere to Victorian coldness. It is not my habit." As she passed along, she shouted over her shoulder. "One day, you might even grow accustomed to my way of being!"

Georgiana chuckled and looked at Margaret Hale.

"I do like open people," Georgiana said to her.

"It took me time to grow accustomed to people of an open nature myself," Margaret Hale said, "for a long time, I did not favor their emotional displays. But time might have proved me in error on that matter."

"Time always tells, Miss Hale. It always does."

When we all fully exited the church and went towards our carriages, Jane, Kitty, and I stood side by side, then we turned around and breathed in.

"On the count of three," I said. "One, two, three!"

All three of us threw our bouquets over our heads.

When we heard the cries of exhilaration, we turned around to see who caught our catches.

The first was Georgiana who raised up her bouquet, her

hand above her head.

"I found my path to a bouquet, it seems," she said. That bouquet was Kitty's that she had caught.

Jane's bouquet was to the Tomlinsons, a family that Lady Catherine had strong-armed into attending our ceremony, despite their small acquaintance with us. The humor of that situation was that a lady was not the one who caught it. Rather, it was their eldest son, Mr. Jeffrey Tomlinson, who accidentally, and instinctively, seized the flowers. For a second, his face was lit with surprise. The next second, it shifted to utter terror. His face was overcome with fright, between the embarrassment, and the fact that, from the little I knew of him, marriage was the last thing on his mind. Ergo, he quickly thrust the flowers to his little sister—who was nine years old.

Happily, she took the bouquet and held it to her chest. This led to everyone laughing, and Mr. Tomlinson did not escape humiliation that he tried to avoid. Rather, he was still in the very center of it all. And he didn't like it by any means.

"He does not take to unwanted attention very well, does he?" I whispered to Mr. Darcy. "An older man at ease would have rolled his shoulders and laughed with the rest of the set. Rather, Jeffrey Tomlinson rolled his eyes, and the mortification hangs about his shoulders like a cross to be born."

"Oh, are you putting him on the sharper side of your wit?"

"Is this where you are out of sorts with me for making someone the sport of a joke?"

"No," he said, offering me his hand as he placed me into the carriage. "Here is where I smirk at it."

"Very good, sir. That is the right answer. Now, who

caught mine?"

I searched around to see who could have been the eager one to hold my bouquet in their hands. Naturally, I did not have far to look, but I also should not have assumed it in any other way.

There, in the middle of the attendees, Margaret Hale stood there, awkwardly with the bouquet in her hands.

"Of course," I said.

"Of course, what, Elizabeth?" Mr. Darcy said, following my gaze. His expression softened as well. "Oh, well now is that not the proverbial image to interest all?"

When seeing us looking at her, Margaret shrugged, a little anxious. She had not intended to catch the bouquet and evidently dreaded the remarks of those around her. But catch it, she did.

"No regret, Margaret," I said to her.

She sighed.

Sitting down in the coach, I looked at Mr. Darcy, enjoying that the weather was warm and congenial on our most beautiful day.

"Do you know," I remarked, "I have stumbled on a most happy thought."

"What?" Mr. Darcy asked, amused.

"I think that I wish to kiss you again."

"Curious."

"What is?"

"I was thinking precisely the same thing."

"Great minds think..."

"Yes, they most certainly do."

Leaning forward, we kissed again. This kiss was even deeper than the one before. It was heavenly.[1]

---

1. Tossing the bouquet after the wedding was customary in the 1800s,

---

As we rode back to Rosings Park, I rested my head along Mr. Darcy's chest, with his arm draped over my shoulder, to maintain my closeness to him.

"Now, I can hold you whenever and wherever I wish," Mr. Darcy said, "within reason, of course."

"Yes, Mr. Darcy, within *reason*."

"You are about to mock my choice of words."

"Your words were correct, possessed logic and restraint. After all, we cannot impose too much on the world, can we?"

"No, we cannot."

I looked at him and smiled.

"Oh, perhaps I was about to mock your choice of words a little."

"I knew it!"

"You actually know the woman that you married? How unique."

"Unique?"

"Not all men and women know each other when they marry. There will always be a little taking in, especially regarding marriage. Yet with us, that is not so. You and I have displayed the better and blunt sides of ourselves to such a feverish pitch, that I doubt that we are even unaware of the childhood illnesses that we once had."

"We do come to the marriage complete. And we have already suffered the worst sides of an argument, and the better sides of overcoming such debates, therefore, there is nothing left to fear. I welcome that."

"Oh, there was something to fear. But not that aspect."

---

but it was a tradition that actually was created many centuries before.

"What is this fear?"

"It is a fear that I possess, but you may not share. With marriage, the second one enters it, it can be supposed that one's cares are over. But sometimes, it feels as if another set of cares has already begun. What if one is ill-prepared for being a mother? What if one is even unable to be a mother? Such things have been known to happen. You worry of not upholding the image that your spouse has of you."

"Truly? Is this where my Elizabeth shows that there are some things that even her courage cannot get the better of?"

"Yes," I replied, sighing, "there. This is my confession on my wedding day. Do you laugh at me in turn? You have my permission to."

"I do not laugh, because nothing in life has any business in being too perfect. If one's spouse is always ideal, then it forces the other one to feel as if one is inferior for not living up to such perfection."

"What a wonderfully logical thing to say. I am glad that we are of the same mind on that score."

"Are we?"

"Of course, we are. For if one is always entirely agreeable, then it forces the other to be such as well—at all times. Well, sometimes, I like to run about the grounds, unleashing my frustration on the world, or sighing at the boredom and dullness of life. If you didn't moan about some matters occasionally, I would feel alone in my flawed state. And misery loves company, doesn't it?"

"Yes, very much so. I love how we can talk so much and say so little simultaneously."

"It is an acquired skill."

"Yes, it is."

Mr. Darcy took my hand.

"Do not be afraid. Ever again, Lizzy. Finding you has been one of the best moments of my life."

"And finding you has been the greatest moment of mine."

"When we go to Pemberley, you shall want for nothing."

"Here is the strangest thing. Whenever I think of this grand estate of yours, of this Pemberley and all the grandeur of its reputation, I often forget it to be a Northern estate."

"It is natural. Everything about my character, from my time being educated in my life, is often spent in the South. I was educated in the South, spent much of my time at Rosings Park and at our London townhouse, and I was even born in the South."

"You were?"

"Yes. My mother traveled to Rosings Park during her laying in, so that she could be closer to her sister, Lady Catherine. I was born in Rosings Park, actually. And I remained there for the first two years of my life. It was not till after I was three that my mother felt it safe to move me back home."

"Truly?" I asked, amazed. "And I still have the pleasure of learning more of the man you are."

"And I think that signified the man that I have become, I cannot help but wonder. I do believe that Southern style of slow life had injected itself into my whole existence. Between that, the constant visits to Rosings throughout my childhood, being at school in the South, as well as usually being at my London townhouse and my social sphere being among Southern society, I rarely act like the Northern man. Sometimes, even I forget that I am a child of both worlds. Besides, my mother is a Southern lady, and father did everything in his power to raise me to that aspect of the aristocracy. And, with the way that Pemberley is established, it is a slice of the South in the North. You will see it soon, and you will judge for yourself."

"Yes," I laughed, "because I married you for your house. Of course, I did."

He chuckled and kissed my forehead.

"No, truly," I remarked, as a joke, "your character had nothing to do with the matter of settlement at all. Not in the slightest."

We arrived at Rosings Park, where Lady Catherine had a dinner waiting for us, along with some other local families who were invited.

"You were married at the same house from which you were born in," I said as we passed under Rosings Parks' entranceway. "What does that feel like?"

"As if everything has reached a completion. Do I sound odd?"

"You sound like a man who has just gotten married. 'Odd' makes sense."

Chapter 2

The Isle of Bliss

When we had returned to Rosings Park, the dinner meal was everything that was delightful and worthy. Also, with it being a wedding, dancing was also the order of the day.

"When a waltz is the dessert," Kitty said to Georgiana as she took her arm, "a person can want for nothing. Who do you dance with?"

"I do not know."

"Do you wish to dance, or do you wish to reflect?"

Georgiana blinked.

"I do not know how to answer that."

"Am I being impertinent again? Oh dear. Never fear, I will leave you to your peace."

"It's not that, I assure you," Georgiana said, coaxing her, "I am merely trying to discover the best way to reply to you. I do not have a partner, am not against having one, but I wanted to say something witty. I could think of nothing."

"I am not witty. I am merely lively. There—now you know. You shall never live up or down to my expectations.

May all the pressure be removed from your shoulders, and you shall just be Georgiana. No more or less."

Georgiana smiled.

"You like me."

Kitty squinted, but not out of confusion. In fact, I felt that she was merely being introspective.

"I suppose that I do," Kitty acknowledged, equally surprised with that conclusion. "I cannot account for why that is my impulse, but yes, I do. Do not ask me to make sense of what I say. Just accept it, and you will be the better for it."

"Very well. You may like me all that you wish. I don't prefer to be disliked, so it is to my advantage."

Before Mr. Bingley and Mr. Darcy could come and take our hands for the first set, Jane stood by me. As we watched this encounter, Jane pressed her face on my shoulder.

"Kitty is accustomed to being two in number, when it comes to friendship," Jane explained. "She will always be very apt and able at drawing in another lady into her life."

"You are worried that my sister-in-law might prefer Kitty than myself," I noted.

"Do I sound foolish?"

"There is no shame in speaking about what ought to be talked of. There is no need to worry on my account, I assure you." I was not speaking from a place of falseness but was truly sincere. "I want Georgiana to like all of us. And I know that she approves of me, therefore, all my cares are over, on that score." Then I realized that maybe Jane had done something entirely by accident. She had revealed herself and then projected her own insecurities upon me.

"Are you worried that Georgiana might favor Kitty's company more than yourself?" I asked her bluntly.

Jane blinked.

"I knew it," I said, smirking triumphantly. "Jane, dear one, you think I did not notice, and would not notice? You were well aware that I am fond of Georgiana, like our friendship with her, and so I am content. Is there any chance that I was correct about you?"

Jane bit her lip.

"I just..."

"What? Speak all, because soon, our worthy husbands are coming to retrieve us."

"I just realized something about myself."

"What?"

"Excepting you, I have no truly close comrades. At Longbourn, you had Charlotte, the Lucas Family, Margaret Hale in London, and the Shaws, and you were even able to establish friendships whenever you went somewhere new. Mary was always very good friends with Maria Lucas, since Mary helped her learn to play. Kitty and Lydia always had each other, and when Kitty followed me into the North, she immediately attached herself to Rasby. And now she does it with Miss Darcy. You have attached yourself to her as well. But when Miss Darcy is around me, I can never think of what to say. Because my company draws no warmth."

"I find warmth in everything you say."

"Because you understand me."

At first, I opened my mouth to protest to this, but upon the swiftness that the mind can work, I made a series of deductions that led to reflections that were worthy of a day but was done in the work of a moment.

It was true. Outside of myself, Jane never did have friendships of true affection. Her relationship with the Bingley sisters, Caroline Bingley especially, proved to be a transient sort of friendship. It was just a bit of amicability passing through, filled with superficiality on their part, and only established because Jane was the handsomest and most harmless woman in Hertfordshire. But once they were free of our society, she meant nothing to them. This must have weighed on her. Then, when going to Milton, the only friendships that she had were the Kirkpatrick children, who valued her general goodness because the traditional governess was hard and stern. In them, Jane found perfect camaraderie until I arrived in the North. Especially since Fanny Thornton's friendship also proved to be similar to Caroline Bingley's as well.

Jane never had a true friend, except myself. Kitty and my ability to endear ourselves to Miss Darcy only cemented something that must have been swelling up within Jane's insecurities all this time.

Once this deduction was reached, my mind rushed to discover the source behind this. Since Mr. Darcy and I had just been speaking on such a matter, I was able to reach the proper conclusion.

"Jane," I said, "the truth is that you are perfect. Images of perfection only intrigue people for but a few minutes before the person needs to rush to a flawed image. Flawed pictures give people something to talk about and reflect on. It satisfies a strange need in us that is perverse and base. But since you are entirely agreeable, always teetering upon always doing the right thing, it forces everyone around you to be entirely agreeable as well. For some people, that is too costly. Always walking around, being perfect, is too much of a weight for them."

She looked at me, her eyes narrowed.

"That is the reason?" she asked me.

"Yes. It might be."

"Oh," she replied, looking ahead. "Who would have known that virtue is my flaw?"

"Jane, I do not want you to go out and manage to contrive defects in yourself. Do not do so. It is not that you must be weaker, but the rest of us just need to become stronger to support you. Besides, I have the delightful suspicion that Mr. Bingley will do the duty most admirably."

And with that, Mr. Darcy and Mr. Bingley approached us both, to take our hands, for the musicians had finally organized.

As we walked to the dance floor, I saw Margaret standing against the wall, looking both calm, cool, and collected, while also uttering the sentence, 'I have no inclination to dance at all' with her air and manner of standing.

She caught my eye, and we looked at each other.

"Tired?" I mouthed the words.

"Yes," she mouthed, rolling her eyes a little. "Very."

I chuckled, and stood next to the Bingley and Fitzwilliam couples, since we were leading the dance. Taking my arms, the music struck up and we all began to dance the waltz.

"What were you both talking about?" Mr. Darcy asked me. "Jane and yourself?"

"Ah, so now I must tell you every aspect of my movements."

"I was merely curious."

"I know. Mr. Darcy, have you ever had to philosophize at a wedding party?"

"You know that difference of location and venue never stops me from philosophizing. Weddings are not exempted from my intense eyes."

"Well, we are two in number there. Jane and I discovered something," I said as he spun me around.

"And what would that be?"

"That humanity is a strange and perverse thing!"

"Oh, do not get me started on *that* revelation. I could spend my whole marriage talking about it."

As we danced, I told him of what Jane spoke of, and he understood my findings. After all, it made sense as to why he always admired my sister but never favored her. He scoffed and mocked Mary, Kitty, and Lydia, but he noticed them. He must have reflected on their actions a great deal, which is why he could not remove their rash behavior from out of his mind. One could even say that despite his stating the opposite, perhaps he was enamored on my family's follies.

When we finished the dance, I moved along the set, kissed Lady Catherine and Mrs. Hale on the cheek, thanked Lady Catherine for this lovely day, and continued my progression toward Margaret.

When I approached her, she was aware of how I would begin.

"You look happy," she said.

"And you look bored."

"Do I?" Margaret asked.

"Yes, you do."

"Tell me truly, what is it?"

"How do you mean?"

"Is it my face? Is there something about it that gave every indication that I always appear to look so much above everything around me?"

"You look and stand like a queen. Queens always feel superior to those around them."

"If that be so, I wonder what Mr. Thornton ever saw in me."

"He saw the woman that he loved. And still does." I looked on her. "And you still miss his presence?"

"Yes." She groaned. "When did this happen to me? Why did this happen?"

"When did my love for Mr. Darcy begin to happen? I cannot tell you because it found me before I found it. All you can do is love who you love."

"I cannot determine that I fully love Mr. Thornton yet. I greatly esteem him, admire him, and am grateful for his love for me. I also do not deny that I am drawn to him."

"Margaret, you are attracted to him."

"Yes, I am. It cannot be denied."

"Then do not deny your heart. Write to him fully about it. Give him warmth in the North."

"But..."

"But what?"

"The idea of it all. Of love. Of attachment. And two becoming one. It is bewitching."

"And also daunting."

"Precisely. I have my freedom, and I prefer my freedom. Am I ready to choose a man, even if I feel for him?"

"Write to Thornton about this."

"I cannot."

"Yes, you can. He is a self-built man who understands the strength that comes from total independence. And I dare say your air of being so much free of all shackles that society has placed on you is what drew him towards yourself. He will appreciate being so wholly into your confidence and be flattered by it. And he will enjoy knowing where he stands."

"Now I feel as if my last letter to him was too sanguine."

"This is England on the second half of the 19th century; everything is expected to be sanguine."

Margaret chuckled.

"You know that I like the vacancy of outrageous emotional displays."

"I know that you do."

"How cruel it is that I am cracking up from within."

"Everyone has the right to be what they despise at least seven times in their life."

"Seven times? Why seven times?" Then she rolled her eyes, amazed that she did not realize it herself. "Ah, yes! Seven."

"A holy number," we both said together.

"Holy number indeed," Margaret replied. "Very well, I will write to him of my perversity. May a plague fall on my head."

"I hope it will not be pestilence."

"No, nothing so little. Perhaps just a river turning red for a couple of days."

Mr. Tomlinson approached us both, bowed to us and asked Margaret if she wished to dance. She smiled gently and accepted. As he led her away, I called out to Mr. Tomlinson.

"Yes, Mrs. Darcy?" he responded.

"Very good bouquet-catching this afternoon. Your seizing skills are remarkable."

A grimace overcame his face, and he barely had enough self-control to give me a forced smile before he led Margaret away.

Marriage changes all of us...but for me, I refused to let it change me too much.

After the second dance, Lady Catherine had an announcement that drew us all to her.

"I had received a letter this morning," she explained, "but since it was the wedding, it was not proper for our heads to be full of anything else."

"Good news or ill news?" Frederick Hale asked. "For this day has been so jolly that I do not wish for the happy couples to have anything tamper their good cheer."

"You protect us, Mr. Frederick," I uttered.

"Once a sailor, always a soldier, I suppose."

"Well, this news will cause a delight for your wedding company on all counts," Lady Catherine assured us. "Colonel, this pertains to your family."

"Oh," Colonel Fitzwilliam said, "then they have returned from the continent?"

"Yes, they have." Lady Catherine turned to the rest of our company to explain. "Your mother has written, they are aware of your honeymoon arrangements, and they have requested that you do not go to Ramsgate or Weymouth, or any other seaside in the county. Instead, they have written to invite you all to break your journey at the Isle of Wight, and the cost of your honeymoon will be their present to you all."

"The Isle of Wight?" Kitty exclaimed. "Truly?"

"I am for it," Colonel Fitzwilliam said to Kitty, "but we are only a sixth of the company."

"I have never gone on holiday to Wight," Jane replied, "how could we say no? Can we say no, Mr. Bingley?"

"No, Mrs. Bingley. We cannot."

They turned to Mr. Darcy and me.

"Mr. Darcy, our judgment hangs in the balance of their

holiday joy," I said. "For the first time in my life, I feel as if I will not take pleasure in being disagreeable."

"And I am not going to be a stone and stand in their way," Mr. Darcy said. "We only have one other party to request."

Mr. Darcy turned to the Hales.

"The Isle of Wight is said to be a superior bathing place."

"It is," Georgiana added, "for Queen Victoria is known for loving to take her holidays there. If a seaside is good enough for a queen, then it must contribute to one's health a great deal."

"I cannot be against such a brilliant plan," Mrs. Hale said. Though she still looked delicate, her spirits were high, and the color had returned to her cheeks. "The only problem is that Mr. Hale has been long away from his pupils."

"Truly, I have been, sadly," Mr. Hale said, resigned. "This is terribly upsetting, and I wished that I could attend. I wish to go—oh, dear, do I wish to go."

"Well," Frederick Hale said, "it will be beneficial to Aunt Hale's health. My wife is aware that my stay in England could be prolonged. Uncle Hale, I would be delighted to attend to Aunt Hale the entire time and see to her and Margaret's safety."

"Oh, yes!" Mrs. Hale said, taking Frederick's hand. "Frederick and Margaret shall look after me. I should like that very much."

Poor Frederick! His mother was there, and he could not call her such.

Mr. Hale, ignoring the dangers that Frederick faced, smiled at the suggestion.

"Very well. Of that, I can agree. But your courage gives

me courage. I will miss my pupils, but how often do I get the chance to be with family? Rarely. Despite the fears of being inconsistent, I shall join you after all."

"And what of you, Georgiana?" I asked. "Will you come with us? I will not pressure you, but regret if you say no."

"I love sea-bathing," Georgiana said, "and now I have more to my family. I always wanted sisters. Therefore, it would seem to be a waste of an opportunity to not attend."

"And what of you, your ladyship?" Mrs. Hale asked. "Why do you not want to join us when we go to Hertfordshire and then to the Isle?"

"I despise the sea," Lady Catherine said, "besides, I have to make the rooms prepared for the married couple when they return."

On the outer circle, Kitty shifted in her place, nervous.

"Aunt Catherine?" Kitty said, "forgive me for being too much of a burden, but I was wondering if you may be willing to have another room prepared for a friend of mine?"

"A friend?"

"It is a companion of mine, from the North," Kitty said, "her name is Raspberry Pitcher. She was a dear friend to our family and is very courageous."

"You will like her," Colonel Fitzwilliam pressed, "Rasby has always been a dear friend to Kitty, the Bennet sisters, and she and my wife are too attached for them to be separate."

"Oh," Lady Catherine said, "I am surprised, Mrs. Fitzwilliam. I thought, when seeing how Georgiana and you have taken to each other, that she would be sufficient company for you."

Georgiana and Kitty gave each other a look. Georgiana was bashful, but Kitty's face displayed an awareness of the obvious.

"But Georgiana's home is in Derbyshire and London," Kitty added. "She will not be able to visit Rosings enough for us to be around each other for as often as we wish. Forgive me, Miss Darcy, I just realized that I was speaking for us both."

"You were speaking the truth," Georgiana assured me. "Our lives do not revolve around each other often, but I will have Elizabeth for a companion, and that is enough."

"You will like Rasby, Miss Darcy," Kitty said to her. "Wait until you meet her." She turned back to Lady Catherine. "Please, Aunt. I should like to have a companion with me on the estate, and I do not wish to leave her behind."

"She is a Northern girl?" Lady Catherine said. "You should prefer a Southern lady by your side. It would make more sense to have it so."

Out of the side of my eye, I saw Margaret Hale shift uncomfortably in her seat before she stood up.

"Lady Catherine," she said, "you must excuse me. I have a pressing letter to write, and I feel that if I do not do it, then I will be most pained of the acquaintance not receiving my news soon enough."

"And who do you wish to write to?" Lady Catherine asked.

"Aunt," Colonel Fitzwilliam said, "that is Miss Hale's affair."

"I have every right to learn of what letter is sent where, when leaving my home," Lady Catherine replied. "Nephew, you will learn that when you take control of the estate."

"Yes, madame," Colonel Fitzwilliam replied, accepting defeat.

"I am writing to the Thorntons," Margaret Hale replied,

unashamed and unnerved. "They are friends that we acquired in Milton."

"What is this charm that you have with these Northerners, I always wonder?" Lady Catherine asked.

"Aunt, Pemberley is in the North," Darcy asked.

"But you are a man of the South and much of your life is here."

"And you love me anyway, despite my affiliations to being close to several counties away from Milton."

"Rasby has been a true friend to Kitty," Mr. Hale stressed. "Believe me, your ladyship, when you see them together, you will wonder how either of them could ever be separate."

"Oh, very well," Lady Catherine replied, waving her hand dismissively, "Margaret, write your letter. And Mr. and Mrs. Hale, remember to inspect the letter's contents. A true parent must always read their child's letters."

Oh, Lady Catherine! Despite all the improvement that she made, her authoritative and imposing manner would always prevail. While it is always bewitching to believe that a person would improve and they would continue along the path to those improvements, it is not always true. The tide of a person's self-reflections flows and ebbs. Therefore, there will always be a side of Lady Catherine that *will always be* Lady Catherine.

"And Kitty," Lady Catherine said, "you will write to your friend and arrange for her to come down. Mind you, she must be subject to inspection. Which I shall do."

"Oh, thank you, Aunt Catherine," Kitty replied, overjoyed. She ran to Lady Catherine and kissed her on the cheek. This burst of affection startled her ladyship, but it did not anger or vex her.

"You have made me very happy this day," Kitty said to her, and then she went back to Colonel Fitzwilliam.

"Well," Lady Catherine said, "I have a habit of saying all the correct things at precisely the correct time."

I watched Margaret as she left the room. I could tell that Lady Catherine's offensive tone toward the North angered Margaret. I saw the offense as it hung about her shoulders.

How much she had changed.

The rest of the wedding dinner progressed pleasantly. There were a few more dances, more refreshment, and laughter.

And after we resolved our affairs at Longbourn, we would go to the Isle of Wight, where we would be greeted by a paid holiday, all made us depart with good cheer.

After all, now it was the wedding night.

Chapter 3

Dirt & Cleanliness

After the days' festivities, naturally one must be exhausted...and we all were. Yet the desire for one's first wedding night, after so long of not being able to act upon one's passions, is enough to bring on a newly found energy to oneself. You transform from your eyes drooping, for want of rest, to being alert, eager, and inviting.

Lady Catherine offered us many lectures on the matter of how to arrange one's wedding night, and we half-heard it, but nodded and agreed all the while. Since we knew that she meant well, we were not in the mood to be disagreeable, but we also understood that all her administrations would go unheeded. When alone with one's husband for the first time, no advice can be enough. One's instincts will fly where they choose to soar to. And since Mr. Darcy and I had longed for each other ever since Jane discovered us on Frances Street, we knew how to proceed.

Therefore, when the party was over, we had to change out of our wedding clothes, for supper, but each of us married couples were not of the sort to be hungry.

"One a wedding night," Lady Catherine said, "I can

understand the desire to be alone with one's new love. If you like, the three happy couples may excuse themselves for the evening. Harold will see to you for the entire evening if you were to require anything. The only thing that I would request, from my own experience, is that you all would perhaps prefer to bathe before falling into your own world."

"That is precisely what I should wish," Kitty inferred, "for I feel as if I am filthy and not fit to be looked on."

"You look lovely, my dear," Colonel said, tugging at one of her curls.

"I will not disagree with you, even if I do look horrid. Lie to me all that you wish, in that regard."

"We thank you, your ladyship," I said, "and it seems we are all in agreement."

And we truly were. For the days' events had worn on our limbs and there was a great deal of perspiration from under our garments. One does not prefer to come to one's husband smelling like the Continental Congress was known for smelling like when they signed the Declaration of Independence in America. Even in Britain, we heard the truth of how that event really unfolded—and how one of the signers jested about how he could *smell* the history they were making.[1]

Lady Catherine outdid herself, truly, for she had predicted

1. This is a report that, in all likelihood, is truth. When the Signers had to sign the Declaration at Independence Hall, Pennsylvania, in 1776, it was reported that they had to do so, in warm weather, with the windows closed and perhaps even the door to the room closed. As such, all the men, wearing two to three layers of clothing, would have sweated terribly.

that we would accept her offer. For as we went upstairs and was undressed by the servants, our baths were reported to be ready. Since there were three bathing rooms, and a plethora of wash bins, the men were able to bathe at the same time, while Jane, Kitty and I were in another room.

As the three of us sat in the hot water, in our three separate tubs, washing ourselves, while our hair was covered in thick rags to remain dry, we reflected on the wedding.

"Who would have thought that the whole day would progress so splendidly?" Jane asked.

"Jane, even when you are exhilarated, you speak calmly," Kitty said, "but I cannot do so. It was one of the best days of our lives."

"And to think," I added. "Months ago, our lives could not have gone any worse unless we had died ourselves. No parents, no home, and only surviving from the kindness of friends. And then there was the matter of you and I almost *actually* dying, Kitty."

"Indeed, I recall every painful moment."

"Yes," Jane said, "it is the most incredible thing in the world to know that there can be such a reversal of everything. In life, how very often catastrophe can occur, and one's life can transform from good to ill. And so suddenly. But for the opposite to occur, for one's life to transform from unfortunate to the very best of situations."

"Achievements are not always meant to be given," Kitty said, "sometimes, perhaps, they ought to be earned. We persevered. We chose to keep going. Very rarely does that not produce its own reward, in some manner or another."

"Very wise," I said.

"Thank you."

I looked at the water in the tub, and on the surface, I saw my life unfold. Or rather, I saw the best moments *of my life* unfold, and flow and ebb with the progression of the water moving where my hand took it.

"Our men are exceptional," I said, "and we walked up to their splendor and grabbed it. That took courage. Fortune truly does favor the bold, as Virgil was famed for saying."

"Well, perhaps his fame does have something to do with him writing Rome's great epic as well?" Kitty replied, joking.

"Yes, perhaps *that* helped his fame as well," I replied, caught in the sentence.

"Sisters," Jane said, her tone soft, with a hint of anxiety underneath, "are you scared at all?"

"Scared of what?" I asked.

"Of this night. Of not knowing how to please your husband."

"Oh," I said, blushing, "that is what scares you? Well, for my part, I can understand your apprehension. This sort of intimacy is all new to you."

"I love our parents," Kitty said, "and I do miss them very much. However, regarding conversations of the romantic side of married life, our parents didn't speak of it much and educate us. We were never even given discussions on how children were produced. Our governess had to tell us the true information that we needed, and even there, she did it ill."

"Yes," I replied, "very ill. She made it seem like it was the worst thing in the world. That is the problem with speeches about carnal embrace; it can't be delivered by a puritan. And our governess was as close to being one as a misinformed person could be."

"Weren't puritans the fools who committed the worst witch hunt in Massachusetts?" Kitty asked.

"Precisely!" Jane and I said together.

"Dear lord," I groaned, "that accursed woman. She ought to have remained teaching the prescribed subjects, and our father never should have subjected us to her extreme views. Well, Jane, you know very well that I do not fear the act, because I have almost committed to the act before."

"Before?" Kitty repeated. "Lizzy, you are not a maid?"

"I am, but Mr. Darcy and I almost fell prey to our wantonness and only was prevented from Jane returning to Frances Street sooner than expected."

"And once more, Kitty is the last to know."

"Oh, Kitty..." I groaned.

"It is well, because I am barely a maid either."

Jane and I looked at her with shock.

"Yes," Kitty said, with a superior look, "now you know how it feels to not be in the other's confidence. I told Lydia of it, but worried about your reaction. Therefore, I thought it best not to reveal anything until after we had performed the nuptials."

"You and the Colonel achieved a level of intimacy?" I clarified. "How deep was the extent of this performance of your passions?"

"Very much so. The Colonel has already seen a great deal of my body, and I am familiar with his form as well. We did not consummate anything, as of yet, but we came quite close."

"So did I," I said. "I am still amazed at how the instincts take over when one is truly attached to a man."

"Precisely. I felt as if my mind was not needed, but rather, my body responded, and it felt so lovely. I could not account for it. I felt ashamed the next day, but the Colonel assured me that it was natural for me to be shy around him for the first time."

"I never experienced that," I said.

"You and Mr. Darcy had a different path to marriage."

"That's true. But I can understand the shame that may come afterwards."

"So," Jane acknowledged, "out of us three, it is my two younger sisters who have gathered more experience than I."

"In some manner, experience can be a good thing," Kitty observed. "I have already disposed of my fears from the first encounter, and so now, all shame has been done away, and I know how to receive the Colonel."

"And I with Darcy."

"I wonder if I will feel shame the morning after," Jane wondered.

"You might," Kitty considered, "but do not let that overwhelm you. Confront it and do not let it serve as an imposition between you and Mr. Bingley."

"And what if I shame myself tonight?" Jane asked. "I am so very much at a loss of what to do."

"Oh," I said, "in that manner, we can neither hold your hand nor give you any advice that will guarantee the perfect outcome. All that we can say is that you should not fear the deed itself. Conjugal embrace is not something to be done out of obligation but is something to find pleasurable. You will be afraid, at first. Afterwards, you will let all fears fall away and trust your instincts. Fall into Mr. Bingley and find comfort in him. But do not, and I repeat, *do not* , lay there and do nothing while he does everything."

"Precisely!" Kitty stressed. "Kiss him back, touch him, and embrace him."

"But that is all immodest," Jane declared, aghast.

"That's marriage," I stressed. "Jane, *do not* lay there and do nothing. It will be the worst sort of wedding night there could ever be."

Jane gasped and she dunked her head under the water.

Kitty and I looked at each other.

"I think we frightened her," I said.

"Yes, I think that we did."

Kitty laughed.

When we finished bathing, the servants helped dry us down, our nightclothes were brought to us, and we dressed in the washroom. When we placed our robes over our nightgown, the three of us looked at each other.

"Ladies," I said, "good fortune tonight."

They gave me the same blessing. Looking at each other with such significance, we knew how important this night was for us.

Then we separated, each to the man that we loved.

Chapter 4

The Wedding Night

The servants led the three of us to our husbands' guestrooms. Since Darcy's was the furthest away, I was the last to be led to the room where I would spend the night.

I thanked the servant who took me there.

Gathering the nerves that filled within me, I knocked on the door.

After a few seconds, Mr. Darcy entered, in his lounge robe and nightclothes.

When his eyes fell on me, his expression softened, and then hardened.

"It's your new wife," I said. "Will you let me in?"

His hard and stern look indicated his preparation for the joy that we were about to be bound in.

"So," he whispered, "this is how it is to begin? With you knocking on my door?"

"Yes. Strange, is it not?"

"Strange looks lovely on you."

Slowly, he reached his hand out to me.

Such a significance to it all. To see his hand there, I saw

now how everything was meant to be. How it all was going to unfold. Of all the heavens we would have together, and the hells that we would have to face. After all, the outside world will always burst in upon domestic joy, and there will always be something to be weathered and tests the strength of a bond.

"Are you afraid to take my hand?" he asked. "Does my Lizzy shy away from me?"

"I fear nothing. I just see everything clearly now."

"Everything?"

"Yes. This is not just a hand being taken. Rather, it is a future that lies before me. A future that I long to see."

I placed my hand in his.

"Let us begin that future now."

"Yes. With great speed."

With a swiftness that I did not know that he had, he pulled me into the room, closed the door behind me, and only a few candles were lit in the room.

It was just enough illumination for us to see the beauties of each other, and enough to feel the romance of the moment.

Quickly, he closed the space between us and kissed me savagely.

I pressed my body against his, wrapping my arms around his back, to hold him closer to myself. I felt our bodies meld into each other, and I wanted to have our skin connect and our hearts end where the other heart began.

The perfect meld!

"Forgive me," he rushed out, yanking my robe off myself, "but I cannot be slow. My eagerness has gotten the better of me."

"I regret nothing of your passions," I said, "my own regret is that you and I are not linked already."

He kissed me once more.

"That will soon be remedied."

With all haste, he pulled me to the bed and practically yanked off my nightdress. I heard the tears and rips of the cloth as he committed to his hasty movements.

Soon, I was bare and stood before him, as revealed as I once had been.

"You are still clothed," I said, grabbing ahold of him, "that will not do, sir."

"I know," he hissed, between kisses, "I know."

I helped him remove his robe, his nightshirt, and I marveled at the strength and beauty of his figure. His chest was the essence of masculine pulchritude.

With harsh thirst, I had the instinct to touch it. I ran my hands down it, with such a savagery, that I worried that my nails would bring scars to his skin.

Mr. Darcy moaned out, then he kissed me again. Afterwards he threw me down onto the bed, falling on top of me with focused determination.

He moved his head down towards my chest, and I finally could enjoy the return of his hands caressing my breasts.

Finally, a return!

His hands moved along my stomach as he pressed his lips against my breasts, kissing them over and over, with such wantonness, that I did not care who heard my moans.

I cried out as I felt his tongue, lips, and teeth, consume the skin along my nipples.

After running his hand down my stomach, he felt along my thighs, before he arrived at the middle. Diving his hand inside of me, he began to run his hand vigorously inside of me, opening me up with his actions.

I cried out!

What else could I do?

With his lips paying such attention to my breasts, with his hand entering further and further inside of me, rocking me from wave upon wave of pleasure, I gave way to the passion that I had been long without.

This passionate position was neither short-lived nor limp. Mr. Darcy only seemed to become stronger the further he progressed.

He did not desire for my breasts to leave his lips, nor his hand to be outside of me.

Rocking against the bed, I encouraged him to continue. My words did the trick, for moments slipped away, but he drove his hand further into me and his lips just kept closing itself over my chest, running his tongue over and under every part of it.

Then at last, he raised himself up.

"Are you ready, Lizzy?" he asked. "The pain has been known to overwhelm a lady."

"I do not fear the pain," I said, "because I am ready. Take me, husband. And leave nothing behind."

"Very well. There will be nothing left."

I wrapped my legs around his body as he fell into me. With a determined thrust, he entered me as I cried out from the agony of it all.

But that agony soon gave way to my body, instinctively knowing how to open myself wider to let him fall further within me.

"Oh, Lizzy," Darcy said, rocking against me. "My Lizzy."

"Do I please you?" I managed to utter, despite being out of breath.

"You have no notion! Nothing in life is superior to this."

Faster and faster, he pushed himself within me, and I felt the exhilaration of trying to be equally as excitable.

I rocked against him, increasing his pleasure. He moaned out, holding my hips in his hands so that he could gather a stronger hold on me. I dug my hands in his back, giving all the encouragement in the world.

At last, I felt him thrust inside of me one final time, and that was when I knew: we had reached the ultimate place.

I was his wife in full.

Exhausted, he collapsed onto me, and I held him in my embrace.

"Now," I hissed, "you are mine. No falling away from me."

"No falling away," he whispered, "I am yours forever."

"You are mine!" Colonel Fitzwilliam cried as he turned Kitty over, in his bed.

They had already consummated their love. However, the Colonel, a man of great passions and endless energy, was not prepared to rest after their first time as man and wife.

After seeing Kitty's nude form once more, he was stirred by the beauty of his wife's face and figure. He wanted to possess all of her.

Since his passions overrode his desire to take his time, he had pushed himself inside of her all too quickly, to satisfy his needs. When he finished, they both were equally dissatisfied.

Kitty did not mention this, but the Colonel sensed her lack of satisfaction, as well as his own.

He had taken her.

But he had not been gentle or considerate.

Happy that her husband sensed her dissatisfaction, she was overjoyed when he continued to kiss her after his body was spent.

Rather, he was still thirsty as he kissed her along her neck, rubbed her breasts vigorously, kissing her nipples with savage eagerness, and moved his lips along her stomach, thighs, and within her.

"You are mine," he said at last.

"Oh, my stars!" she cried. "Richard, I... I..."

There were no words. Such an incredible moment could not be described but felt and loved.

After Kitty reached a level of ecstasy, Colonel Fitzwilliam had his fill of pleasure. As she laid down on the bed, Colonel Fitzwilliam wrapped his arms around Kitty.

"Colonel?" Kitty asked.

"Won't you call me Richard?" Colonel Fitzwilliam chuckled.

"I will call you that in the morning," Kitty said, "but for now, Colonel, Colonel, Colonel!"

Kitty turned around, wrapped her arms around his back and pressed her face under his chin, nibbling his neck. Colonel winced, feeling a little ticklish under the administrations, but soon, he enjoyed the sensation of her affection.

"Well," Kitty said, "you are a treasure."

"So are you."

"And I must thank you again."

"For what?"

"For helping me with Rasby. We have reached part of the journey to having Rasby come to Rosings Park."

"I am happy that Aunt Catherine agreed. But as you say, we have only achieved half of the battle. The other half is having her stay."

"Still thinking in battle strategy?"

"It's a difficult habit to be rid of."

"I am not against the tendency to do so. I would like it if you talked of your wartime activities. You did not talk of them often. Especially now, where Rasby's coming is half-success. We do need a military mind to contrive how to keep her here. If she even wants to stay."

"You don't think that she would want to leave you?"

"Me? No. But Rosings Park, perhaps."

"She would want to leave all this grandeur and luxury?"

"That is the wonder of it. When a person achieves a certain level of freedom, autonomy, and the liberty of urban living, it is hard to turn away. I was born to the world of the South. Therefore, it is not difficult to fall back into this life. But Rasby is something else. She is a child of sound, noise, bustle, and activity. I worry that she might like this world for a little, but then the North might call out to her again. Pemberley is not too far from Milton, but even there, I suspect, it would feel like a whole world away from all that she is accustomed to."

"That is the strange thing of human nature: give them all the riches in the world, but if their liberties are limited, they will prefer a hovel instead. She ought to be grateful to us, though."

"Don't talk like that. We owe her nothing and she owes us nothing. I hope she will be happy with us, though, for I would prefer to have my friend with me. Our bond is too tied together, and I do not have the ability to create another sort of friendship like that again. I am not able to gain and lose friends so very easily. I have not that talent. I am not you, O' Beautiful One."

"You call me beautiful?" Colonel Fitzwilliam laughed.

"I am born like Henry V. All the meanness was born on the outside."

"You are not ugly. Your beauty is unorthodox. You are beautiful and let me dote on you. And, evidently, I am not alone. Your loveliness is felt by your aunt as well."

"Ah, my aunt. She likes you, Kitty."

"Does she?"

"Yes. My dear, she does. I thank you for always considering her. Kitty, normally I would never ask you to adhere to the whims and worries of others, but with my aunt, it's very different. She is accustomed to ruling her domain, and she is a woman without a daughter. The more you both agree on matters, the more that there will be peace here. I know that you have promised me before, however..."

"However, I made that promise before we were married? And now we are married, and you wish to reaffirm it." Kitty was not offended by this, nor surprised. On the contrary, she understood his need to reiterate the promise.

"Do not be upset with me," the Colonel requested.

"Indeed, I am not. I've met many a man and woman that made a great deal of promises before they married, and once the wedding band was placed on the bride's finger, all those promises were quite thrown out of the window, with all haste."

"Precisely. With you, I knew that I didn't have to worry of marrying a lady who changed as soon as she secured me, but I just want all to be well."

"Well, I make the same promise now as I made then. When it comes to domestic matters, and estate business, I will leave the matters entirely to her and yourself. You can conspire together all that you wish, like two chattering geese."

The Colonel laughed.

"But when it comes to everyday manner and dress, I am my own lord and master, as well as who I choose as my friends. When it comes to important engagements, I will always adhere to her preferences as well. Our marriage might very well be me always shuffling between being as I am and submitting to the whims of a great lady." Kitty looked in the Colonel's eyes. "Will you support me?"

Colonel Fitzwilliam smiled.

"To the very end."

"Then onward to glory we go," Kitty said, kissing him once more. "Sir, you are mine."

Under the sheets, Mr. Bingley held Jane as she rested her head on his chest. After fully becoming man and wife, Jane was so exhausted from the activities that she fell upon him, her beautiful hair falling on Mr. Bingley's chest.

Mr. Bingley was equally as exhausted, but he was too overjoyed to give way to sleep just yet.

Seeing Jane with him, in his bed, he had to reflect on all that he had won.

Seeing her bare form resting against him, he analyzed every aspect of her figure. From her perfect legs, her curves and elegant arms and neck. He married a woman whose body was as lovely as her face and person. Stroking his hand down her back and along her stomach, he caressed her skin lightly. At last, he ran his hand along her breasts and felt complete with the deed.

"You are mine," he said, satisfied, "after all the trials and tribulations, you are mine at last. Remain in my life, Jane. Without you, what is Bingley?"

Thus was the wedding night of all three ladies and

gentlemen. No words of anger, contempt, or discomfort. All was as it ought to be—and no sooner or later than it ought to have been.

Over an hour ago, Margaret Hale had sent the letter to Marlborough Mills, in Milton. Knowing how long it would be until she received any reply, she retired early to bed.

And yet, rest and sleep eluded her.

Her mind was too full. Her heart was too awake. Yet her sensibilities antagonized her too much. She did not prefer emotional displays, and yet, at the wedding party, she found herself not adhering to her traditional proscriptions.

She had wanted to smile.

She had wanted to dance merrily.

She had wanted to laugh.

She had wanted to roar out.

She had also wanted to cry.

Everything about the day proved to be silently provocative. And that was the horror of it. This was the happiest day of her friends' lives.

And yet, her mind was thinking away.

It drifted over hill, town, village, bridge, railroad tracks, and found its way into the cloud and activity of Milton. Having spent so much time romanticizing the South while in the North, and now she found that she missed being amongst the hardships and redemptions of Milton Common.

And one man especially.

She wanted Thornton to be there. She wanted him to be beside her, and to dance at the party. Every part of her mind wondered at what he was doing.

And it made her angry with herself once more.

She did not despise him. She despised needing him so.

That was another reason for why she retired earlier than any other. She did not want to betray herself, nor did she forgive herself for not focusing on her friends' happy day. Nor did she want them to ever learn of it. She wanted them to only know that she was overjoyed for them finding each other and quieted down the part of herself that perhaps... might have been wishing to obtain the very happiness that they achieved.

And the wedding night that proved so very satisfying to others gave a sleepless night to Margaret Hale.

Chapter 5

Economy

Meanwhile, at Milton, the chimneys smoked, the ceaseless roar and mighty beat, and dizzying whirl of machinery, struggled and strove perpetually.

Senseless and purposeless were wood and iron and steam in their endless labors, but the persistence of their monotonous work was rivalled in tireless endurance by the strong crowds, who with sense and with purpose, were busy and restless in seeking after—what?

That is what Rasby travelled along, going to the hotel for her daily shift.

The riding along the omnibus did not upset nor disturb her, for rarely did anyone take notice of anyone else around them. However, when she arrived to work, Rasby once more understood the great truth about her life.

She was alone.

Sometimes, there is no great evil, no terrible ill, in being respected through association. Especially if the friendship is genuine.

Due to her level in life, her race, and her station, she was an invisible servant as well as an invisible employee. To those who remained at the hotel as guests, to those who worked amongst her. Kitty had been more than just the greatest friend she ever had. But rather, she also had been Rasby's protector.

Kitty had come to Milton with blindness. Blindness to the follies of the world around her. Blind in having vain preferences for a friend. Kitty came to Milton wanting a comrade who would remain fast and true.

Rasby had wanted a friend who cared neither for who nor what she was.

And now, her chief friend, her main ally, had been swept away, back to the South, from where Kitty had sprung from. Their friendship had given Rasby a confidante who never deemed her inferior, and whose groundwork of their bond had not been founded on vexatious pity on Kitty's behalf. Rasby would have despised herself if that had been why she was kind to her. No. She and Kitty merely wanted friendship in its simplest form and had found it. This gave them both importance and significance in the world. Now she was one in number, and the cold eye of the world was upon Rasby.

Before the Bennets had come to Milton, Rasby had been accustomed to being invisible and unnoticed by the world. It was to be expected, for her mother had raised her not to take any notice of that sort of thing.

But when the sisters had fallen into her life, the comforts of camaraderie had been awakened and Rasby discovered something about herself.

"Miss Pitcher!"

Hearing her name being called rose her out of her musings and Rasby stopped on the street that she had been walking down.

Turning to the caller, her shoulders slackened in relief when she saw Nicholas Higgins and his daughter, Mary, approaching her. His step was eager, and his eyes were insistent.

Rasby very well understood why. Despite that she had no news to bring to him, the familiar is always welcome.

"Nicholas and Mary!" Rasby replied, merrily walking toward them, and feeling the comfort of someone looking on her in a congenial manner.

"How are you?" Mary contrived to ask as they met her.

"In truth," Rasby said. "A little lonely."

When she said that, Nicholas and Mary looked at each other, warily.

"Oh dear," Rasby said, "I just realized that I made you all uncomfortable by telling you blunt truth."

"No, it ain't that, pray," Nicholas Higgins said, "yer were thinkin' away about the Bennet lasses, weren't yer?"

"Yes," Rasby replied heavily as she walked alongside them, "I was, I confess."

"We were thinkin' of them the night be'fo, is all," Mary said. "Tha's why we looked on yer so funny-like."

"You miss them too, don't you?" Rasby asked.

"Yea, I reckon that we do," Nicholas admitted.

"That makes us three in number. And for my part, time has taught me a harsh lesson."

"What sort of lesson is that?"

"Well, I had made a skill of being alone or being ignored. But once the Bennets fell into our lives, Kitty especially, I find that I cannot..."

"Go back?" Mary guessed. "You cannot go back to the way things were."

"Precisely," Rasby acknowledged. "That is what

happens when you stumble on a better way of life. You realize...that there is no going back. There cannot be."

"It cannot be denied," Nicholas acknowledged, "that when we were all together, it was a merry time. If only my Bessy had been well, she might have even eventually been invited to the South to visit them. Margaret and Lizzy liked her so."

"I'm sure that they would have."

"Has Kitty called for yer yet?" Mary asked.

Rasby bit her lip, evidently dismayed.

Feeling foolish for putting her so much on the spot, Mary bit her lip and looked down at the ground.

Wishing to smooth the situation between the ladies, Nicholas Higgins decided to change the direction of the conversation.

"We do feel incomplete, no matter what. In fact, as selfish as it may seem, however, I do so much wish that they all would return. It cannot be ignored that we do feel somewhat incomplete without 'em."

"Yes," Rasby said, smiling, "we do, don't we?"

"I reckon that we cannot help it. They certainly left their mark on Milton. They came, made a lot of joyous noise, and then they left us to the quiet. The noisy quiet."

"And four," Mary said suddenly.

"Four?" Rasby asked, confused. "What do you mean, pray?"

"Oh, well, I was speaking out of order, garn." Mary looked a little uncertain, but then she always spoke in such a fashion. "I was meanin' that we were not three in number, when it comes to missin' the Bennet ladies. Rather we are four. After all, Mr. Thornton misses them, right and proper."

"Oh," Rasby realized, interested, "And how does Mr. Thornton do?"

Through the streets, Mr. Thornton walked home on an errand to bring his mother some more ink.

When he entered, he heard a noise from the parlor, and he heard his sister giggle. Distracted, he walked in, to find Fanny deeply in confidence with Mr. Slickson. Faith, that was a euphemism for his actions.

Rather, he really saw Mr. Slickson kissing Fanny's hand and Fanny blushing. When they heard his footsteps, they turned, felt ashamed and moved away from each other.

Sighing, Mr. Thornton straightened his jacket, looked at his pocket watch to appear unobservant, and then he entered.

"Thornton," Slickson acknowledged.

"Slickson, how do you do, man?"

"Well, thank you."

"I didn't know to expect you visiting at this time."

Mr. Slickson looked at Fanny, who smiled and looked at the floor.

"Yes, but you know how it is with lovers and all that. Time is not our master."

Thornton breathed in heavily. "Yes, I suppose that it does not."

"Fanny!" Mrs. Thornton called from up the stairs. "Come here for a moment!"

Fanny rolled her eyes, excused herself from them and as she passed Mr. Thornton, he handed her the ink to give to their mother.

Giving Mr. Slickson a significant glance, she left the men alone.

"Some port, Slickson?" Mr. Thornton said, going to the decanter on the table under the window.

"Thank you, good fellow," Slickson said. "I'll have a glass. But only one glass. Your sister does not like it if I drink more than one glass at a time."

"Prudence is something she values and is right to."

"Yes. She might make a practical man out of me yet."

"My sister?" Mr. Thornton laughed. "Fanny has been driven by her sensibilities since I can remember. When you marry, make sure to set up an account to any music shop that you can."

"A lady must have her interests."

"Yes, she must. I think you both will suit each other very well."

"Nice to have the older brother's blessing, when one cannot have the father's."

They both drank the port.

"Thornton," Slickson began, "I have been thinking."

"Thinking? With us men, that can be a dangerous pastime."

"Yes, it can. But with this, with us being family, I cannot help but wonder and assist where I may."

Thornton's face hardened. He sensed what was about to happen.

"Oh?"

"Well, it is on the subject of our wedding," Slickson began.

"I thought you wanted my blessing, not my permission to remove yourself from the engagement."

"Not at all," Mr. Slickson said, raising up his arms. "Fanny and I will marry. Believe me. I am certain of that. It is merely that I am aware how expensive a wedding can be. And I know that, like myself, the strike has driven a shocking blow to both our businesses."

"Yes, it has."

"Thornton, we must face the matter, man. We are in desperate times. And one either thinks and acts or sinks and drowns. Well, I have no inclination to drown."

"Neither do I." Thornton rubbed his eyes, looking out of the window. For one moment, his brain played a dirty trick upon his sensibilities.

An image of Margaret Hale, walking along the street and waving at him through the window, had flashed across his vision.

For a second, hope spread across his features. The sight of her was like food to a starving man. Passing across his mind was like that of a mirage, a feint dream that drifted along in the most intoxicating of manners.

"Thornton?" Slickson asked.

Hearing his name drove Mr. Thornton from out of his revelry. Turning back to Slickson, the stubbornness of his usual appearance returned.

"Oh," he replied.

Turning back again, he looked out of the window, and Margaret's image was no longer there. Passersby crossed along the street, and the dream had all but faded.

"Nothing," Thornton replied, somber, "nothing at all." He rubbed his face. "Were we talking of drowning?"

Slickson guffawed.

"We were, by way of a metaphor. I have heard rumor of

Marlborough Mills. You and I both have suffered from that foolish strike, and we are all behind on our orders."

"I don't pretend that *that* is not true. I have been trying to fulfill those orders and needed the finances for the new machinery. I did not expect to not be caught up by then."

"None of us did. And that's why I have undertaken it to find other means of recompense."

"What means?"

Slickson folded his arms, feeling a sense of triumph.

"How else does any man make a fortune in the work of a week?"

Thornton was interested for a second, but a second only. Once he realized Slickson's meaning, he was dubious.

"Speculation?" Thornton asked. "Do you mean a quick money scheme?"

"Well, yes. Of course. In the war of the economy, one must be the victor, mustn't we?"

Thornton sighed.

"Naturally so. I am not against the pursuit of wealth... but Slickson—the speculation?"

"I can understand your apprehension, Thornton, but there has been known to be miracles."

"And tragedies. I will not try to influence you, but I would advise against it."

"Economy, sir, and I will win that battle. But I take no offense to your advice because I will give you some in return."

"What would that be?"

"If fortune does fall in our favor, then it could be a delightful opportunity for us both."

"You expect me to join you? Even when you know what the speculation led my father to."

"Things are different now. There is a stronger likelihood

of success. Besides, when it comes to business, there will always be some level of duplicity there. The trick is to be properly cautious. Which we will be."

"But there is no definite chance of success. You know this as well as I do. I cannot risk Marlborough Mills, my workers' wages, on some fragile enterprise."

"What I do know, Thornton, is that if we are diligent and meticulous, we will not be duped or swindled. And we shall be wiser than your father."

This was the final nail in the coffin. Despite that his father had speculated wildly, and had abandoned them to his grief, he was still his father. To hear anyone else shove him aside did not rest well in Thornton's mind.

"Speculate as you wish, Slickson," Thornton said, "I will not risk anything."

"Are you certain, man? The opportunity will soon pass you by if you wait too long to accept."

"Be it today or tomorrow, or the day after, I cannot follow you. But thank you anyway."

Seeing that Thornton would not be moved, Slickson took his leave of Marlborough house. Before doing so, he gave Thornton one last parting advice.

"Your father is gone, Thornton. Don't follow him into the grave."

"I aim not to," Thornton had replied.

Slickson left Thornton alone and Thornton was able to reflect.

Father! he cried, in the depths of his mind. *Why did you have to do this? So much of my life has been shaped and torn down by you. Why must you haunt me now?*

Before returning to the mill, he went back up to his bedroom to get his warmer gloves. As he did so, he was curious about Fanny.

Going to her room, he knocked on the door.

"Come in, Mother!" Fanny said.

Thornton opened the door and Fanny looked at him in surprise.

"No, it's not Mother," Thornton said.

"You are going to lecture me," Fanny said, about to pout. "You are about to lecture me on letting Slickson take too many liberties. Well, I can assure you that I have not allowed anything vulgar in any way."

"No," Thornton said, "that's not the reason that I came."

He sat down in a chair by her desk, and he rubbed his hands together.

"He is about to undergo speculation, Fanny."

"Yes, I know."

"You do?" Thornton asked, surprised.

"He told me about it the second that he visited."

"And what do you think of it?"

"I think that I ought to trust him. If Mr. Slickson says that he has taken every precaution and that he is planning on making certain that there will be no swindling in the case, then I support him. He has considered every option and left no stone unturned."

"Fanny, the speculation is not a guarantee. There is too much risk involved."

"And my beau also says that all business has some risk attached to it. And he is correct. You took a risk in being Marlborough Mills' master. And that worked. You took a risk in importing the Irish workers, and that broke the strike."

"The speculation killed our father."

"Our father killed *our* father," Fanny said, with finality. "You know this as well as I. Yes, he was swindled, yes, he was ruined, but he chose to kill himself. He chose to leave our mother to make a life for us, because he could not bear the shame. He chose to make life hard on you, and you had to save the family before you were ready. He did all that. I cannot live under his shadow. I will not. So, I will decide as I may."

"There is no convincing you about trying to persuade Slickson against it?"

"No, there is not. Also, he is going to speculate before we marry, and not afterwards. If he loses the money, then he will not marry me. If he does become wealthy, then I will want for nothing, and we will wed. I lose nothing, in this situation."

"Very well. Then he does right by you."

Thornton stood up, walked to the door, but he had one last request to make.

"Fanny, I still have to ask. As your brother and protector, I must ask...do you love Slickson?"

Fanny laughed at first, and then her chuckle became a sad one.

"I am—well, I am very fond of him."

"And have you forgotten your love for Darcy yet?"

Fanny's lip turned into a tight line.

"Yes," she answered, "I am recovered from that sad part of my life."

"Are you being honest with me? I am not here to judge you. But I just must make certain again. I do not want you to attach yourself to a man, to recover from another man. It will only lead to you hating Slickson and then hating yourself."

"John," Fanny coaxed him, "I want to get married. I

truly do, and I do not regret this impulse. I like Mr. Slickson. And I can see myself growing to love him. Do not expect me to wait around for my love for Mr. Darcy to fully disappear before I move on to life in another direction. A woman ought to be allowed to recover, as you men do. We have a right to have a second love, for very rarely do women marry the first man that they dote upon."

"But are you fully recovered from Darcy?"

"I do not think that I shall ever fully be if I were to be wholly honest. I cannot help but wonder if all of us are often tied to our first affections for the rest of our lives. Some will spend the rest of their lives looking for that same sensation. Others of us are wiser and know that it may never come for us. So, we move on. We adapt. And we recover. I aim to recover."

"But will this make you happy?"

"Happy? Me?" She chuckled. "I daresay that it will make me as happy as anyone else when entering the married state. For what is marriage, truly? How can anything bring total happiness to anyone? We humans are not ready nor prepared to be wholly content. There will always be something else tugging away at us. In fact, from what I have noticed, we humans are always in a habit of rushing to make ourselves miserable. I will not go on such a voyage."

"Nor would I have you do so."

"Besides, you know what I speak of. You have been in love, John. I know how you feel about Miss Hale. Did that love always make you happy either? Or did it tug at your confidence? Love does that, you know. Yes, I am familiar with the agonies that love brings with it. Does that surprise you?"

"It does. But perhaps, it should not have." Thornton

smiled at his sister, happy that they finally understood each other. In one way at least. "Very well, Fanny. Marry him and be as happy as you can find it to be so."

"Thank you. I believe that I will be."

"I support you."

"Are you certain that you do not want to join him in the speculation?"

"I am sure. I do not want to be our father. I will not be."

"I understand."

Thornton left his sister, to the grace of her own reflections.

As he walked to his factory, Thornton considered what his sister had told him.

Yes, love had brought him pain. Agony. But he was not afraid of it. Especially since Margaret's heart had been changing so suddenly in his direction. Even when he did not have her love, he was willing to still have his love for her.

So certain was he that there was no other woman for him, that he would prefer a broken heart and all—rather than to align himself in any other avenue of affections.

"Margaret," he uttered to himself as he walked to his office, "where are you now? Do you think of me?"

Chapter 6

Home Again!

Two days after our wedding marked our time of departure to Hertfordshire...and to Longbourn. Lady Catherine gave us leave, and there was one slight change. Since we were to enjoy our honeymoon at the Isle of Wight, it was arranged that Mr. and Mrs. Hale would stay at Rosings Park until our business in Hertfordshire had been done. We all would meet in London, our parties would be joined, and then we would progress to the Ilse.

Of course, this was not our idea.

"I have been talking with Mr. and Mrs. Hale," Lady Catherine said, "and I have instructed them that they ought to remain here until your holiday begins. All that hustle and bustle of traveling will not do for Mrs. Hale at all. It will undo all the recovery that she is evidently undergoing. She will remain at Rosings, and they are quite in agreement with me."

Not being by his 'mother's side' was a little aggravating for Frederick Hale, but we all understood the logic of the situation.

"My aunt does it for more than just Mrs. Hale's consideration," Darcy had whispered to me. "She does not want Mrs. Hale to leave. She still will not fully admit this, however, but she is very attached and finally has a proper friend in her elderly years."

"It makes sense. Elderly women need friendship as much as younger women do."

This true bond was very evident because Mrs. Hale did not only tolerate Lady Catherine's authoritative manner but welcomed it. She had returned to the life that she knew and felt the flattery of having such an illustrious friend.

Thus, we set out from Rosings Park early in the morning. Mrs. Hale was still in the invalid chair, with Mr. Hale behind her. They, along with Lady Catherine, bid us farewell with much kindness and joy.

"When you are at the seaside," Lady Catherine said to Kitty, especially, "avoid walking in the sand as much as possible. Fisherman often stomp up and down the place in their dirty boots. You have no notion of what they bring onto the shore."

"Yes, Aunt Catherine," Kitty assured her, "I promise, I will do everything to keep in good health. I have a husband to care for now."

"And, with any luck, soon you shall be eating for two. Consider that."

"I will, aunt."

"Good. Nothing like having a child of one's own."

Lady Catherine kissed all us ladies on the cheek, including Margaret Hale.

We climbed into the carriages and set out, waving from the windows.

"Kitty," Colonel Fitzwilliam said, "I do believe that if you return from our honeymoon, not with child, my aunt will be very cross with you."

"She may do as she pleases," Kitty said. "We humans always need something to complain about. Tis the way of the world, Colonel. Who am I to stand in its way?"

The fifty miles journey from Rosings Park to Hertfordshire was achieved in the late afternoon.

"Lizzy!" Kitty cried, "look, we are soon to arrive to Meryton."

"Yes," I said, amazement in my eyes, "we have. After all this time, we are near home. I... I cannot believe it."

There it was before us. The familiar hills, trees, and dales that we were accustomed to. Soon, we would roll into Meryton, and it was as if I could get out of the carriage and walk it blindfolded.

"Of course," I said, "it would feel as if there was no significant change, and I should have expected it to be so. I am glad of it. Some things ought to never change. Meryton and Hertfordshire ought to remain as they were, as a constancy."

Eventually we did ride through the main road in the market, and there were shopkeepers who were beginning to close down their stores.

Since we had ridden into the town, in an illustrious set of carriages, the shopkeepers turned to look on us, as well as the villagers.

"Let's wave to them," I said to Kitty, "and show that the Bennets have returned at last!"

Kitty and I leaned out of the carriage window and waved to the shop boys that we once knew so well. When seeing us, their eyes lit up with familiarity and they waved at us.

"Miss Bennets!" they cried. "You are returned to us."

"We are!" Kitty cried. "Did you really think that we could stay away?"

"There is Mrs. Long and her nieces," I said, seeing our neighbors. The ladies waved at us, also happy to see us once more.

"Call on us soon!" Mrs. Long cried.

"We will," Jane cried, from the other carriage.

Further along the road, we passed houses that we saw.

"We have to visit our Uncle Philips soon," Kitty uttered to me. "He will be happy to see us, especially with him being so lonely now."

"We will," I assured her, "never fear. We will do right by our relatives. Of that, I can assure you."

Kitty looked at me shrewdly.

"You're thinking of Mr. Collins now, aren't you?"

"Yes, I am." I turned to Mr. Darcy and the Colonel. "My love and Colonel, you have to understand something."

"What?" Mr. Darcy asked.

"Sometimes, a lady must abandon being a lady, when regarding matters of family. I have a cousin who threw us out of our home and now depends upon us again. He will greet us eagerly, and flatter himself for having such connections, because of our marriage to you both. He will brag and boast if he has not done so already. And he will not think himself in error on any matter. When we arrive at Longbourn, I shall be cordial, for a brief period, before I begin to cut him down in every way that an angry harpy can."

"Will you do it in the house and behind closed doors?" Mr. Darcy asked.

"Yes. I shall never believe in washing one's dirty linens in the street."

"Very well. Chastise Mr. Collins all that you wish. I will not stop you from shouting some common sense into him."

"Thank you, my dear. That is of great comfort."

On the road, we passed along Lucas Lodge, and we marveled at it—while also dreading the reception.

"Ah," Kitty said, "soon, we shall have to meet Sir William and Lady Lucas and deliver Charlotte and Maria's delightful news to them."

"They will not thank us for that."

"No, they will not."

"Hopefully," Colonel Fitzwilliam said, "they have adopted the philosophy of 'do not shoot the messenger'."

"Yes," I said, "hopefully, they have."

At last, we arrived at the lane that led to Longbourn.

My heart was in my throat.

My thoughts were awake.

My mind had replaced the anger I felt toward Mr. Collins to joy of seeing the familiar lane and walk that always had been when I made my way toward home.

At last, the trees cleared away, and—

"Home!" Kitty cried.

"Yes," I said, breathing heavily, "there it is. Longbourn."

Our home, where there was so much great comfort, so much simplicity of life and beauty. Of a home that once was filled with so many great voices inside of it.

Five voices of five very different sisters.

Two voices of two entirely different parents.

The noise that my father often complained of. That, in truth, I think he found pleasure in hearing, to give himself something to scoff at and feign superiority over.

All that sound was in Longbourn's walls.

We were home.

As we rode up to our past residence, the door opened, and two characters emerged. The first was Mr. Collins, who greeted us as if he had been sprung up from out of a puddle. He even gestured for someone to quickly follow him.

Soon, I saw Mary exit the house, with a child wrapped warmly in her arms.

For a second, my eyes switched scenes and I saw my parents waving at us. But that was not to be.

Rather, it was a half-image. An image that brought on joy and internal grumbling. Joy of seeing my sister, after all those years, and anger of seeing my father's elegant walk replaced by Mr. Collins' bumbling way of presenting himself.

Our carriage stopped, servants emerged, and our gentlemen helped us down from the carriages.

"Mary!" Jane, Kitty, and I cried. We rushed to her and embraced her, despite that she had a child in her arms.

"All these months," Mary declared, "and my sisters have found me, through it all. Even employment could not fully best us."

"No," I said, "it could not."

"Let us look at you," Kitty said, standing back and analyzing her. "Oh dear, Mary, you've put on weight."

"Have I?" Mary asked.

"Yes," Kitty said, looking at the child in Mary's arms, "twenty-five whole pounds, I declare."

"Oh," Mary laughed. "Yes, I suppose that I have. Let me introduce you to our lovely cousin."

Despite that Mr. Collins was standing right there, Mary ignored him and introduced us to his child herself. Since the infant was not at the stage where talking was learned, we received our greetings with gurgling sounds—and even a smile was managed.

"Lovely," I said to the child, "this bodes well for you to possibly be of good cheer and optimistic spirits as you grow."

"Yes," Mr. Collins said, at last, "my child is a healthy one. We have been making sure to always give it the right amount of food. Even Lady Catherine writes to me, weekly, with her advice on how to raise our child. My poor and late Mrs. Collins had always been willing to listen to her advice with proper respect that was due to her ladyship." He looked at Mr. Darcy and Colonel Fitzwilliam. "Your aunt may be fifty miles away from Longbourn, but I declare that her authority is as respected in this house than as if it had been right next to Hunsford Parsonage. Mr. Darcy and Colonel Fitzwilliam, this is a great honor to have you visit Longbourn."

"Thank you, Mr. Collins," Colonel Fitzwilliam replied, diplomatically, while Mr. Darcy merely nodded his head. "And how do you do, sir?"

"Very well, but I have recently lost my wife."

"Yes, we heard. We are very sorry for your loss."

"Truly, as you can see, I have had the good fortune for Miss Mary to come here and perform the duty that ladies are meant to perform so very well."

I groaned inwardly. He assumed that Mary came to help, not because she chose to come out of familial loyalties, but because it was expected of her. He was as conceited as ever.

"And Mr. Bingley," Mr. Collins said, "you are very welcome as well."

"Thank you, sir," Mr. Bingley said.

"And you all have married my fair cousins," Mr. Collins

said, standing back and looking at us all. "And my dear cousins, you are returned to Hertfordshire. Welcome to my humble abode."

Jane, Kitty, Margaret, and my eyes widened in disbelief. First, he still had not acknowledged the Hales, and now he was welcoming us to the very house that he drove us out of. Did he have any sense?

"Sir, that is kind, but not necessary," I replied, "after all, it is hard to welcome a set of sisters to a house that they were raised in. For most of *their* entire lives."

"Mr. Collins," Mary said, "it is more prudent to be glad to see family and assure my sisters that you have been doing your best to maintain Longbourn and that the estate is being properly run."

"Well, of course," Mr. Collins said. "Oh! Have I offended my cousins? Believe me, I am mortified."

"Margaret and Frederick!"

"Mary," Margaret Hale said, going up to her and kissing her on the cheek. "It is a delight to see you."

"You are looking as well as ever," Mary said, then she looked behind her. "And this is a face that I never thought that I would see again."

Frederick Hale came forward, smiling merrily.

"Miss Mary Bennet," Frederick said, "this is a great pleasure to see you."

"The Spanish weather appears to agree with you."

"And I have the pleasure of seeing four of the five Bennet sisters together," Frederick said. "If only Mrs. Denny was here, then the perfect picture would be complete."

"And how is the baby of the five of us?" Mary asked Jane and me. "Just as lively as ever, I'd imagine."

"It's Lydia's skill," Jane said. "She is still the healthiest of all of us. Denny dotes on her as much now as they did when they were first married."

"She married the right officer."

"Yes, she did."

"Mr. Collins," I said, "you have not been acquainted with the Hales, as of yet. I shall remedy that. Mr. Collins, this is Mr. Frederick Hale and his cousin, Miss Margaret Hale. Margaret and Frederick, this is our cousin and the present master of Longbourn, Mr. Collins."

Mr. Collins welcomed them both.

As we walked up the steps, to enter, Mr. Collins directed our attention to the front of the house, under the windows.

"Do you see there? I had the gardener plant a particular set of flowers under the windows, and it has been said to bring great enhancement to the place. Are they not the very essence of aesthetic superiority?"

"They are very lovely, indeed," Jane said.

"Yes, they are. They are."

I looked at Mr. Darcy. My eyes showed my mortification. Darcy was sympathetic.

When we walked to the door, Mr. Collins turned to us.

"And once more, I welcome you all to my home," he said to us, welcoming us to our old home—for a second time.

It was as if Mary and I had said nothing at all to him. The tedious fool!

When we entered, Mr. Collins immediately began to regale us with all the 'improvements' that he made to Longbourn. Many of them, he made certain for us to know, were always given under Lady Catherine's express wishes. And even if he made a choice that he did not ask her about, he made it assuming that she would have made the same suggestion.

"Even though she is no longer his patroness," I whispered to Margaret, "he still acts like she watches every move he makes."

"And that he ought to answer to her," Margaret responded, equally as quiet, "as if she were the queen and her reign was supreme. Was he always like this when he courted you?"

"Yes."

"No wonder you rejected him. At least, Mr. Lennox was respectable."

"Yes. You rejected a logical man. Wait? Margaret, does that make you feel better or worse? I felt no remorse rejecting Mr. Collins because he is so obviously ridiculous. Did you feel upset for having to reject a better man?"

"No, I confess that I did not. Besides, it is evident, in many ways, that I was right."

"We both were."

Mr. Collins was everything that I remembered him to be. An odious creature who was an odd blend of humility and conceit. One moment, he was apologizing for saying something wrong to Mr. Darcy, Bingley, and the Colonel for a quarter of an hour.

The next moment, he was boasting about something that he had no right to boast about.

When the moment came, Mary and I had a chance to speak alone as one of the servants came and took the child back to the nursery. While the rest of the company was by the fire, with Mr. Bingley, Frederick and Jane dominating the conversation.

Mary told me about her time working in Uncle Gardiner's factory.

"As strange to admit," Mary said, "I found completion in working for my uncle. And he was not ashamed for employing me."

"Understandable," I said, "we all became ladies of profession, and it was humbling. That humility led to a new respect for the working class."

"I cared not for society looking down on me," Mary continued, "I just enjoyed not being idle. And I found that about myself. Some of us are made for lives of leisure. Others of us were made to toil and work. It fills up our days and brings purpose to our lives. We do not have to always be at home, letting our emotions prey upon us. Activity breeds distraction. One can learn to love distractions."

"Yes. One can." I took in her look and her attitude. She was looking better than I had expected in every way. "Age and labor have helped you. Amazing. Work can easily diminish one's good looks, but with you, it has brought a bloom to your skin."

Mary smiled.

"Thank you for flattering me, but I am aware that I will never be as lovely as Jane, you, Kitty, and Lydia. I forgave life for making me the plain one long ago."

"Beauty is subjective."

"And the world would have it be objective. I know what I am."

"And I know what you are as well. Mary, I must know, what prompted this? This decision to come to Longbourn and assist Mr. Collins when his wife died? I know that you had more respect for him when he first visited us. But once he took possession of Longbourn, and took it away from us, that respect turned to contempt. What changed?"

"Faith, Lizzy, I did not do it for him. In truth, my feelings for Mr. Collins were as cold as ever. I did it for selfish and selfless reasons, God forgive me."

"He forgives you. Now proceed."

"If I had not any moral and disinterested reasons for coming, then I would not have let my selfish side win out. But since my flaw was equal to virtue, I did not despise myself. First, I had a notion."

"What sort of notion?"

"Notion of envisioning Mr. Collins with an infant of his own and having no mother to assist him. Can you imagine what that image would be like? He might be of landed gentry and no longer needs employment and therefore had time to raise the child—but still."

"Oh," I said, grimacing, "I understand you. Mr. Collins, as a sole parent, would have made a terrible single parent."

"Precisely, Eliza. Or, out of desperation, he would marry a woman, just for the sake of supplying a lady to be the mother. Never mind making sure that she was the proper candidate. Not all men and women are equipped at loving another child as much as loving their own. He could make a foolish match, where the lady has no maternal skills, or she would never love the child as much as any children she might later have with Mr. Collins."

"To be sure, to be a stepmother is a skill. Not everyone has it."

"Precisely. I didn't want Mr. Collins to raise an even worse child than himself. Some vicious cycles must be brought to an end. If I could come and assist in raising the child until Mr. Collins had chosen the correct wife, then all would be well. And if he does not find the right woman, then I am here for as long as he needs. I could raise a child who does not throw defenseless women into a life where they have no home."

"You wanted to give the child good principles."

"Yes. And now, for my second reason."

I leaned forward, curious.

"Well," Mary said, "selfishness cannot be helped all the time, now can it? I offered to come because...I wanted so much to be at home again. Even if it was temporary. I wanted to see Longbourn, Meryton and Hertfordshire. The shops in the marketplace, our friends, our neighbors. One cannot go one's entire life, out there in the world, without stumbling on the concept of there being no place like home, sometimes."

"It is natural. Our parents' voices are caught in the walls of this house."

"Yes," Mary said, her eyes lit up. "You feel the same?"

"Yes, I do."

"How wonderful to know that you understand me, Lizzy. I did not think that you would. When I returned, I saw all our history, laid out before me. I saw our parents' image, with my waking eyes."

"Home," I uttered, "Longbourn."

"Yes. Longbourn."

"And then there is the second part of my selfishness," Mary continued.

"I like it when things come in twos."

"You quibble, Lizzy."

"I always quibble. Accept and be accepting."

"I know." Mary laughed. "Believe me, I know. Well, this was something that I did for all of us."

"For all of us?"

"Yes. If I came and assisted Mr. Collins, making myself

indispensable to him, then Longbourn would be our home again. Lydia has Denny, but at the time, I was not wholly aware of your romantic prospects. I thought, in this way, I could save our family and bring us back to Hertfordshire. For this is where we belong. You may have done well in the North, but we are people of the South."

"I married a man of both the North and the South," I said, "not always remembering the Northern part. I wonder what that says of me. Or that we fall in love wherever we may."

I took Mary's hand. "Mary, for the first time, it can be said that being selfish did nothing but good."

When hearing me say this, she smiled.

"If our lives had turned out differently," I said, "your coming would have saved us all. We may not have been saved in the beginning, but you would have protected us at the middle and secured our lives for the end. Looking after our cousins' child would be a certain way of bringing us back home again, while doing right by the baby. After all, Mr. Collins would have felt indebted to us, while you had given the child many ladies to look after it."

"Yes. I had attempted to save as many as I could at one time. But, as usual, I am no hero."

I looked at her, curious.

"Were you trying to be the hero, Mary?"

"Well, as vain as this sounds, yes, I rather think that I was. Everyone has the right to be, at some point or other. To be the hero. One feels like one matters. I wanted to matter. And to be the hero...well, what feeling is better than that? I never had to save anyone before. When our parents died, our aunt and uncle took me in. Denny married Lydia. Then Mr. Bell helped Kitty, Jane and you find employment in the North. Your exploits in Milton were the stuff of legend.

And then there was me, as always. Mary in the middle. Not right in one direction, nor right in the other. And her good intentions rest where they always do: in the middle. Well, I was repaid for my vanity."

I took her hand.

"Mary," I said, "you were heroic."

"You tease me, Lizzy."

"No, I do not tease you. I speak sincerely. You were a hero. If all other plans, our dreams, had come undone, and we had not found our good fortune, then yes, you would have brought us home, safe and where we were happy, hearty, and whole. While also being a mother to the child. But that is more important than anything else now. You are looking after an infant that is not your own, doting on it, and giving it the love and care that it deserves to have in this world. That is more heroic than anything else."

Mary smiled, a genuine and truly grateful smile. Her eyes were misty with emotion, and she felt as if she would not go ignored, as she perhaps might have been, once upon a time.

"You really think so?"

"I know it."

Mary and I were interrupted by Mr. Collins directing his attention to us.

"Dear cousin, Elizabeth," Mr. Collins said, "now I can very well comprehend where your mind was about."

"About, sir?" I asked him, confused. "Pray, I know not to what you were referring?"

"Well," Mr. Collins said, a little sheepish, "naturally, you will recall a certain event betwixt yourself and I over a year ago."

I rubbed my cheek, discomforted. He was referring to when he had proposed to me.

"Oh," was all that I cared to utter.

"Yes, that event. I shall not put full words to it, but you know the event that I mean. But the matches that you three ladies have made make all other past engagements feel miniscule. Lady Catherine wrote to me of the event. She was overjoyed to be the one to arrange your wedding, and I knew that my cousins would make me proud of them. She mentioned that you were friendly and diverting, and I felt so very proud that I had three cousins who I need not be ashamed of."

Looking over my shoulder, I looked at the others in our company.

Margaret Hale looked at her lap.

Frederick Hale looked pointedly at him.

Mr. Bingley looked a little repulsed.

Jane drank from her tea, pretending not to hear.

Colonel Fitzwilliam groaned silently.

Kitty was subtly angry.

And Mr. Darcy's eyes were filled with venom.

Mr. Collins was happy that we were not a shame to him. Never would he even realize that, when it came to the distribution of shame, it would always be the other way around.

"Therefore," Mr. Collins acknowledged, "know that I am aware that you were saving your choice for such an illustrious set of persons...well! Let us just say that it all makes a great deal of sense now. You made three very fortunate alliances, and prudence is properly maintained."

"Sir," I said, icily, "I thank you for my share of the compliment. But when you refer to that incident that we share from over a year ago, my decision was not swayed by another match from another quarter." In this next bit, I looked at him with such direct contempt. "On the contrary, when I made the decision that I made at the time, there were no prospects that I knew of. I made the decision because the request asked of me was too much of an inconvenience and was against every proper feeling that I had. I chose that course of action because it was the *only* right action to take. Nothing else influenced me but my firm belief that to do the reverse would be wrong in every respect."

No matter how foolish he was, Mr. Collins could not ignore the fact that I deliberately said that I rejected him, without the expectation of a better match eventually. But rather, I had rejected him because the thought of being married to him was the most disgusting thing to imagine. Sometimes an indirect insult was as cutting as a direct one.

Mr. Collins' face drained of color, and he felt ashamed.

And I was just beginning.

Chapter 7

Oh

"Oh," Margaret Hale said as I was helping her unpack her clothes. It had been nighttime, supper was over, the family had mostly retired, and Margaret was sleeping in the guestroom.

Coincidentally, it was the same room that Mr. Collins had been a guest in when he first visited Longbourn.

"So," Margaret said, "this is the very cousin that you warned me about."

"And now that you have met him, what do you think?" I asked.

"He is everything that you described. You rejected a ridiculous man. Imagine if you had not known what you were about, and you had married him."

I grimaced and made a sour face.

"Oh, do not imagine it!" I exclaimed. "For I refuse to even picture that alternate reality."

Margaret laughed.

"Marriage is too tricky a sacrament, isn't it?" Margaret asked.

"Yes. One must be careful."

"And even then, a person can still make a mistake. That's what I fear. First, I think one thing of Thornton, then lately my mind has been shifting about more and more. For my part, I feel as if it is shifting from indifference to respect, then respect to admiration, then from admiration to affection too quickly."

"You wrote him that letter."

"Yes, I did. And I have been regretting it in one moment. Then I do not regret it in the next." She sat on the floor and rested her back against the bed, leaning back and rubbing her eyes.

"I do not know what I want. That is disconcerting. I have always known what I wanted, there was no cause for alarm. Now, I am in a state of..."

"Being wholly in love?" I hinted.

"Yes."

"Only being wholly in love produces such confusion. I was there myself."

"I think I could adapt to the principle of it if it wasn't so provocative," Margaret said. "Why did this have to happen? Things are so perfect by living with father and mother and being able to go about as one wishes. When you are in love, and the man does share the same sentiments as you do, you have more to care about. You have to consider both of you. Not you yourself—but you both."

"Tears away at your autonomy, doesn't it?"

"Yes, like the very devil. But it can't be helped. I am now falling in love, and there is nothing else for it."

I laughed.

"Well, there is some joy to this all."

"What is that?"

"We are all in love together. When it comes to friendship, when so many of us conveniently fall in love at the same time, it spells nothing else but convenient."

"Yes, I suppose that it does."

"But I suspect, while you are in love, you are not altogether ready to resign yourself to marriage just yet."

"No, I am not. I feel as if there is some other burden out there, waiting for me, or some other bridge to cross."

"Will you write to Thornton of that as well?"

"Yes, I will. But only after receiving his next letter. I would not want to look too pressing or too obsessive." Margaret Hale looked at herself in the mirror. "I refuse to lose my sense of control. *Not in the slightest.*"

"When it comes to love, communication is never easy."

"No, it's not. *Not in the slightest.*"

"Until the day that it becomes so. If both sides reach that ideal point, both sides understand each other so very well, that they can say anything and everything, and the other comprehends."

Margaret breathed out and in, considering.

"Happiness in marriage really is a matter of chance," Margaret said, "But from what I have seen and experienced, is too stark a reality."

"And what is that?"

"That I am not you. Nor am I Jane. Nor am I Kitty, or Lydia. You four seem to be born in a way where you are a groove, the man you meet is a joint, and you all fit. What if I do marry Mr. Thornton, and we prove to be each other's undoing?"

"These are difficult questions that you must consider and confront. But if your growing affection for the man is not larger than your doubts, then continue to take the time to reflect. But there is one bit of advice that I can give that I am sure shall be right."

"What is it?"

"Well, wait for his letter back to you. Only then can you make the next move. Until then, there is no need to carry the woes that one carries when one is greatly unsettled."

"True."

Margaret closed her eyes and then opened them again.

"Life was much simpler once," she said, "wasn't it?"

"No, it was not," I disagreed. "Our lives have always been complicated. Either we were always being obliged to do something that we did not wish to do in a drawing room, then we were traveling somewhere we did not want to travel, for survival. Be you poor or wealthy, there is always some sort of complication somewhere that keeps us from achieving the constant bliss that every human is owed."

"I suppose so. But even when we were walking along the Milton streets, even when we were dashed against the unknown, I knew that we would persevere."

"How did you know that?"

"We were friends, and we owned ourselves. When you love, you do not own yourself anymore. Someone else owns you, and you also own them. That is true love, as it ought to be."

"Margaret," I said heavily, "you only compromise your freedom if you choose. Being married does not change that. Darcy would never mistreat me. I married a great man who the adoration is mutual. But if he did hurt me, abused our love, oppressed me, and I felt trapped, I would divorce him."

Margaret blinked.

"You would?"

"Of course, I would. Just because I love him does not mean that I would stop loving myself. There would be no power in this earth that would have me ignore my own sense of self. We are not in a time where we are confined to a room and are forced to endure our lives. I've been in situations where I have had to uproot my entire life, change my station, and I think I could do it again."

"And what if you had children?"

"I would take them with me. Of course, the courts might not let me, but I would try. I will not be oppressed by anyone. Even the only man that I love. Nor will I oppress him. We rely upon each other, but we were all independent once. I'm certain that he and I could find our way back there again."

"Therefore, if I choose Mr. Thornton, and eventually discover that we both were in error to love each other, we could always arrange something."

"Very few people in life are in situations where they have no exit. Nowhere to run. Remember, we are the lucky ones who have an exit. Use it when the time is able."

I stood up, walked to the window, and looked out at the night sky.

"However, this advice that I give you is not a decision that should be the first one that you have. It's an action that should always be the last scenario that you use. Always try to understand your husband and attempt to have him understand you. Only cut and run when no other solution has been achieved."

Margaret sighed.

"Well, then I suppose there is only one thing for me to do."

"What?"

"Be happy that I know what I am about. And not grumble at the worst outcome—an outcome that might never happen."

"You and I have the same flaw of believing in the worst

thing possibly happening, and then everything sorts itself over time."

"Well, we've been given our share of adversity. But I daresay that everyone has, excepting spoiled people."

"Never fear. Spoiled people tend to go out and create their own adversity, since they have little else to occupy their time."

"True. Thank you, Lizzy."

"For the advice?"

"Yes. But also, for giving me a way out. I cannot get out, as the starling said.[1] That's what I was afraid of. But now I can get out. That's all that matters."

There was a knock on the door.

"Come in, husband," I said.

The door opened and it was Mr. Darcy.

"Forgive me for intruding on a conversation between two ladies in each other's confidence," Darcy began.

"But you missed me," I teased. "Do not deny it, or I shall be hurt."

Mr. Darcy looked on me, fondly.

"Very well. I missed you."

"Good."

I looked at Margaret, smirking.

"I can get out," I replied, smiling at her. "As the starling did not say."

Margaret laughed.

"Very well. I shall rest easy. Now be off with you. I hate how often you challenge my logic with another logic."

1. This is a reference to a quote that was used in 'Mansfield Park'.

"Call me purgatory's advocate."

I stood up, Darcy and I bid Margaret goodnight, and we went to our room.

"You left me for too long," he said.

"I know. Ah, I love torturing you."

"I knew it!" He hissed. "Woman, really?"

"You knew the woman that you married. Why are you always surprised by the things that I do? I thought that you would have had my character properly analyzed, properly catalogued, and properly determined."

We entered our guest room, and I helped him out of his robe.

"Yes, my dear. What was I thinking?"

"Lay down on the bed, on your stomach."

Mr. Darcy raised an eyebrow.

"I beg your pardon?"

"You have had a long day and have had to endure my cousin's constant vulgarity. This is my way of helping you find some level of relaxation."

I sat down on the bed.

"We are newly married. Do you not trust me?"

Giving in, he laid down on the bed, on his stomach.

Preparing, I pulled up his nightshirt, to reveal his back. I rubbed lotion on my hands and stretched my fingers.

"Mr. Hunnicutt told me about something that his mother would do to his father, and it seemed like it would be a pleasant thing.

I poured a little bit of lotion on his skin and began to rub it along his shoulders and back, massaging him.

"Oh! Oh..." he uttered.

"You said those 'ohs' in two different ways. The first was shock, and the second was gentle. That leaves me to assume that you are enjoying yourself now."

"Well, yes. Thank you, Mr. Hunnicutt! This feels delightful."

"Yes. Massaging one's back and one's shoulders is very good at relieving a person's anxiety, he told me. But he always declared that after his mother paid such attentions to his father, his father felt his limbs improve in some way. So that leads me to assume that it does give some health to the body as well."

I ran my fingers up to his head and began to rub his scalp and hair.

"Oh, I love that!" he cried.

"Good."

"Lizzy?"

"Yes?"

"You must do this to me very often."

"Very well. As long as you *return the compliment.*"

"Eh?"

"Of course. If you take pleasure in it, is it not natural that the female body would feel the same?"

"Correct. I just worry that I would do the deed ill."

"Practice makes perfect."

"Yes, it does. Tell me if I get too rough."

"I will, without hesitation. So, when are you going to ask me?"

"What?"

"About what Margaret and I were talking about?"

Mr. Darcy's body tensed up.

"Oh, I see that I stumbled upon a nerve," I noticed.

"You knew that I wanted to ask about that?"

"Oh, I very much knew. You are intrigued with any discussion that we have."

"Because it inevitably returns back to discussion of Thornton. I cannot help but be curious. I know that you told me that she has softened greatly towards him, but she can always change her mind. Young people have been known to do that, you know. Especially when their thoughts are in a constant state of confusion."

"And hers is. But she knows now. She is fully in love with him. And it hurts her so very much."

"Hurts her? How?"

I told him everything that she said, knowing that he would not repeat any of our discussion.

When I concluded, Mr. Darcy remained on the bed, hoping the massaging would never end, but he had many things to say.

"I doubt that marriage to Thornton would make Margaret miserable. But she is right, Elizabeth. They are not us. They are shades of us, but *not* us. They are very much themselves. You and I are both headstrong, but there is a similarity to the turn of our minds. With them, there is much difference that they have done their best to overcome. Margaret does have reason to worry, so I understand why you showed her that one can always escape a bad situation. But I believe that they would be happy."

"She just needs a little longer."

"Precisely. After all, we did."

"True, we did."

"Elizabeth?"

"Yes?"

"I will never do anything to make you have to leave me."

I leaned down and kissed his neck.

"I know that you won't. And I will never do anything to make you have to leave me. But it was nice hearing that promise."

"Yes, it was."

Chapter 8

Neighbors

The next day, there was not a moment to lose. All of us were very insistent to visit Lucas Lodge, for what ought to be done could not be done too quickly.

Afterward, we requested to continue into Meryton to visit our Uncle Philips, who was now a widower.

"That is another thing that added to my coming," Mary said to me as we arranged for the carriage to come. "Our uncle was happy for one of us to return to his life. I visit him three times a week."

"And how is he?" Kitty asked, truly concerned. "Our aunt and him were married for thirty years, and recovery from such a thing is difficult."

"And it still is," Mary informed us. "He still has not fully recovered from it. While I have not seen him do so, the servants have told me...he cries sometimes. Especially when he sees the chair that she often sat in."

"I cannot wait to see him," Jane said. "Poor uncle."

When we arrived at Lucas Lodge, say what you would of the situation, but Sir William would never be anything else but pleasant and jovial at receiving such company.

Ah, to see Lucas Lodge, Sir William, and his wife!

They looked the same as they had when we had left Longbourn all those many months ago.

In a world where everything was changing, where the proverbial rug always seemed to be pulled out from beneath our feet, it was nice to see some constancy.

I can very easily forgive change, as long as there is some tradition, some custom, that even change cannot fully remove. Lucas Lodge was still here, and still under the reign of the Lucas family. For Sir William had three sons, and therefore, he was safe, by way of inheritance.

He and Lady Lucas greeted us with such amiability that we fell back into our old ways without even mentioning Charlotte and Maria's decision to remain in Milton.

"I knew it, didn't I?" Sir William Lucas cried, slapping himself on the knee. "Mr. Bingley, when you arrived at Netherfield Park, I declared that there would soon be a marriage and Miss Bennet—forgive me—Mrs. Bingley, would soon be properly settled. Did you all not hear me mention it to your mother often?"

"Oh, we heard it, sir," I said, "and mama marked it down as definite. How happy that she was to have another ally on her side. Especially since father was quite indifferent on what happened."

"And you can boast of taking the credit for being the gentleman for determining it," Mr. Bingley replied, looking at Jane. "In this matter, you anticipated me."

"But we did not anticipate other such matches," Sir William said. He turned to Colonel Fitzwilliam and Kitty. "Sir, in my defense, I had never made your acquaintance, so

I could not make any delightful predictions. But what I was right about was that Kitty and Lydia could not bear a life lacking in excitement. Lady Lucas and I always declared that they would marry officers."

"My dear," Lady Lucas said, "we look so uncouth in the presence of our company for speaking of their future."

"Oh! Have I caused offense? I had no notion that I was."

"It is well, Sir William," Kitty encouraged, "for you are correct. Our spirits would not allow us to marry a man without spirit and courage within himself. And what horror is there in preferring men who defend their country? None at all. Sir William, you were correct, sir."

"And for the most pleasurable surprise of all," Sir William said, turning to Mr. Darcy and me. "Who would have thought? When I first offered Mrs. Darcy as a dance partner to you, Mr. Darcy, I never would have known. At first, I felt a little upset with myself for trying to force you to dance with our local beauty, but now I see that it was all for a good reason."

"I should have not been so against the activity when you suggested it," Mr. Darcy said. "That was a product of my stoicism."

"And I should have accepted. That was a product of my stubbornness. Well, Sir William, your forcefulness did you credit in that moment."

Sir William clapped his hands together.

"Good, good. Capitol, capitol!"

At last, the moment came when the adventures and exploits of the Lucas sisters finally had to be disclosed.

"And how are our daughters?" Lady Lucas began. "In their last letter to us, they seemed to be well."

"And they are," Jane said, with a fragility to her tone.

"However," I said, "the truth must be confronted. Sir William and Lady Lucas, I know that you raised your daughters to be genteel ladies, and they are. However, when it comes to their independency and their desires to remain in the North for some time, things are very settled."

Sir William and Lady Lucas looked at each other, a little anxious.

"Yes," Lady Lucas replied, "we have suspected as much. But in truth, we had assumed that their decision was made from being so swept away by the novelty of being in a new place. Of the exhilaration that comes from being hurled into the unknown. But soon, we assumed that they would tire of the concept."

"And then we have done our best to understand that," Sir William smoothed over, "after all, our daughters are very obliging creatures. We realized that they would stop at nothing to assist you."

"At the expense of their own happiness," Lady Lucas said, and then wished she unsaid it in the next second. Sir William looked uncomfortable, and Lady Lucas blushed and sipped her tea.

I began to prepare myself to speak, but to my surprise, Margaret intervened.

"Your ladyship," Margaret said, "Charlotte and Maria love Lucas Lodge, and Hertfordshire. Nothing could ever replace their love for home. But they are also very determined women, and I can assure you that their decision to remain in Milton was as much about their own personal desires for gathering a wider acquaintance with the world, than about their assisting the Bennet girls. I was able to witness their daily activities. They loved the activity of the North. Despite its rougher edges of existence, there was an eagerness to everything they experienced. In fact, I daresay that their willingness to stay was focused just as much about their own character development. I think they wanted change in their life because they don't fear it. Some of us do. We are not accustomed to change happening in our lives when we find a preferred way of living. We do not like the outside world coming in and bringing difference. I confess to being that sort of woman —much to my chagrin. I am happy that I am aware of it now. But your daughters quite surpassed me. They did not fear the difference, and the different sort of people that they met with. They understood that a change in environment was not something to shy away from, but rather was something to accept and embrace. That is what makes them admirable, I can assure you. In a strange way, the Bennet sisters gave your daughters the chance to show their skill at adapting to differences of lifestyle, of society, and other customs. You have every right to be proud of them."

"Oh," Lady Lucas said, eager to agree with anything that would ease the tension that she had created. "I confess that I had not thought of that. You put it very well, Miss Hale. I am glad that Charlotte and Maria have found their joys in the North. It is just very hard not to be biased, you see. We are so accustomed to viewing the North as being so very coarse and people being harder."

"There is that aspect of it," Margaret said, "for it is a place of industry. However, the Northern factories are what keep English society functioning. I see the importance of that now. And your daughters see it. They want to see the wheels that makes the vehicle of Britain move. They are part of it all. They are involved. And when one finally becomes involved, you cannot go back."

"You make our daughters sound like heroines, Miss Hale," Sir William said. "That is just delightful."

"And the Bennets are the catalysts through which they are able to display their talents of survival," Lady Lucas said. "A toast then, to adventuresses."

We all drank.

"Upon my word, Margaret," I whispered to her as we rode into Meryton to visit my Uncle Philips, "I never thought that I would see the day."

"The day of what?" she asked me.

"The day where you compliment the better aspects of the North, speaking well of it, to Southern society. This is a turn of our lives, I declare."

"You mock me, Lizzy."

"Of course, I do that. Why are you surprised by this? I lay my character out for you to always see, plain and tall. And yet, you are still surprised."

"Call that one of my charms; I am always underestimating your wit. You must remember, those of us who are witless, always do not understand the turn of a witty mind."

We arrived at Meryton and knocked on our uncle's door.

A servant received us, and we found our Uncle Philips in the parlor, looking very much not surprised at our arrival. When we entered, Kitty ran to him, he wrapped his hands around her and they embraced.

I had to stand and watch them, unaware of if I should attempt the same amount of affection.

"Kitty and Lydia had always been uncle's favorite," I whispered to Colonel Fitzwilliam, "and there is no wonder for it. They always exerted themselves to be more familial."

"You sound like you did not?" Colonel Fitzwilliam asked me.

"It's because I did not, now that I come to think of it. In fact, I always was a little harsh on my judgment when it came to my aunt and uncle Philips. Since I had set my aunt and uncle Gardiner as the ideal marriage, everything else paled in comparison. Now I realize that there are various forms of proper marriages, and that maybe my shame towards the Philips' was not understanding the foibles that make family life well-rounded."

"Every family has fools. Your uncle does not seem like one of them. He just seems to have an open temper."

"I know. People of open tempers have a purpose in this world."

When he finished speaking of his joys in seeing Kitty again, Uncle Philips turned to Jane and me.

"And there are my other two flowers of niece-hood. Jane and Lizzy, you look as lovely as ever."

"Thank you, Uncle," I said, walking up to him and kissing him on the cheek. "I am sorry about our aunt."

And true to his open nature, Uncle Philips' face shifted from pleasant to melancholy.

"Thank you. So am I."

For the first time in my life, I felt my heart reach out to him. I never pitied our uncle before, but now, in the shadow of such a loss, his heart had fallen out, displayed in front of us.

"Yes, uncle," Jane said, "when we heard the news of our aunt's passing, we wished that we would have been here to have been with you at the time."

"It is not your fault," Uncle Philips said. "I am to blame for it."

"Blame for it?" Kitty asked, confused, "how so?"

"If I had been more successful in my business, I could have had the money to take you all in when your parents died, and Mr. Collins had taken possession of Longbourn. But I did not. You had to leave and find your own way in the world and were hurled into the whims of the world's plans. If I had been rich..."

Kitty took his hand.

"Uncle, this was not your responsibility."

"Yes, it was. I was so very fond of you all being close by to always come and visit. You kept your aunt, my wife, always with company. She was never lonely. Then you all moved away, and she was sad over it. Loneliness found her, in ways that none of us suspected. Sometimes, she walked around, wondering what she could do with her time. Yes, she visited neighbors, but she was not accustomed to the silence that occurred when Longbourn was lost to you. She preferred the noise that you all exuded when you came here. She relied on it, and come to think of it, so did I. And I cannot help but consider that the loneliness ate away at her, and maybe a part of her gave up. And that helped the sickness on. Sometimes, a want of spirits can help an illness get worse."

I was humbled. Truly humbled. My uncle was such a sturdy man whose roughness never unveiled any human frailty. And now, to see him, his shoulders hunched over, so broken, that it amazed me that I could spend my life feeling that sometimes, we can know someone and never fully know them.

"Uncle," Jane said, "I..."

"No," he shushed her sentence with his hand, "I should not speak of that when I have not met the new acquaintances and received your husbands properly."

We introduced the Hales and introduced our husbands. After all, technically, our Uncle Philips had never met the Colonel, and never actually spoke one word to Darcy or Bingley. He sometimes was in their company, but they never exchanged words of any kind. I assumed it was because Darcy thought it was beneath his dignity to speak with my relations, and maybe he would have done so, at one time or another. But time had changed him, and now he would meet my uncle, fully, at a time where any man could relate to the other.

Mr. Darcy's words were sparse, but I could tell that it was merely that he had no notion of how to address him.

Colonel Fitzwilliam, Mr. Bingley, and Frederick Hale were more verbose about offering their sympathies, and Margaret was silent. She discerned that Uncle Philips would want to talk to us first, especially since it had been so long since he had seen us. She remained in the back of the group, so that we could be in the forefront, and it would allow my uncle to focus solely upon us and the comforts of his nieces returning.

"We missed you as well, Uncle," I said, as we sat down, and Mary arranged to have coffee brought in. "Leaving Hertfordshire society was hard, we can assure you, especially since you and Aunt Philips were such a fixture in our society. Where one went, the other was not far behind."

"Our aunt and uncle were wed in their youth," Jane

explained to the Hales, "and they remained married for thirty years."

"Thirty," Margaret repeated, "oh, such a long and happy marriage."

"And it was, Miss Hale, believe me," Uncle Philips said, getting a faraway look in his eye. "Not many men and women can say they knew every aspect of their spouse's character before they married them. But that was the case with us. In fact, when I called on her one day, when she was a young beauty, do you know what she said?"

"What?" Mary asked, coming in and setting the coffee and cakes down.

"She said, 'Mr. Philips! I want you to know me. Not know me a little but know me entirely. I am going to tell you every awful thing about myself, every awful thing that I have ever done, so that you know the sort of woman that you call upon'. And she proceeded to tell me every lie she ever told, every flaw to her person, her jealousies, her prejudices, the things she despised, and even the people she hated. Then she concluded with saying this one thing: she said, 'Mr. Philips, I tell you this now, because I want you to know that no matter what happens the day after this, and after that, you are the only man that I will always be honest with and owe the truth to. I will never deceive you or manipulate you. I will simply be your wife'."

We all were silenced for a time. Until I just had to speak.

"Our aunt said that?" I asked, amazed.

"Yes."

"And what did you do next, sir?" Mr. Bingley asked.

"I was so flattered, that I decided to return the compliment. I told her every sin I had ever committed. We just sat there, for hours—talking. There was no silent moment. And by the time I was done that social visit, I declared that I had never had a more comfortable day in my life. And when I was alone, I whispered to myself, may this woman marry me. May she marry me!"

This memory brought on the frightened creature within him.

"Now I cannot say that it is we two in life," he said, his eyes growing wistful. "And I can only say that it is just me."

Suddenly, he began to cry.

And the cry was not a brief and simple one. His face and whole body shook with grief. He was a widower who had never expected to be in this predicament. We all know how life is supposed to end, but we still cannot help but be utterly shocked when the inevitability occurs.

When he wept, Kitty and Mary immediately rushed to him, and he fell into their arms.

This sudden outburst astonished all of us. Aware that our uncle would not want an audience for his sudden outburst, I gave our company a look. Margaret perceived and ushered the gentlemen out of the room.

When alone, Uncle Philips went even more into Kitty and Mary's arms.

"Why did my Jane have to leave me!" he cried, for our sister was actually my aunt's namesake.

Jane and I went to our uncle and embraced him as well.

"Why did she have to go where I cannot follow her?" he asked the air, hysterical. "I was selfish, you see? I always wanted to die first. I knew that she would be taken in by you all. I had not planned any of this. I was a fool for not planning."

"Uncle," Jane uttered, "this is not your fault."

"It is!" he cried. "If I had been rich, I could have provided for you all. I could have kept you all here, safe, and your aunt would never have let the loss of her family affect her. And your aunt would have had her nieces with her, even if her illness was too strong for her to live. I could not have been alone to bury her. What sort of ending is that for my poor Jane? To die when her sister was gone, her nieces were far from her? Is that justice!"

He cried this, grabbing my face. Forcing to look into his heartbroken eyes, his bewildered expression, could not help but influence myself. The full weight of his grief had captured my focus, and I was humbled even more.

He loved my aunt, and now he was without the one stable element of his life. The great love that was like a fire keeping him warm had gone out. And now, he was left to the coldness of the remainder of his days without waking up next to her.

"No, it's not," I said, whispering. "Uncle, it never is."

"She was beautiful," he uttered. "She was so beautiful. You all don't remember it. She is part of the reason you all are so. You inherited she and your mother's looks."

"I am certain that she was Aphrodite remade," Jane assured him. "I am sure that she was."

"And I... I was the one to walk right up to that beauty and grab hold of it. I did that! I was a courageous man, standing in the presence of a lady who was so much superior to myself. And taking hold of all that beauty and making it mine."

"Uncle," I assured him, "we are sorry to have left you all. But we are here now."

"Yes," Kitty stressed. "We are here."

"And I will not leave," Mary uttered, "I will be in Hertfordshire, to stay with you."

"And we'll invite you to our homes often," Jane assured him. "We shall remain as a part of your lives now."

He smiled sadly, tapping our hands.

"You are good girls," he uttered. "Such good girls."

We remained a little longer, but we could tell that it made our uncle uncomfortable to speak to the gentlemen after such an outburst.

So, we assured him that we sisters would revisit him often, which he agreed to.

As he escorted us out of the house, to offer our farewells, he looked at our husbands.

"Colonel Fitzwilliam, Mr. Bingley and Mr. Darcy," he said, "you have my nieces' happiness in your hands. Do right by it."

"We will, sir," Mr. Darcy said, "we assure you."

"Good. It would break my heart to see them unhappy in their life. Protect them...in a way that some of us were unable to."

"Their predicament led them to finding us," Colonel Fitzwilliam assured him. "You did not disappoint anyone, or fail anyone, sir. It is merely that everyone has their path to walk down. And as you can see, your nieces found the path themselves. You have done well, Mr. Philips."

"Yes," Mr. Bingley stressed, "very well, sir."

On our way home, I whispered to Mr. Darcy.

"How do you feel?" I asked him.

"As if I have misjudged your uncle for too long."

"We are both guilty of that. Our uncle, all this time, was a true romantic. Much must be said of him. We must invite him to Pemberley. If we do not, he will give way to his sadness, and we might lose him to his grave before his time."

"We will."

I kissed his hand.

"Well then, to the proper path, we go."

Chapter 9

Where One Door Closes...

After taking notes for Mr. Hunnicutt's class, Charlotte Lucas was sitting in the library, copying the notes for the records.

She did not look up as the door opened, guessing who it was.

"Mr. Hanley," she said, over her shoulder, "that had better be you."

There was no response.

Charlotte, however, was no fool, and did not leave everything to chance. When she was met by silence, she lowered her pen and held a letter opener in her hand. Especially since she heard the footsteps grow closer and closer.

Turning around sharply, she was met with the sight of Mr. Hanley and little Molly Gibson tiptoeing toward her. When she had turned to them, they grumbled, halting in their steps, and sighing out in frustration.

"Oh!" She laughed.

"Told you that we could not sneak up upon her," Mr. Hanley said to Little Molly.

"Well," Molly said, animated, "it was worth a try."

"And a good try too," Charlotte said, putting down the letter opener and opening her arms. Molly Gibson ran into them, and Charlotte lifted her on her lap. "Truly, I give you full marks for your manner of secrecy and subterfuge."

"I want to be a spy when I grow up," Molly said.

"A spy? Oh, but that is so dangerous!"

"I like danger."

"You are a child. Danger makes you feel brave. When you get older, you will learn that pirates are not that romantic, soldiers never get the dirt from their uniforms, adventurers always discover lands that other people are already on, and that prodigal children always return home eventually." Charlotte laughed.

"Forgive me, Miss Lucas, but that all cannot be true."

"Perhaps it is, or perhaps it's not." Charlotte gave Molly a face. "I will never tell you what part that is the truth, or what part is a lie. By the by, how is little Cynthia, Roger and Osborne?"

"Cynthia is learning to sing and play the pianoforte very well. I cannot learn like she has. I don't understand how to play."

"Oh, never fear. It does not do well to measure your talent at the speed of someone else. We all learn at different speeds. Education is about proficiency and not competition of timing. Remember that. It took me ten years to perfect my playing."

"Did it?"

"Oh yes. My friend, Elizabeth, and her sister, Mary, were always better than I was. In fact, they were better at me in many ways. And you know what I learned?"

"What?"

"That I ought not to care. Not at all. I had my own speed of life to follow and that was enough."

Charlotte pinched Molly's cheek, affectionately.

"And what of Roger and Osborne? You still have not mentioned them."

"I think...Roger still favors me."

"Does he?"

"Yes...he..."

"He what?"

"He asked me if we would marry when we grew up."

Charlotte's eyes widened and she looked at Mr. Hanley. This announcement clearly was news to Mr. Hanley as well because he looked at Charlotte and Molly, with alarm in his eyes. While his shock was intense, Charlotte's was brief. After all, she was accustomed to this sort of talk from children.

"Molly?" Charlotte asked. "Did you say yes?"

"I told him that he might hate me when I grew up. Especially since I might get ugly when I get older."

"You won't be. That was your answer to him?"

"He said that he thought I was pretty, and so I said, that when we grow up, I would marry him."

"Well, you have all the time in the world," Charlotte said, "and did Mr. and Mrs. Kirkpatrick learn of this engagement?"

"Yes, they do. Mrs. Kirkpatrick laughs, calls it a lot of nonsense, and Mr. Kirkpatrick grumbled and said nothing about it, except to tell our governess to give me a lecture. But Miss Maria has not talked to me about it at all. Besides, soon Roger and Osborne are going off to university eventually, so she says that he will not be worried about that."

Charlotte and Molly spoke a little while longer before Mr. Hanley interrupted.

"Molly," he said, going to the window, "the carriage is here to take you back to the Kirkpatrick residence. Come, little one, and I'll see you out."

"Will you come to dinner this Saturday?" Molly asked Charlotte before they parted.

"Oh, yes," Charlotte said, "and tell my sister that I will see her soon. Promise me that you will be kind to her. I know how children look at their governesses."

"She is nice to us, so we are nice to her."

"Very good, Little Molly."

"Well, not all governesses are kind. Miss Maria is, and that is all that we want. She is...rosy!"

Charlotte laughed.

Molly took Mr. Hanley's hand, and he led her out. Abandoning her seat, Charlotte walked to the window and looked out of it. She observed Mr. Hanley escorting Little Molly to the carriage, kissed her forehead and helped her into the carriage. He offered her some kind words before they parted.

Smiling, Charlotte returned to her task, and soon Mr. Hanley entered.

"Working on notes?" Mr. Hanley asked as he began to pull some books from the shelf.

"Yes. Mr. Hunnicutt's. His lectures are like honey, Dennison's are like a rapier, and yours..."

"Yes?"

"Are like air. It flows naturally."

Mr. Hanley smiled bashfully, looking down and cleaning his spectacles.

"Thank you, Miss Lucas."

"For what, Mr. Hanley?"

"For how you treat my niece. After she lost Miss Bennet —" he cut off when he realized that he labeled her wrong. In fact, the new title gave him pain. "Forgive me, I meant Mrs. Darcy. Well, after losing her, little Molly was in a bad way. I worried that she would never have another friend when the Bennets left. But she loves learning under your sister, and you are so very good with children. I thank you for that."

"You're welcome, but it's my experience that helps me through. When in Hertfordshire, I had quite a few siblings. So, I'm used to talking to children. It helps to have brothers and sisters. And the attempt is mutual. A woman can be kind to a child all that one wishes, however, the child has to like us in turn. Molly gave me a chance, and that helped a great deal. Also, I appreciate how you treat her."

"Me?" Mr. Hanley asked, putting his spectacles back on his face.

"Yes. You are not severe with her, and you talk to her in the right sort of way. I've seen fathers and mothers not understand such gentility towards their own children, let alone uncles. But you do talk correctly to her. That means a great deal."

Since Charlotte had been copying her notes all the time that she had been talking to Mr. Hanley, she didn't notice that he had been studying her.

Mr. Hanley did not presume that Charlotte was any great beauty. Her looks were nothing in comparison to Elizabeth's, or the other Bennet girls. However, it did not signify much. A person can be as plain as paper, however, there is something electric about their look—an attractive quality that strikes a person's eye.

Charlotte struck Mr. Hanley.

He felt a charm radiate from her, especially since she displayed her usefulness time and time again. She helped

Elizabeth marry, filled up the notetaker position nicely, supplanted Mrs. Darcy in Little Molly's eyes, and usefulness always has an attraction to the prudent.

Mr. Hanley believed in prudence. He cherished it.

And yet, he was also logical. Was he growing to feel for Miss Charlotte Lucas? Or were his sensibilities shifting from one lady to the other to repair his damaged heart? After all, a part of him was still in love with Mrs. Darcy. His heart was awake, and there was nothing for it.

He loved, and now he would love.

But love can transition so easily, and so wrongly. There was the possibility that he was shifting his affections because he might have wanted revenge on Elizabeth, and what better way than to choose her friend to do it with.

Mr. Hanley wanted to believe that he was better than that. But when leaning back, and considering everything, he had to acknowledge that he was as human as any other.

When she didn't hear any sound from him, Charlotte dipped her pen in the ink and looked at him.

"You are like a statue, Mr. Hanley."

"Oh," he said, shifting, "pray, forgive me."

"I do not imply that you must speak to entertain me. Naturally, one ought not to speak unless one feels compelled to. However, I am not accustomed to you being so very still and contemplating something without offering one word. I just had to inquire in case something was troubling you."

"You think something is troubling me?"

Charlotte looked at him, innocently.

"Am I wrong?"

He looked a little embarrassed.

"I am not wrong, am I?" Charlotte asked.

"No, you are not. But it is something that is wrong to discuss. At least, not at present."

"Then don't tell me. Never unveil anything because you have been found out."

"Oh, believe me," Mr. Hanley chuckled nervously, "you know that I believe in discretion."

"Because it is the better part of valor?"

"Indeed, it is the better part of valor."

"Well, whatever it is, I am willing to listen to anything, provided that it is something you wish to share. And when you wish to share it."

"Are you trustworthy?"

"Do you know that you always ask me that?"

"Yes, I do," he confirmed.

"And I always say yes."

"Yes, you do."

"And then you never tell me what ails you anyway." Charlotte smiled. "We like talking in circles, don't we?"

"Is there any chance that you find amusement in it?"

"Don't worry, I do. Now, I must finish this before Mr. Dennison's class."

"Is he still hard to you?"

"Yes, but I am accustomed to it."

"Do you want me to speak to him?"

"If his tone gets too harsh, then you can. Until then, I will handle him in my own way. But thank you for caring to protect me."

Mr. Hanley did not smile, but his eyes were gentle, showing his affection.

"Of course."

Charlotte was early to the lecture hall, so she was already setting up her desk at the back when Mr. Dennison entered.

When he did so, he grumbled when seeing her.

"Good afternoon, Mr. Dennison," Charlotte said, "I see that your disposition has not improved since yesterday, or the day before that."

"I will not suffer that sort of talk from a woman."

"But you will suffer me."

He walked to the desk and began to arrange his notes.

"Is that friend of yours married yet?" he asked, harsh.

"Yes, she is."

"They will be divorced by the end of the year, and she will return to Milton."

"What makes you predict that sort of nonsense?" Charlotte responded, losing her patience.

"She has tasted the life of independence. She worked for herself, earned her own income, and made her own decisions. Women who do that can't return to being idle housewives who are not given such liberty. They know what the other half of life is like."

"Elizabeth is very good at adjusting, and she loves Darcy." Pause. "Why can't you just admit that you miss Elizabeth? Would it be so hard?"

He looked at her, venomous.

"It is merely that her handwriting is superior to yours. If I am to suffer our notetaker being a woman, I prefer to have one who's writing is legible. Unlike yours."

"Oh, Mr. Dennison, you are always so *polite*."

"I speak the truth, whereas others are too soft toward you."

"You call it soft. I call it congeniality."

"When it is really all just a façade."

"You like me, sir."

He gasped, banging his fist on the table.

"What did you say?"

"I did not mean romantically. I meant as a person. You like me. That's why you are so cruel to me. It's because you feel comfortable enough to do so. In a sad and sick sort of fashion, that is your way of showing affection."

Mr. Dennison's lip turned into a fine line.

"Don't speak nonsense, Miss Lucas. It does not become you."

"Beg your pardon."

As Charlotte continued to arrange things on her desk, Mr. Dennison continued to sort his notes and massage his throat, for his voice box.

Indirectly, he did not take his eyes off her. There was a question that he wanted to ask her, that was burning in his brain. But he knew that it would be best to go about it indirectly.

"I have not seen your sister come as often as she used to."

Charlotte bit her lip. She knew where this conversation was headed towards, and she did not want to approach the subject. But now there was nothing for it.

"Has she forgotten you?" he asked.

"No," Charlotte responded. "She is a governess. Her time is not her own as much as she would like. Instead, the Kirkpatricks have invited me to dine with them every Saturday. It's easier for me to visit them, as opposed to her seeing me here."

"Well, she ought to come around more."

As the eldest, Charlotte felt the defensiveness rise within her, and she decided not to avoid the subject. Rather it was time to face it.

"No," Charlotte declared.

"No?" Mr. Dennison responded, stopping his actions, and looking at her.

"No."

"No what?"

"Maria is too young for you."

Mr. Dennison turned a redder shade of bitter.

"I beg your pardon? When did I ever say—"

"You didn't need to. You think that I never noticed how you look at her when she visits me? If you thought that you have been discreet about it, you are mistaken. Even the other professors have noticed."

"You are wrong."

"Am I?"

With his lips like a tightline, Mr. Dennison took a few steps forward but stopped soon after.

"I do not... young women have married older men than myself."

"That practice only works if there is a great deal of compatibility and mutual affection. I will not let my sister align herself to a man who would disrespect her so. And forgot what true love was long ago."

"Let me tell you something, Miss Lucas. Sometimes a man can be old and still know what true love is."

"But do you know it? My sister is kind and gentle, as well as pretty. You don't need a woman like that. You would devour her. You need a hard woman who can face you."

"You are wrong. You know nothing."

"I know my sister, and I will do right by her. So, I know

everything. She is a young woman with her whole life ahead of her. I will not see her life be ruined. Not by you or by anyone."

"I—"

He was cut off by something in the doorway.

Charlotte followed his gaze and saw Mr. Hanley standing there. Though he was still, there was a power that radiated from Mr. Hanley's figure. Especially from his eyes. There was a simple ferocity to his look, and it spoke volumes of the passion underneath.

"Dennison," Mr. Hanley said, "is your tone and discussion fit for a lecture hall? It is not. Go to your lessons, man."

Mr. Dennison groaned and returned to his preparations.

Looking at Mr. Hanley, Charlotte Lucas gave him a grateful look. He received it with a kind look of his own and left the doorway.

Charlotte felt the comfort of knowing that, no matter what, she was never alone.

Once more, Charlotte had to sit through Mr. Dennison's class, angry that he was a magnificent teacher.

When he finished, and the students were all filing out of the hall, Charlotte did the best she could to pack up her items quickly into the desk.

Despite her efforts, naturally Mr. Dennison finished packing his briefcase, and he began to leave. As he passed her, he stopped and turned to her.

Unable to ignore his look, Charlotte turned and looked at him.

"Is this where you tell me that you will continue to

watch my sister's every move when she visits me?" Charlotte asked.

He rolled his jaw, back and forth.

"I..."

"Yes?"

"What do you want from me?" he asked, sincere.

Naturally, this unnerved Charlotte.

"What do you want from me?" Charlotte echoed. "To respect you?"

"Yes."

"I cannot do that until you respect me."

"I am not that old."

"Whether you think so or not, your spirit is. And something within it died long ago."

Mr. Dennison put his hat on and left her.

Charlotte breathed out. Excepting for Mr. Dennison and his temperament, life in Milton had been kind to her.

Chapter 10

Discomfort & Decision

At Longbourn, I found myself with a natural inclination to go to my father's library and see the room that he spent so much of his life in. I felt compelled to do so, as if a force drove me to believe that a part of his soul was still there. Like a spirit that dwelled amongst the books.

Never had I been one to believe in ghosts. However, sometimes, a person can go back on a constant belief of theirs and accept the idea of the fantastic.

As if an invisible force pushed me onward, I walked to the library. When doing so, I saw my father's image eagerly walking down the hall to the door, with my mother walking in the neighboring room, calling out for him, but getting no reply.

Even though that image conjured all sorts of evidence to their disjointed union, there was something bittersweet about that memory.

It was another memory to be missed and had gone unappreciated at the time. Now it meant something.

When I reached the library's door, I placed my hand on the doorknob, turned it, and entered it freely.

For a brief moment, I looked forward to the smell of the books, of the scent of familiarity to find its way to me.

All those hopes had been dashed to the wayside when I was not met with a memory of my father.

Instead, there was Mr. Collins, sitting in my father's armchair, with the fire raging beside him, reading a copy of *Fordyce's Sermons.*

Fordyce's Sermons!

That old, outdated, primitive, and demeaning strict book of maxims that had been overlooked by generations since its initial publication decades ago.

It was strange, but something about that image had unleashed a wrath and seething contempt within me, adding fuel to a fire that was already ignited.

I was angry.

And now I knew what had driven me there.

What ghost had ushered me onward.

It was the spirit of Retribution.

"Mrs. Darcy," he uttered, closing the book, and placing it on the desk. My father's desk.

"Good morning, Mr. Collins. I had come to the library to seek a favorite book of mine."

"Well, my library is open to anyone."

"My father's library."

"Beg your pardon?"

"My *father's* library."

My eyes were like slits as I closed the door behind me.

Despite that I was a great deal shorter than him and not as strong, I detected fear in his eyes. He was afraid of me. Good. That was as it should be. I wanted him to be afraid. I wanted him to shake in his boots and feel the agony of being so wholly intimidated by a smaller creature, such as myself.

And I took pleasure in it.

"My father's library," I repeated, even stronger than before.

"We-well," he stammered, "naturally, you must think it as such, since you are accustomed to calling it thus."

"Because in my mind, it still is his. It always will be because his soul is here. And every intention of not seeing a man come into his house and drive all his children out of it, like a cold and cruel devil who had no sense of feeling, no understanding of God, and any of the teachings that our holy book contained. The same holy book that you swore to uphold, Mr. Collins. And that you failed to do so."

"Mrs. Darcy, I am astonished to hear you address me as thus."

"I address you in the way that you deserve." The wrath in my eyes was replaced by somberness and sadness. "How could you? How could you drive us out of our home? So soon after we lost our parents, our protectors, and call yourself a man of God? Did you not take anything from the book that you studied so long? A book about exerting peace, charity, kindness, and love. And vengeance on those who commit such atrocities as hypocrites like you have done. Tell me, William? How could you do it?"

Hearing me call him by his first name seemed to be even more alarming than all the other aspersions that I cast at his feet. His face blanched and he looked uncertain.

"I was within my legal right."

"Yes, your legal right. But what of your moral one? What of that?"

"I attempted to do right by you all, as you had seen. I came here, with every intention of marrying one of you, to save the family, and I was repaid with denial."

"Ah," I said, "here it comes down to it. You wanted revenge, didn't you? You wanted revenge upon me for not accepting your hand."

"That was not it."

"Yes, it was. The only reason that you deny it now was because it would show you in a demonic state, and your sensibilities cannot face that. It cannot face the reality that your soul has the ability to be as dark and sinister as any other."

"I am no such man."

"You are no more or less human than us, Mr. Collins. Your piety is not a cloak that can hide that. You did something evil. You were angry that I would not have you, despite that I did us both the greatest of favors. You were angry at Charlotte because she would not forsake me or my feelings. You wanted revenge on not only Longbourn, but Hertfordshire as a whole. And you got it. I was not the woman for you, and I saved you from an obligation of virtue. I gave you the freedom for us both to choose the right person. But when our parents died, I never would have imagined that you would have driven us out so quickly, like a fury. You had your work, your patroness, and you could have given us time to find new homes for ourselves and taken Longbourn when we had settled in a permanent place. But you arrived two weeks after their passing, stressing us to leave your house. Your house! Did you earn it? Did you strive for it?"

"I inherited it. I was born into that role. You cannot blame me for that."

"I don't blame you for your inheritance; I blame you for how you obtained it. You could have been congenial. You could have been a proper clergyman."

"Very well, since you want it to be plain and true, I will speak truly. It hurt that you rejected me."

"It hurt your pride, sir. That is a sin of the top seven."

"It didn't just hurt my pride," he said, affected. "It also hurt my heart."

"Your heart?"

"Yes."

I sighed, angry that he was willing to insult my intelligence.

"Is this where you expect me to believe that your affection for me was anything other than transient and disinterested?"

"It was. I was fond of you."

"Of me?"

"Yes."

"You only noticed me because Jane was already chosen for Mr. Bingley. Do not think me ignorant of the shift in your attentions and transferred preferences from her to me?"

"Of course, I preferred her first. She was the eldest. Seniority is the first thing that we are told to consider in life. As a clergyman, it was my duty. But when she was chosen for another, I shifted to you afterwards."

"Because I was the second oldest."

"Yes. That was it, at first. However, soon, Elizabeth, I... well, I grew fond of you."

I blinked.

"William, is this some form of a trick?"

"It's not a trick. I am not doing this to gain any sympathy, but that you should know me. I developed a passionate attachment toward you. I began to find you beautiful. Therefore, it hurt when you rejected me."

Oh, no!

Why did this have to be what he said? Why did there always have to be some form of excuse, and some desire to seek pity from another quarter?

But then I realized all the rest of it. All the moments afterward. His moment of victimhood would not distract me.

Turning away from him, I walked to the window and steadied myself.

Mr. Collins, on the other hand, viewed my hesitancy as a means of him gaining ground.

"Can you not see that I am as human as any other? As you said before?" he asked. "You spurned me."

"I did the right thing," I responded. "And this is not the silence that you expect. This is not a woman suddenly turning around and feeling pity for you. I thank you for growing to care for me. It is kindly meant, it is. But it does not justify all your actions afterwards. First, you never distributed your affections toward me in any way other than obligation and disinterestedness. You even mentioned that in your proposal. You never mentioned love."

"I spoke clumsily. I was not accustomed to proposing to a woman before."

"I feel sorry for any pain that I caused you, but since you never showed me your heart, how could you expect me to understand it? And whatever your heartbreak, it does not justify how you acted the day after that, and every day afterwards. I rejected you properly, and you cursed my family's name up hill and down dale. You proposed to my friend the next day, to gather your wounded pride, with no affection for her. Then, like a vulture, you swooped down upon our tragedy and picked at us like we were carcasses on the road. And you were rude to Charlotte. All of this is not justified by a wounded heart. In the back of your mind, surely you know that. If you say that you once cared for me, then do you show no proper feeling?"

"Proper feeling?"

"You could have left us in a place where we were destitute, homeless, no man would marry us, and we were lost to the whims of relative's plans. Was it right that my sisters had to suffer because of the revenge you took out on me? Is that right? Is that fair?"

"I—"

"No," I said for him. "Do not excuse yourself, do not justify cruelty exerted on casting out a family, do not explain your evil away, and lay it all down to you being a creature of pity. If you had loved me properly, then you would have never made my sisters and I homeless. I have seen what true love is, and when it is such, the man doesn't ruin your life because he can't have you. That's not love; that's obsession. I was an obsession of yours. Not a great love of yours. That's the difference. The man I married loved me. And he would not have made me homeless. He would not have made my sisters homeless. That is love. Look what you did."

I walked up to Mr. Collins. He tried to back away from me, but that did not stop me at all. I approached him to the point where there was barely two inches between him.

I wanted him to see the fire in my eyes.

The anger that fueled me and startled him so.

"Look what you did! You acted, under the pretense of love, as a devil. You threw women to the wind and called yourself a man of God. The same God that defended Mary Magdalene. Who died loving the world! And now you are a shame to that same lord. You embarrassed him, because your vanity was hurt, and your heart was affected. You don't know what true love is, William. True love ought not to be a weapon to destroy. You used it as a hammer to bring down upon my family. And is this the man who claims to have loved me? The man who practically threw us out of our door and did not even look at us as we cried as we left. That is you, sir?"

Mr. Collins began to weep.

I crossed my hands in front of me, finally happy that he showed some sort of shame. Or at least, I hope that it had been shame.

"You are not the hero that you think you are, William. It is time that you saw it."

"You are cruel to me."

"You were cruel first. And you hurt because you hear me. You hear my words, and now they are affecting you. This is good, sir. Because now, you are truly listening to the pain of others. Go forward, William, and be a better man."

I went to the door and placed my hand on the knob.

"I want to say that I am grateful for any affection you may have grown to feel for me. And I want to say that I am sorry that I hurt your heart. However, that is not what you should know, because it would make you pity yourself again. And think that you are in the right. But no jilted affections justify the villain that you became."

Mr. Collins sat down, overpowered.

"Remember that, sir. And if you are disposed to try and

force me from this house, my husband will have none of that, and his aunt would punish you for it for the rest of your miserable life. I didn't come to destroy you, William. I just came to force you to realize that you almost destroyed our lives. And you now have to live with that knowledge."

I left him alone to accept that he was a villain of his own story all along.

Chapter 11

Another Failed Proposal

"He felt for you?" Mr. Darcy repeated the question.

After my discussion with Mr. Collins, I went to Mr. Darcy and told him everything that had transpired between me and my cousin. I wanted him to know everything about my life, and that there would be no secrets between us. If I had to start a life with him, I knew that I had to make the first step. Too much of our history had been disheveled from us not speaking plain truths to each other. A resurgence of that habit was not going to start with me.

"Yes," I confirmed. "It turns out, in that perverse mind of his, he did."

Mr. Darcy walked away from me, walked up to the fireplace, and banged his hand slightly on the mantel. I did not flinch. I had suspected he would do something like that.

"And knowing him, he had to justify himself in that manner, didn't he?"

"Yes, he did. Darcy, I doubted his affections since it led to malicious intent. But Mr. Collins is a man and knowing other men is your province. Do you think there was anything sincere about his affections, or were they flimsy at best?"

"Oh, it was real."

I blinked.

"It was?"

"Yes. In our world, seniority is the natural preference. There are even still places where a woman cannot receive gentleman callers until the elder siblings are already engaged or in some form of courtship. Once he shuffled off that obligation, and he could transfer his affections, you were natural. We men value reserve in this world, but many men secretly still value a woman of spirit. He probably did grow to feel for you and your conversation. And with some men and women, spurned love is destructive. As frightening as it is, love has launched military ships, it's killed, it's burned. It's a powerful emotion, and when it takes hold, it can set a fire within that sets everything ablaze. It can drive a mind to insanity."

"So, Mr. Collins is justified?"

"No," Mr. Darcy replied, "not in the slightest. While love can do these things, any true person, of steady character and proper feeling, should never justify their evil. Even if they commit it, they should own up to their villainy. Mr. Collins used his heart as a justification for abandoning you to the unknown. He was at an age where he should have eventually defeated his sensibilities and acted out of compassion. He did not do that. He submitted to the evil sides of himself and there's an end of it. Eventually, one must seek atonement. Do not regret your harsh words toward him or expect that you must allow his sinister behavior because of his wounded heart. It is never wise to make excuses for cruelty."

"Thank you," I said, kissing his hand, "for a second, I was about to doubt myself."

"Do *not* do that. That's how the wrong people always win: because others justify their actions, out of pity. Stand firm, Lizzy. Stand firm. You committed no evil, except make the right decision for your heart and peace of mind."

Still angry, Mr. Darcy sat down beside me.

"I just despise all of this."

"Yes, I..."

"No, you do not know what I mean. Lizzy, I know how Wickham favored you once. I know that Mr. Hanley was in love with you. For all that I know, perhaps even Nicholas Higgins might have felt something. Maybe even Plato for all that I know, as well as Robert, Liam and Colin."

"Nicholas and Plato looked on us as family. Robert, Liam, and Colin simply admired us as people who cared for their people."

"Robert, Liam and Colin favored you. I saw it in their eyes. And with Plato and Nicholas, with us men, you never fully know the depths of our hearts, because we keep it shut away. With those men, at least I have the comfort of knowing that they felt a fondness for all you Bennet sisters, and Margaret. But with Wickham, Mr. Hanley, and now Mr. Collins... I just don't enjoy men preferring the woman that I love."

"Oh," I replied, assured. "Well, you had better not enjoy it."

"Oh," He said, amused, "you are not upset with my overprotectiveness?"

"I want you to be protective. You have no need to worry

about me being whisked away. Not today, not tomorrow, and not ever. However, that does not mean that you should lay back and be indifferent. I want you to care and not be complaisant about that sort of thing."

I took his hand.

"Care, Mr. Darcy. Always care."

He leaned forward and kissed me.

Our moment of earned intimacy did not last long, because suddenly we heard some determined footsteps on another side of the trees that were near where Mr. Darcy and I sat.

Mr. Darcy and I separated, I stood up and straightened my gown and placed my hands in front of me.

From around the green, Margaret Hale entered. When seeing us, her cheeks reddened, out of embarrassment.

"Lizzy and Mr. Darcy," she said, perturbed, "forgive me. I intrude."

"No, it is well, Miss Hale," Mr. Darcy said. "Perhaps I ought to leave you both alone, for I see that you have something of import to discuss."

"In truth, you both ought to remain. I was in the house when I heard the news, and I thought that it was best that you learned of it."

"What is it?" I asked. "Is something wrong?"

"No one is hurt, but there is some difficulty. A spot of bother if you will. I know it's not my news to tell, but I know that Mary would want you to know."

"Know what? Where is she?"

"In her bedroom. She has just received a proposal of marriage from Mr. Collins."

Mr. Darcy and I were aghast.

"What?" I asked. "He proposed to her?"

"Yes. And she refused him."

At first, Darcy and I could scarcely believe what we were hearing.

"Mr. Collins proposed to Mary, and she refused him?" I repeated.

"Yes," Margaret said.

"Where is Mary now?"

"She is in her room, and when last I was in the house, Mr. Collins has retreated into the library."

Immediately I began to run to the house, dragging her along. Darcy, instinctively, ran alongside us.

"I can't believe it," I said to Darcy and Margaret, "what is Mr. Collins about?"

"He was probably feeling some ill-placed insecurity from your argument," Mr. Darcy explained, "and he needed to find acceptance somewhere. I've seen such behavior before."

"What argument?" Margaret asked me.

"I will explain in a moment. How did Mary look when you saw her?"

"Perturbed and very out of sorts."

"I wonder what Mr. Collins had said to her..."

Twenty minutes earlier...

Mary was playing with Mr. Collins's child on the carpet in the parlor when she had felt eyes upon her. Sensing a shadow in the doorway, Mary had looked up and she saw Mr. Collins watching her successful attempts as a mother.

He smiled at her, and Mary smiled in return, until she looked into his eyes. There was something anxious about his expression. In fact, there was almost a quiet and subtle apprehension to him.

"How does Miss Bennet do this afternoon?" Mr. Collins had asked her.

"She does well," Mary said, kissing the child's forehead, "and so does our little lion here." She made a face at the child. "You are a lion, aren't you? Rrrroooarrr!"

The child echoed the chant, Mary had laughed, and they embraced.

As Hill entered the hallway, pouring some water in a vase of flowers, Mr. Collins had called to her.

"Hill, take our little lion upstairs, will you? Miss Bennet deserves a rest for today."

"Yes, Mr. Collins," Hill said, taking the child upstairs. "Come on, let's see if you can roar for me? Rrroooarrr!"

The child roared again, and Hill laughed as they had disappeared upstairs.

Now that they were alone, Mary straightened her dress and began to put all the toys away in a chest.

"Your little lion gets stronger every day," Mary said.

"Oh, come now, Miss Bennet. After all this time, I would think that you would begin to think of my child as *our* little lion."

Thinking nothing curious about this comment, Mary laughed as she picked up the rest of the toys, packed them away and began to put the chest aside.

"Well, if a woman is to be a cousin, she ought to do it properly."

"Mary," Mr. Collins said, standing near her, "I have to thank you."

"Oh. That is very kind of you. I am happy to help family, at a difficult time."

"That is another thing that I find about you, that makes you superior to your sisters."

When hearing this, Mary squinted. While she appreciated the comment, she found that she did not like that Mr. Collins was about to disparage her sisters, for the sake of building her up.

"Really, Mr. Collins," Mary said, "I thank you for whatever you are about to say, but you do not have to puff me up by setting my sisters down."

"Naturally, of course, of course. But you must understand, Mary, and I am certain that you see it yourself, being so keen. You must see that your sisters don't always understand the proper role of a lady in society."

"I do not think that I understand you," Mary said, sitting at the pianoforte. "My sisters are all married to great men. They are more ladylike than I am."

"Well, of all of you, you are the most congenial, for you are obedient and understand the proper role of a lady is to be a proper housewife, and mother to those forsaken in the family. And to practice temperance and attentiveness to when a man requires a lady to assist him in all matters of the household. The way that you came to my aid is something that I never forget, cousin Mary. And I am sensible to it."

When Mary had heard this, she found that she did not take much comfort in it. At one time in her life, she might have been flattered. But experience and a wider acquaintance with the world had enhanced her mind and self-purpose. Her place in life was not blind obedience, and it never could be again. Mr. Collins's mindset was still one of the past, and she was now beginning to look to the future.

"You were a man with a child of his own," Mary said, "I merely knew that it would be difficult until you can stabilize your household. If you are telling me all this because you feel that you have reached that place, then I am not offended. I have no scruples on returning to London and attempting to find employment somewhere."

"Employment!" Mr. Collins had responded, sneering at the word with disgust. "Oh, that I would save you from such a fate."

"Save me?"

"Yes. Cousin Mary, you will never have to work and be put in a demeaning situation of life again. I give you the greatest gift, Cousin Mary."

Mary smiled.

"Well, what gift would that be?"

"I give you myself!"

"And not only myself," Mr. Collins had said, "but the life and welfare of my child, and you shall also take your mother's place and be the mistress of Longbourn."

"Mr. Collins," Mary had remarked, "Are you proposing marriage to me?"

"Yes, I am. My fair cousin, you have proven to be vital to the running of this house, being a proper lady of going where you are needed, being obliging, and possessing such piety as well as economy. And therefore, there is nothing left but for me to offer you my hand, my income, and my house."

Mr. Collins took Mary's hand and got down on one knee.

"Therefore, when we are married, you will make me the happiest of men."

"Mr. Collins," Mary blurted out, removing her hand

from his and standing up, "you asked me while not asking me at all."

"Oh, forgive me. Due to the importance of your place in the household, I thought that your answer was already given and implied."

"No, it was not implied." Mary walked to the other side of the room, breathing heavily. This was a day of great anxiety that she had not been prepared for.

"Mr. Collins," Mary said, "a proposal is something that every woman looks forward to with anticipation. At one time in history, I would have welcomed your attentions. I would have been flattered by them." Then, at the turn of her countenance, Mr. Collins saw the answer. And it was the last thing that he would have wanted. "But today, I cannot. Forgive me, Mr. Collins, but I cannot marry you."

When hearing her rejection, Mr. Collins grew still. Naturally, this was neither the response that he expected nor needed. Since part of the inspiration for his rushed and sudden proposal was also due to his need for a restoration to his wounded pride.

Elizabeth Darcy had set him down and he needed to have his sense of security and pride return to him. Therefore, something that he had considered lightly now was rushed, to help lessen his insecurity and hasten the balance in his life.

Therefore, not imagining that maybe his proposal was not coming from the very best of intentions, but rather selfish ones, the hasty stroke went awry, and he was ignorant as to why that was.

But Mary knew. And no more was she blinded by his folly.

"You cannot?" Mr. Collins repeated.

"No, I cannot. We are family, Mr. Collins, and I come

to assist you. However, I think that you and I are in two different places. You speak of blind obedience, but I have developed myself in a way that I do not think you understand. My assistance to your situation was not done for the sake of submitting to you as if you are a superior power. It was not done for the sake of adhering to your standards, but rather out of my own morality. Also, the way that you speak of choosing me it is because I am of use. No woman wants to be chosen for that reason, solely. It must be an enhancement to her charms, but not her only charm. I may be serious, but I want to be chosen because I want to be loved by the man. You have not mentioned love for me, because love is not what you feel. It's something that you have never felt. And I don't fear having a vanity about me, in that I do not want to marry without it."

Mary went to the door to leave.

"Mary," Mr. Collins called. "I do believe that you are mistaken."

"No!" Mary cried, wielding on him. "I am not mistaken! I face reality. And when I say reality, I refer to the reality that is, and not the reality that you would have me see—an untrue one. And the truth is that I am not your first choice for a wife, nor your second, or your third, or fourth. I am the fifth, chosen out of desperation. Well, I do not want to be your fifth choice. I don't want to be any man's fifth choice. I want to be his first. What am I to you, but a tool to be used as? I am not a function. I am a woman, who has a heart. A beating heart! I feel. As strongly as any woman or man that lived, do I feel! Do you know the truth? The plain truth. When you came to Longbourn, I admired you. I admired your profession, your pursuit of morality, to the point where it blinded me from your flaws. I adored you, Mr. Collins. And then I had to watch you choose every woman besides me, then harden yourself against our situation and throw us to the wolves of uncertainty. And now you want me to be grateful? For what? For being nothing but a function to you? And to be the greatest mistake that my heart ever made? I do not choose you—because I am too good for you, sir. You are no gift! And until you understand my self-worth, until you come to me because you see a wonderful woman, do not come to me at all!"

Having given her final word, Mary dashed out of the room and rushed up the stairs.

When doing so, she found Margaret Hale on the landing, who had looked a touch embarrassed: she had overheard it all.

"Mary," Margaret said.

"Don't look at me now," Mary cried. "I do not want anyone to look at me."

With that, Mary had rushed into her room and closed the door behind her.

'Poor Mary!' Margaret had thought.

When I rushed back into the house, with Margaret beside me, I looked at Mr. Darcy.

"I must go to my sister. What should be done about Mr. Collins?"

Mr. Darcy rubbed his lip, aggravated. "Well, this will be another trial to my life."

"What do you mean?"

"I must go and speak with him."

"You will talk with Mr. Collins?"

"I must. He has proven to not always make the best

decisions after he has received a rejection. I fear what he may do."

I touched Mr. Darcy's hand. "When you married me, I brought much useless baggage along, didn't I?"

He smiled. "No, you didn't. You did not bring it at all, but it merely suffered itself to be chained to you. I will do the best I can."

"I know that you will be splendid."

Kissing him on the cheek, I joined Margaret as we went upstairs.

"Poor Mary," I said.

"Yes," Margaret said, but she grabbed my arm before I knocked on Mary's door. "Lizzy?"

"Yes?"

"Hear everything that Mary has to say. She is not like us."

"Not like us?"

"You and I have received two offers of marriage from men who we were the first choice of. And the men that we have chosen were our first large love. With Mary, it is harder on her. She was no one's first choice and was passed over, often. We were loved, properly. I do not think Mary was, and she simply hid the pain of it."

I was a little disconcerted by this revelation.

"Oh. I had not thought of that."

"Her character is not as fortified as ours is. Under all that reserve is a fragile woman. Appeal to that side of her. She might need it."

"Very well."

Preparing myself, I walked to Mary's door and knocked on it.

"I want to be left alone," Mary cried from the other side of it.

"Mary?" I asked. "Please, let me talk to you."

"Oh, is that you, Lizzy?"

"Yes."

"Forgive me, come in."

I opened the door and was confronted with Mary's tearstained face. Never had I seen her cry since she was a child. All sense was gone and only sensibility was in its place.

"Oh, Mary!"

"He sees me as nothing more than a tool for use," Mary cried. "That's all I will ever be."

Closing the door behind me, I rushed to her and held her as she shook.

"Lizzy, why did he have to propose?" she cried. "He ruined everything. And he only plans to use me. I am tired of no one seeing my heart. I am tired of it."

"I know, my dear. I know."

"It's not fair. It's not fair."

"No, it's not. Mary, you are loved."

"But never by the man who would love me."

"You are young. There is time. Do not care for Mr. Collins' words. You have family. You will never feel alone or useless. You have worth, dearest. You have worth."

I continued to hold her as she told me the entire story of how Mr. Collins proposed. With every bit of the narration, I grew even more sour at our tactless cousin.

I was almost resolved to speak with him again, until I remembered Mr. Darcy.

I wondered what both men were saying to each other.

Chapter 12

Humility

When Mr. Darcy went to the library, he braced himself for either false reports of how the proposal went, or Mr. Collins would speak all sorts of foolishness.

He knocked on the door and Mr. Collins said 'enter'. When seeing Mr. Darcy, Mr. Collins's face turned red from embarrassment. Doing his best to overcome his shame, Mr. Collins began to speak of Lady Catherine de Bourgh.

However, not wishing to spend more time with the man than he had to, Mr. Darcy raised up his hand and closed the library's door, to give them privacy.

"Sir," Mr. Darcy began, "My aunt does well, but I presume that you are speaking of her because you do not want to approach a subject that might give you pain. Well, I come to speak with you on that score. I have heard that you offered Miss Mary Bennet a proposal of marriage. And that she refused you."

Mr. Collins was silent over this.

"I do not take pleasure in my secrets being so easily bandied about," Mr. Collins said.

"If you are unsettled at my impertinence, I do not regret my frank way of speaking. I do it for your benefit, sir. You have proposed to a woman and were refused. I think it best to talk about it."

"A proper gentleman would not wish to speak of such matters."

"We are family, sir. What ought to be done is not wrong to do. I am your cousin now, and Miss Mary is my sister too. You both are a part of my life, and so I ought to care." Even though it hurt Mr. Darcy to acknowledge any sort of familial relation to Mr. Collins, it had to be done for the sake of making Mr. Collins feel obliged to reveal much to him. "Also, Mr. Collins, you have received rejections before."

Mr. Collins looked at the floor, hiding his apprehension.

"You are neither the first man nor the last," Mr. Darcy answered smoothly. "Many a man has received rejections. It is not the end of the world. However, I come to you because your reaction to rejections has often led to you making hasty decisions. Mr. Collins, I think, as man to man, you ought to discuss what happened, and how you feel."

Mr. Collins rubbed his face, nervous.

"Sir," Mr. Darcy said, "if you respect my aunt, then I request that you respect me. And tell me what happened."

Mr. Darcy was such an intimidating force that Mr. Collins slowly began to unveil everything that had occurred with his third failed marriage proposal.

When he finished, Mr. Darcy was as analytical and objective as he had been with Thornton's proposal to Margaret Hale.

"Mr. Collins," Mr. Darcy said, "I am sensible to the agonies that a man feels when he has been refused. I understand that you may be upset. But I need to offer you advice to help you now."

"Help me? Oh, Mr. Darcy, you are too good, sir! Too good of a man! As good and proper as your aunt."

"You may not think so when I distribute the advice. But please, I request that you hear me. For in matters such as this, I know myself to be right. First, I will stress upon you to be kind and courteous to Miss Mary when you see her again. She has been like a second mother to your child, and that alone makes her above reproach from you. You were a clergyman. I advise that you remember the forgiveness that you preached of."

"If you think I was wrong to take over Longbourn, then—"

"Mr. Collins, you *were* wrong. It is time that you see that about yourself. Now here comes my next bit of advice. Sir, I cannot order you to listen to it, but I ask you to. You expected Miss Mary to be honored by your proposal and were shocked when she was not. It's because she had every right not to be honored by it. No woman wants to be chosen as a last resort. That's how you treated her. It makes her feel as if you view her as less than nothing."

"That is not what I meant."

"I think it is, and you cannot separate that *intention* to your *intention* of doing your duty. Marriage is not a duty; it's a choice. She was your fifth choice. There is nothing flattering about that. Also, no woman ought to be obliged for being chosen. You look at ladies in such a fashion. This is something that you must accept. You offended her when you proposed to her."

Mr. Collins was about to speak but Mr. Darcy overrode him.

"Do not speak. But listen. You have a tendency, Mr.

Collins, to try so hard to be obliging that you accidentally cause offense as you do so. You hurt her. And you need to reflect upon that. It is not her that must aspire to be worthy of you. It is time that you aspire to being worthy of her. And until you choose her because she is the chief object of your affections, and because she wishes to choose you in turn, you cannot expect anything but the response you were given."

Mr. Darcy stood up, obligingly patted Mr. Collins on the shoulder and went to the doorway.

"But again, sir," Mr. Darcy continued, "I must stress that I will not allow any woman in this household to endure any unpleasantness. My aunt favors the Bennet sisters and would not take too kindly to hearing any harsh words said against them. However, again, I am aware of the pain of being rejected. I am sorry for you, but that is as far as it goes. Think of my words before you make any action. And apologize to her."

"Apologize?" Mr. Collins repeated.

"Yes. Apologize for every offense you gave to Miss Mary. She deserved better than to be overlooked by you for so long, as well as for you to have abandoned her to fate. Now there's a good man."

Mr. Darcy left Mr. Collins alone, wondering if any advice he gave would be put into action.

Chapter 13

The Apology

That day was also the day we were to dine at Lucas Lodge for a dinner party. This was a welcome relief, for it drove us from the house for a duration. It was even greater relief because Mr. Collins made his apologies that he could not attend. And even then, he did not deliver this news himself, but used Hill as his messenger, where we were well aware that he had retreated to his bedroom, as sanctuary.

This was precisely how it ought to be.

Mr. Collins was not in a state where he could gather any pleasure from the sight of us, we would be awkward around him, and he would be in no mood to be a charming guest at Lucas Lodge.

When we made his excuses to Sir William and Lady Lucas, there was not even a lamentation over his absence. Somehow, Mr. Collins and his late wife really had found a way to sour the Lucas' opinion of them both. They were company that everyone withstood but took little joy in seeing.

Through the dinner party, I observed Mary, worried

that the earlier events of the day must have worn on her, rendering her quiet and reflective.

Rather it was the reverse. She was more outgoing, more open to conversation and easily submitting to when she was called on to play music for when the younger people wished to dance. Since it was difficult to hold very private discussions in such a social scene, I was afraid to ask her about anything too intimate.

Kitty, on the other hand, was entirely different on the matter.

"She is stretching her legs of liberty," Kitty informed Jane, me, Margaret, Georgiana, and Frederick Hale.

"Legs of liberty?" Frederick asked. "To what are you referring?"

"Sometimes, when a person experiences a tragedy of sorts, or a very difficult moment, they feel trapped at where they are. Even if that place is their house. So, in times like that, they feel as if they must get out. Over and over, they tell themselves, 'get out'. Even if it was just a dinner party at Lucas Lodge, she had a moment where she had to tell herself that she was free of something that she wants to put behind herself. Even if it's just a moment, this time gives her levity. And she is probably taking every opportunity to enjoy that."

"You were able to discern that just by observing her."

"Actually, not really. I know because she told me."

I rolled my eyes.

As fate would have it, truer words could not have been spoken. For when we returned to Longbourn, Mary's transition shifted the very minute we arrive back home. Her expression and whole countenance dropped, she grew somber, and when we stepped through the front door, she didn't utter a word as Hill, and some other servants came to take our things from us.

"Mr. Collins is in the sitting room," Hill informed us, "he is expecting you all."

Everyone looked at each other, apprehensively.

"Does he wish that?" Colonel Fitzwilliam asked for us all.

Hill looked at us, heavily. She knew everything, even without us having to tell her.

"Yes, he does. He was most insistent that you come and tell him how the evening went."

"Well," Colonel Fitzwilliam replied, diplomatically, "it is the proper thing to do."

"Very well," Darcy answered, always willing to tell the absolute truth. "After all, whoever said that life was easy?"

Bracing ourselves, we walked toward the sitting room, where we saw the fire blazing from. Instinctively, I looked at Mary, and Jane had stood by her. They whispered to each other, in each other's confidence. Lord knows the agony that Mary must be enduring.

When we entered, Mr. Collins was sitting in Father's armchair, by the fireplace. He had a book in his hand, and once more, I was antagonized by the similarity of Mr. Collins's appearance to how my father would have looked when he once stationed himself in such a fashion. The similarity of image was too unkind.

When seeing us, he lowered the book and did everything in his power to control his nerves. He smiled gently, but there was a great deal of uncertainty to every gesture that he made.

I found that I enjoyed that aspect, at least.

"Ah, you are returned. How was the dinner party?"

"Well," Mr. Bingley answered, "I can easily say that I enjoyed myself as thoroughly as I had on the very first dinner parties that I had experienced when I first came here."

"Yes. They are gracious hosts. I never understood their ability to always survive the social scenes that they know how to envelop themselves with. Do you need any refreshment?"

"Thank you, but merely some pitchers of clean water in our rooms would suffice for the evening," Mr. Darcy said for us all. "Parties are delightful experiences, but they are very tiring ones."

"Oh, you all must be exhausted," he responded, and yet he looked more tired than we did. "Very well, I..." He looked around at all of us. "Before you retire, I do believe that I must speak to you."

"Sir," I asked. "Is it all of us, or one of us in particular?"

"While I wish that it were one in particular, your expressions indicate that you all seem to be aware of this day's incident. Am I correct?"

That could not be denied. All our faces indicated that we all were feeling the same thing and possessed the same amount of knowledge. No one was in the mood to lie.

"Well," Mr. Collins said, his hands a little shaky, "your faces say it all. Often, I am not accustomed to reading expressions correctly. Recently, I have discovered that about myself. However, since my past actions concern more than just one in this party, I suppose that it is correct to address everyone."

"Since Margaret and I are not kin to this family," Frederick offered, "would you prefer if we retired to our rooms while you all discuss private affairs?"

"That is very good of you, Mr. Hale."

"Come, brother," Margaret said to Frederick, and they

went upstairs. As they did so, the rest of us collected around the room and sat down or stood near the window. Perhaps, out of a natural impulse, Mary sat at the bench at the piano forte. Mr. Collins looked at her, through the side of his eye, before he turned his attention back to us.

"When we go upstairs, you are going to tell Margaret everything anyway, aren't you?" Kitty whispered to me.

"Of course, I am. Yet still, protocol must be followed."

When we heard the door upstairs close, Mr. Collins was prepared to speak.

But, of course, even when he preached sermons at his parish, there was an awkwardness to his delivery. But now, he no longer was preaching about morality, religion—to speak plainly, he was not reading from a script that he had prepared. Now, he was speaking matters on family, his personal trials, and how it connected to everyone in the room.

This was an altogether different sort of thing, and no amount of preparation could render him *prepared.*

He opened his mouth but was so overpowered that he stuttered a little.

"Mr. Collins," I said, "you may speak, and we all will listen, and react when we will."

"I know. You must all forgive me. This moment is rather difficult."

"We are here," Mary said to him.

As she spoke, Mr. Collins's cheeks reddened, and his nerves clearly were more awake than ever. Now, he reminded me of our mother.

"We will listen," Mary said patiently, folding her hands over her lap.

"Thank you," Mr. Collins said heavily. "I never thought to find myself in such a position."

Gathering the little bit of nerve that he had left, he began to speak...

"Well," Mr. Collins elaborated, "this has been a strange year, for many of us, as well as myself. For a long time, I prided myself on my ability to discern everything around me and declared that I was a man of correct views and viewpoints. I deemed that I knew the world and was so certain that I always did right. How much I was in a hurry to do right, that I never learned what right truly was." Mr. Collins turned to me. "I confess that I believed that I was justified for my actions. I declared that my actions were correct, but I see that I was exchanging one honest rejection with a cold-hearted one. You were right, Mrs. Darcy. Whatever pain I felt for you rejecting me was no justification for throwing five ladies from their home—the chief home they always had. I did have my profession, my living, and I could have given you ladies the time that you needed, or at least lived here with you all, as your cousin and protector. Under the excuse of being a man of God, I did a heartless act. I daresay that I am not the first man to use religion to justify my actions, but it does not excuse it. Bennet ladies, I stand before you, sorry for what I once was. What I did was deplorable, perhaps even unforgiveable. I do not ask for you to forgive me now. Time is the only thing that can help. And in *time*, maybe that forgiveness might be obtained."

Then he turned to Mr. Darcy.

"Mr. Darcy, at first, my behavior naturally made me submit to your advice. But not for the right reasons. I submitted because you are Lady Catherine's nephew, and you are superior. But I now reflect and realize that is not the correct reason to submit to any sort of philosophy. At first, I did not listen to Mrs. Darcy or Miss Bennet, believing still that I was the one correct. Mr. Darcy, your advice should only have been confirmation of who I ought to have been listening to, from the very first. And not as law, but as further assurance. The person that I ought to have been listening to, to have been paying closer attention since the beginning, is now seated at her favorite instrument."

Finally, he turned to Mary, who was shaking a little.

"Earlier this day, I proposed to you, Miss Mary. I do not regret it, for you were the right woman to propose to. The evil was not in the deed, but in the delivery, the lateness, and the intention behind it. I have been raised to expect women to accept a man eventually, and now I realize that it was the thought of conceit. No one is obligated to marry anyone. Gratitude is not a part of the bargain, in such matters. And you are correct, Miss Bennet. I should have noticed you long ago, rather than looking everywhere else, other than the place that I ought to have looked. All of that is in the past. I cannot change it. Yet, I wish that I could. I should have noticed you long ago, appreciated your consideration of me, your respect for me, and such economy, practicality, and propriety. I should have seen the beauty of these things that I preached so much on. Virtues that you have long possessed. Convinced that I was doing right, I was wholly blind to them all. Until now, I feel as if I never knew myself. Miss Bennet, I have hurt you. Your sisters, yes, but you especially. You came to help me, out of a genuine heart. And I took it for something that was owed to me.

"What a selfish creature that I was. But no more. Miss Bennet—Mary, you have come to mean so much to me. I do not deserve you. I know that now. However, I confess that I am lost and have fallen down. I do not oppress you with any more unwanted and unworthy proposals. I only ask that you help me. Stay with me and help me look after my child. I do not have it in me to look for another wife. The idea frightens me. But I hope that being the mistress of Longbourn is enough to give recompense for the life you left behind to come and assist me. My child loves you. Do not let the child suffer for the sins of the father. Can you find it in your heart to stay with me and help me raise my future?"

With tears almost falling from her eyes, Mary let out a cry, raced out of the room, rushed up the stairs and retreated.

Now, it could be supposed that we all would feel a slight tinge of awkwardness. After all, we had experienced a man lay his heart and humility out before us, and the recipient rush away, but that was not so.

Rather, excepting Mr. Collins, we all were intrigued by what we just saw. Gathering my presence of mind, I decided to make an excuse for Mary.

"Mr. Collins," I announced, "your apology is very heartfelt, but there is no need, at present, to be alarmed by Mary's swift exit. You must understand that she has a great deal to consider. The anxiety from the moment must be immense."

"I can understand so. I feel the weight of it myself. Forgive me, but I must retire to my room."

"Of course," Mr. Bingley said. "We all perhaps shall do the same."

We all dispersed to our room, except for Jane, who volunteered to be the one to inquire after Mary.

Later that evening, Mr. Darcy and I were lying under

the bed sheets, holding one another and still we were discussing what occurred that day.

"It is agonizing," I said to Mr. Darcy as he rubbed his hand along my stomach and thighs.

"What is?"

"Mr. Collins' apology. I was content to hate the man for the whole of my life. And then he had to go and spoil it by repenting. Now I cannot despise him at all. As horrid as that sounds."

"It does not sound horrid, but merely human. The fact is hate is a sensation that humanity was plagued with. And even more so, it is a defect that we all love to possess. It has a satisfying effect on us."

"It is such an incredible thing, to have a dislike of that kind. Now I feel that I ought to forgive him and cannot hate him again."

"While it is never wise to rush into a hatred, you might be leaping before you look. Mr. Collins has given a wonderful apology, but many people in the world are actors. He could very well mean his repentance today and then revoke it tomorrow. Just because we all say things, does not mean that we all put it into practice. Mr. Collins cannot be wholly forgiven just yet. He has to take the time to prove it."

"True. It is best not to walk through life blindly. And since I have two eyes that are fully functional, I really have no excuse."

Mr. Darcy laughed, then he looked up at me.

"Lizzy?"

"Yes?"

"Tell me that you love me."

"Never," I teased.

"Oh, yes, you will, yes, you will...you will, you will, you

will," he insisted, nudging his face against mine, making me laugh.

"No, no," I lied, completely in jest, "how could I love such a man? You must have taken leave of your senses."

"Tell me that you love me, you harpy."

"Casting aspersions at me?" I chuckled. "Well, I guess I have no other choice but to rebel."

I rolled on top of him, biting him on his neck.

"I love you, you worthless cretin," I answered, grinning. "I love every fiber of your doomed soul."

"Yes, I will burn. And you are going to burn with me."

"I never liked being cold anyway."

We fell asleep in each other's arms.

Chapter 14

Facing the Fact of Affection

The next day, Mary found herself willing to brave anything. She had spent the whole night shut up in her room. However, she was not in the habit of playing the lady who was overpowered by her sensibilities. Finished having her cry out early in the morning, she was resolved.

When she finished dressing, she left her room to go down to breakfast.

The first person that she met at the top of the stairs was Jane, who also had just finished dressing herself. Seeing Mary stirred every maternal instinct that Jane had, and she immediately appealed to her.

"Mary," Jane said, going up to her little sister, "I am happy to see you awake. You look well."

"I do not," Mary said, sighing. "I am certain that my eyes are still a little red, and my face must look affright."

"I never knew that you were the sort to be so interested in your appearance."

"I am not. But it is always right to look respectable."

"Yes, it is. I was not judging you. Just making a deduction."

"Oh." Mary was ashamed, accepting that she had turned defensive. "Yes, forgive me. I still am not fully myself yet, am I."

"Well, after a day such as the one you had yesterday, I daresay that no one would be. I was just thinking, maybe you would like to go with the rest of us for a holiday at the Isle of Wight. I am certain that it would do you a great deal of good."

"I had actually wished that you would invite me," Mary said, "I thought about it for quite some time last night. At some point, the invitation would have answered all my prayers. I would be able to be with my family again, we would be united, and I would have the chance to recover. But Jane, I don't think that I can do so. I think that I have come to a decision. I will tell you all at breakfast."

"Are you certain?"

"No, I'm not. But I also know that I am doing the right thing. Even if it hurts me a little."

Marveling at her courage, Jane accepted this, and they went down to breakfast.

At breakfast, the entire family had arranged themselves to dine. With the table being filled with her sisters, Mr. Collins, Mr. Darcy, Colonel Fitzwilliam, Mr. Bingley, Georgiana and the Hales, she had an audience that she knew she must answer to.

At first, the family began by being silent. Afterwards, they began to talk of their plans to go to the Isle of Wight, and how they were looking forward to the excursion there.

For a moment, Mary lost her nerve. She felt that maybe she did not need to explain anything. After all, did they truly need to know what she was feeling and the decision that she had made? She could explain herself to her sisters, individually, and they could make her excuses for why she had no inclination to join them—or why she had chosen this particular path to take.

However, in the next moment, she knew that if she did not speak now, she would be a coward and would remain as such.

Therefore, as the discussion on the beauties of the Isle was the main source of delight to look forward to, Mary spoke for the first time since she had sat down at the table.

"I hope that you all shall enjoy your time on holiday. I wish that I could have joined you."

"Oh, but Miss Bennet," Frederick Hale invited, "surely you can join us? The Isle will be my last place to see in England before I must leave for Spain. It would be nice to part with many friendly faces."

"I thank you, Frederick. And I wish that I could have come. In fact, Jane had already invited me, and I do wish to join you all. However, sometimes, one feels compelled to go where one is needed."

Mary looked at Mr. Collins when she said this. His eyes were hopeful, but still a little wistful.

"The fact is," Mary replied, "that I cannot escape the reality of what happens when one chooses to be helpful. When one chooses to care, you cannot undo that sort of link —of binding time. I have grown rather affectionate towards our little cousin and wish that Mr. Collins has someone to look after his child with him."

"Miss Bennet," Mr. Collins said, "you have been of great use to me, when I did not know how to be a proper father. Yet, I do not want this obligation to hang about your head in a way that it withholds you from the pleasures of your family."

"Thank you for understanding that. And yet, I find, that I do not want to go, because I will be upset if I leave Longbourn. I want to stay and help you look after that little Lion of yours."

Mr. Collins chuckled at the reference, sadly, but genuinely.

"I've come to care for this part of my family," Mary continued, "and I think that my heart would break if I were to leave at this time. Even for a little. Even for my own selfish desires. Mr. Collins, again, I thank you for your proposal. But, at present, I cannot forget the pain I have endured, from our past with each other. If you care for me at all, then I need you to give us both time. Time for me to adjust, and time for you to try to help me understand any sincerity you might have. Put simply, sir, if you want to marry me, you have to earn it. I have done my duty, and my care for your welfare. You must show complete admiration for me in turn."

"I will," Mr. Collins stressed heavily. "I assure you, I shall."

"Good. Now all we can do is submit to time. When we are ready, maybe more will come from our circumstances."

"But when will we know when that time is?"

"We shall just have to see." Mary looked around at all of us. "Forgive our constant displays of sensibility. Discretion, of course, is always the order of the day. Yet, since we are family, I knew that this all was information that ought to be distributed."

"Of course," Colonel Fitzwilliam assured her, "and we appreciate that you have been willing to entrust us with your sentiments and your situation. Now we all feel as if we are on equal standing with each other. And, in time, I do believe that all wounds will heal."

Kitty chuckled, pointing to her husband.

"Yes, that is *my* husband," she declared, proud. "Mine. I obtained that."

Colonel Fitzwilliam blushed.

"She's proud of me," he boasted. "Yes, she is."

Chapter 15

May the Isle of Wight Be Our Refuge

As the rest of the family finished up their visit in Hertfordshire, the day soon arrived when we were to depart. Eager to confirm that Mary had not wanted to change her mind, I asked her again if she was certain that she did not wish to come.

She confirmed that, while she missed the opportunity of traveling with us, she was adamant.

"I think she still cares for him," Kitty whispered to me, "after all, we know that she respected him from the first day that they met. For some of us, it is not easy to remember all the offense when someone seeks a reconciliation."

"True. And it's better that way. Implacable resentment is not the most attractive ornament to wear about oneself."

"It's true. But I still need time to adjust. Mr. Collins is the sort of man whose quest for morality masks a selfishness. Now, we are all selfish, from time to time, but we defeat that part of ourselves, eventually. What if the selfish aspect of his character returns?"

"The answer is simple: we all come back and fix everything."

"Ah. Yes, that ploy!"

The moment of our departure fully arrived, and with hope in our hearts, we bid farewell to Mr. Collins and Mary as she held the little *lion* in her arms. The child was spirited, and I found that I quite liked that.

We all got into our carriage and rode off, back to London where we would meet the Hales.

As we waved goodbye, we had to accept something. Lord knows when I would see my home again. For there was much to do, to go to, and to resolve, that being homeward bound was something that we would be unable to look forward to for quite some time. There was the holiday, Frederick's departure, the return to the North to resolve things in Milton, settling into Pemberley, and Kitty and the Colonel's settling into Rosings Park while helping the Bingleys find a new home.

Home!

Another memory, come and gone.

As we journeyed to London, we had the luxury of meeting the rest of our party halfway.

Lady Catherine, worried for Mrs. Hale's health, did all in her power to help Mrs. Hale have a comfortable journey as they traveled to London, and had her settled into her townhouse, awaiting us.

When we arrived, Lady Catherine received us, animated.

Despite that she would have loved to have ruled our holiday, she was adamant about not attending.

"I do not like the sea," Lady Catherine said with determined finality, "And I hate sand. It gets everywhere."

And, at last, all three married couples boarded the ferry that was to transport us to the destination where we truly could enjoy the delights of the warm air, and the sea.

Chapter 16

News of Good & Bad

Through the Milton streets, Rasby ran eagerly. Aware that it was one of the days where both Lucas sisters were home, at Frances Street, she knew that she could share her good fortune with two women who would not disparage the path that life had taken.

When she knocked on their door, she saw Maria look through the window and she waved at her. Eager to see Rasby, Maria Lucas opened the door.

"Rasby," Maria said, rushing to the other side of the room, "come in. I have to show you the good news."

"You have good news as well?" Rasby responded, closing the door behind her.

"Yes, I do. Charlotte!" Maria called up the steps. "Rasby is here, and she has something to discuss with us."

"I don't mean to override you all with my news," Rasby said, removing her bonnet, "therefore, you may begin first."

"Well," Maria began, "the news just came yesterday. Our parents sent us a letter."

"Judging by how animated you look, it does not bear bad news?" Rasby observed, sitting down.

"Not in the slightest." Charlotte came down the stairs and began to make them some tea. "All of that fear was for nothing. Mama and papa completely understand why we chose to come to the North and wish to remain for a duration."

"They do?" Rasby asked. "Wholly and completely?"

"I am surprised in my own way," Charlotte said. "Though I cannot help but suspect they enjoy the prospect of not having two daughters who will die old maids who bring no income to the household."

"Miss Lucas," Rasby responded, "really? You are being gloomy."

"Charlotte embraces practicality, and I do not," Maria said. "Our parents would not view us as such."

"But our brothers might," Charlotte said, completely unaffected, "besides, having a profession builds up the Lucas economy. At the end of the day, our eccentric decision does makes us less of a burden."

"Do they understand that you both like being here?" Rasby asked.

Maria looked thoughtful.

"I am not certain. It was explained that they regard our new lifestyle with no contempt, but I'm not certain that they fully understand why we would prefer to live in such a place."

"The North is practically a whole other side of the world to them," Charlotte explained. "And you said that you came with good news?"

Rasby raised up a letter.

"Kitty wrote to me of the wedding."

When seeing the missive, Charlotte and Maria looked eager.

"How did the wedding fare?" Maria asked. "Oh, I wish

that I could have seen the gowns that they wore. We should write to them and tell them to bring the gowns to the North with them so that we could see it."

"They are on holiday now," Rasby said, "with every intention of returning to Pemberley by the end of the month. We'll send our letters there. They ran to the church."

"What?" Maria and Charlotte said in unison.

"They both arrived at the same time. And the brides thought that it would be comical to dash toward the church steps. So, the husbands chased them."

"How romantic."

"Did Kitty write Lady Catherine's reaction to that episode?" Charlotte asked, amused.

"Oh, she did. Apparently, the great lady was in the mood for some amusement. Kitty said that she chastised them for only a minute before she gave into the jollity of the spectacle."

Maria shook from being nervous.

"Oh, I could never imagine doing something so bold in front of her ladyship. I barely even know how to form words when she looks at me."

"Is Lady Catherine really that imposing?" Rasby asked, a little worried.

"She scared me to death," Maria observed.

"Maria," Charlotte responded, "you would think that Lady Catherine was an ogre who ate people. We're giving Rasby the wrong impression. Rasby, Lady Catherine is no different than any other wealthy knighted lady who is used to getting her own way all the time. She owns a large estate, and rules it like a queen. Perhaps, when not in a position of power, she is as comfortable an acquaintance as any other. But since she is a ruler of her own world, and in a viciously aristocratic society, she is a tough character. Life perhaps has made her so."

"I don't know what she will think of me," Rasby said, wondering away, "especially since I would be the last sort of guest that she expected."

"Guest?"

"Yes," Rasby replied, breathless, "that was the last bit of my news. Kitty wrote that Lady Catherine has accepted my role as her companion. I am going to the South."

"You will go to Rosings Park? Well, that is wonderful."

"Told you that Kitty would not forget you," Maria stressed.

"Yes, you were right. It's just, now that my excitement is over, I am scared."

"Why?"

"They didn't tell Lady Catherine what I am. How do I know what will happen to me when I get there? If all falls apart, I know one thing."

"What?"

"I will lose Kitty as my closest friend. And then, very swiftly, the Bennets will abandon me. In Kitty's effort to give me a better life, I could lose everything."

Maria and Charlotte looked at each other, apprehensively. They knew that Rasby was not overreacting.

"Rasby," Charlotte admitted, "I cannot pretend like your views are not an overreaction. You are correct. You are going into the unknown. I cannot predict what is going to happen. Neither of us can. But the advice that I can give is that where people see evil, it's very easy to become that evil. Do not let any ill treatment overpower you or affect you. When it does that, it affects everything that you are doing. It leads to you becoming every wrong that you might be accused of. Let your courage rise with every one of anyone's attempt to intimidate you. Do not let your confidence be shaken, or they will win. And you do not want them to win, now do you?"

"No, I do not. I want to see them lose."

"Good," Charlotte said, "then pretend like you do not care a fig for whatever slight may come your way. Do not let their wrong affect you, or you will become the wrong they label you as. And good luck. You've got your friends on your side. Kitty will not abandon you. She's faced too much adversity to be afraid of a little more."

Rasby sighed, relieved.

"Then I will go to Rosings Park," Rasby said. "My friend is there. I'll take comfort in that."

"Oh!" Maria cried. "I forgot about the roast!"

She went to the kitchen, to see to the meat that she was cooking in the oven.

When they were alone, Rasby looked at Charlotte.

"And how are you?" Rasby asked.

"Work at Granger Hall is tolerable, and I enjoy it. From how I have been received, it is evident that they miss Elizabeth, but they are very kind to me."

"And what of Mr. Dennison?" Rasby lowered her voice. "And his love for Maria?"

Charlotte blinked, utterly aghast and shocked. Never had she mentioned Mr. Dennison's perverse affection for Maria to anyone.

"How did you..."

"Mr. Hanley," Rasby explained. "I passed him on the street. He expressed some concern about Mr. Dennison's curiosity for your sister. Does she know?"

"No," Charlotte said, whispering equally as low, "she doesn't. And I want to keep it that way."

"I can understand why. Just prepare yourself."

"For what?"

"For the day when Mr. Dennison tells Maria that he cares for her. When men like that finally do fall in love, it is hard and heavy. It's like a gavel that comes crashing down. Dennison may be horrid, but you don't have to worry about him doing any real harm."

"Are you certain about that? I do not trust him."

"Who knows? I have been wrong before."

"Either way, I don't care. He's not good enough for Maria."

"I know. But he will still hope. And he will tell her. And then, either she will attempt to understand, or she will be repulsed. Either way, someone will get hurt. She will enter a match where her husband might be vicious when they argue about anything, or he will be angry at the sight of her."

Charlotte sat down, resigned.

"This is, altogether, too frightening. Perhaps, if we are fortunate, his affection for her is merely because she is a novelty. After all, we are still new to Milton, and something must always be said for the exotic. Perhaps, in time, it will be nothing more than a passing infatuation on his part, and in a month or two, his affection for her will be entirely at an end. I suppose I ought to tell her soon. Of course, from a practical standpoint, he would offer her a home."

"But you do not think from a practical standpoint, in this case."

"Usually, I do. But not now. I'm too much of an older sister. If it were me, then I would think differently. But it's Maria. I don't want any serpent to seize and devour her."

"I would say that Maria might be able to change him, but Dennison would have to change on his own."

"Should I mention that to him?" Charlotte asked, then

retracted it immediately. "No never mind. He would not listen to me. Maybe I should ask Mr. Hanley or Mr. Hunnicutt to speak to him? Or am I being too dependent?"

"There are some things that must be spoken about between the same sex. That might be one of those things. If you like, I can speak to Mr. Hanley and Hunnicutt on your behalf. I have known them longer."

"Thank you, but if I am to stand on my own, I really ought to start acting like it."

"Well, happy hunting. Also, have you seen Mr. Thornton recently?"

When entering Marlborough Mills, Nicholas Higgins thought to check in with Liam, to see how he was faring. However, he halted when he saw Mr. Thornton exiting the mill and rushing to his home.

In his hand was a letter. In Thornton's face was an urgency that Nicholas could not get the better of it.

Worried that his looks displayed worse news than what rumor said, he walked onward, to the mill, for his post. When he walked past the carding room, he met Liam on the staircase.

"Nicholas?" Liam declared. "How goes it?"

"Well enough." Unable to resist, Nicholas could not help but inquire. "Liam, have yer seen Mr. Thornton lately?"

"Yea. I saw him walking out of the factory. It looked like he had some heavy news that he got."

"That's what I reckon that I saw too. You don'..."

"Don' what?"

"You don' think e' received more bad news, do yer?

Now, what I'm 'bout to tell yer is just rumor, and all. Ain't nothin' full certain about it, but from what I've heard..."

"The mill is in danger of closin' down."

Liam winced, seeing that Nicholas had heard the same rumor. If Nicholas had heard it, then there was something credible about it, Liam had assumed.

"You heard?"

"Yea, I did."

"And what do you reckon?"

"That where there's smoke, sometimes, there usually is a fire a-brewin'. I've overheard some conversations with the overseers, and by the sound of it, we are not able to make up for the orders that were left behin'..."

"From when the strike happened?" Liam guessed.

Nicholas Higgins looked down at the floor.

"I'm not sayin' that it's your fault, Nicholas," Liam responded, "I just am the sort who speaks by fact. That's all. It's natural to be wantin' a better life. That's all that anyone wants."

"No," Nicholas responded, "I am not afraid of the truth. War costs money, and masters and men always will be at odds with each other. If this is true, Liam, then did I cause this?"

"It's impossible to know. Take comfort in that. Besides, how are we to know if it's even true?"

When going inside of his house, Thornton placed the letter on a table in the parlor, next to his decanter. He removed the cork, poured himself a glass, and he drank vigorously.

One half of his mind was heavy, and the other was light.

Or rather, his heart was now light as a feather, while the

prospects of a future would be as heavy as a stone that pulled him to the bottom of a lake.

His prospects felt as if they were drowning, while his passions felt as if they were flying above the earth. If only one could save the other, but he felt as if the latter only doomed the former.

He had his love! He had so much!

But now, he might very well lose his wealth, the mill, and property that he built up so much over the course of his life.

What world could he damn his wife to? Surely, not this one. For truly, he was hard pressed. He felt it acutely in his vulnerable point—his pride in the commercial character which he had established himself.

As he drank, he considered all this, falling into the comforts and woes of his own world. Little was he aware that he was being observed.

Turning his head, he saw his mother standing in the doorway, and he flinched.

"Sorry, Mother."

"You come from the mill sooner than expected," Mrs. Thornton said, entering the room with some sewing.

"Yes, I did."

"And I think it's time," Mrs. Thornton told him, putting her items down.

"Time?"

"Time for you to tell me. Time for you to tell me how badly we are off."

Thornton looked at her, ashamed, and then looked ahead.

"Fanny is fortunate. Slickson will marry her, despite how badly off that I am, currently. Mother," he said, sitting down, resigned, "I know that you are about to tell me that I was wrong, and that I ought to have joined him in the speculation."

"You did what was right, and you did not want to endanger your workers' wages. I understood that. There was too much risk taken, so you did the honorable thing. No one could ask for more than that. Nor would I."

Sad, Thornton walked up to his mother and took her hand. She wrapped her fingers around his, to offer him comfort.

"I just," Thornton sighed, "after everything that I had done, that I had built up, and for it all to come to this."

"How much are we owed to the bank?"

"Four hundred pounds."

When hearing this, Mrs. Thornton grimaced at the thought of it. However, she did so while looking away from her son, for she did not wish for him to see the worry in her face.

"The fact is," Thornton said, "there is no hope. The strike has prevented me from completing some of the large orders that I had on hand. I also had locked up a good deal of my capital in new and expensive machinery, and I had also bought cotton largely, for the fulfillment of these orders taken under contract. That I had not been able to complete them, I had not expected. All of this I could not foresee. And now I feel..."

"None of this was your doing. You did the best you could, in a world that seems fit to always bring levels of imbalance and injustice pouring around. To be a world where some build themselves up to be masters, and so everyone else must seek to bring them down—but with you, John..."

"It's not fair!" Thornton cried. "I do not understand. First Father loses everything, he rips himself away from us, and then just when I raised us up again, life has to bring us down to where we once sunk to." Thornton collapsed on the sofa, and Mrs. Thornton sat down next to him, attempting to ease his grief. "I do not think that I can do it again."

"Do what again?"

"Rise again. When I sell the mill and the machinery, I will have just enough to pay the workers their last wages, pay the bank their loan, and then afford to marry Fanny off properly. Mama, I am sorry, but we must leave this house."

"I do not care about the house," Mrs. Thornton insisted, "I can manage. You know that I can. I merely don't like seeing you cast low, in a place below what you deserve. Too much has been taken from you, John, again and again. I am tired of seeing the world cause you pain. As your father did."

"And it's more painful than ever," Thornton responded, "but I finally gained her love, and now I cannot bring her so low with me."

He raised up the letter, to show his mother.

"Miss Hale wrote back to me. She is in love with me."

Mrs. Thornton leaned back, alert. The pain of her son losing everything was overcome by knowledge that the young harpy had finally realized what she was about.

Snatching up the letter, Mrs. Thornton began to read it. This sudden act shocked Thornton, only for a moment, because he wanted his mother to read it. He was happy that she had done so, for he wanted her to see that he had achieved the love of such a superior woman.

"She writes to me plainly and beautifully," Thornton whispered as his mother read. His tone was masculine, deep and true. "She wishes to be by my side, her heart warms at the thought of me, and that her love is mine." He wiped his eyes, for fear of a tear leaving it. "After all this time, trials, and conflicts that we have gone through, she loves me. I won her affections."

When finished reading the letter, Mrs. Thornton lowered it.

"She loves you now," Mrs. Thornton said, "but what's to say that her mind won't change when she sees you again?"

"It won't," her son responded, "she's not that sort of woman. You know that. When Miss Hale says that she is in love with me, she speaks truth."

"Yes," Mrs. Thornton said, resigned, "she does. I will say this for her; she does mean what she refers to. She loves my boy. That is why I always was apprehensive around her; I knew. Even before you did. I knew that she would take you away from me. A mother cannot help when she no longer is the first in her son's heart."

"I will always love you, Mother," Thornton said, "you know that."

"I do. But that does not keep a person from being irrational. I admit that I did not think her worthy of you. But if she accepts you through all this, then I will think her worthy at last."

"She will not have me, because I will no longer make her an offer."

Mrs. Thornton looked at him.

"I will not marry Miss Hale."

When hearing this, Mrs. Thornton needed no explanation, but she awaited it. After all, she knew that her son wished to elaborate more on the subject. Therefore, she let him continue.

"Why should I doom her to my life?" Thornton continued. "She is a queen. Even when she hated me, I knew that she was a queen. She deserves a man who does not come to her, in debt. I will release her."

"But you love her."

"And that's why I'm letting her go. She deserves a better chance at life."

"From the state of a husband, I will say that she could not do better than anyone else in England. However, it turns out that everything is correct. If she had accepted you when the time came, you would have had a wife on your hands, who might even have a child on the way, and you would still be in the state that you are in now. With all your woes. Perhaps, she did right when looking in hindsight. And maybe you do right, in foresight."

"I am," he replied heavily, "for now has come one of the eras of bad trade, when the market falling brought down the value of all large stocks. No orders are coming in now. I've lost the interest of the capital I had locked up in the machinery. And then there is the constant strain of running the business."

Thornton rubbed his eyes.

"I obtained her love. I wanted it so much. Now I finally have it, and I can't take her in my arms. I cannot have her walk alongside me for the rest of my life. You don't doom a woman to such a fate. But I don't have the courage to write her such a letter."

"I do," Mrs. Thornton offered. "But not right now. Tonight, think on your actions. If you feel the same way tomorrow, I will take dictation for you and send it—since I know that the matter will be hard for you to write. However, think about it before you commit to any rash action. Maybe you can go to London, where you might be able to raise capital again. Miss Hale made you wait before she found her love for you. I daresay she can wait a little longer herself. Especially since she will be in the South for some time."

"True. Maybe I do not have to be rash now. Perhaps I do have time. Maybe, maybe, maybe..."

"Yes. Maybe."

Thornton looked at his mother.

"Take heart in one thing."

"What?"

"You were right. She was in love with me. She just needed some time to see it." He smiled sadly.

"Yes. I told you."

"Oh, Mother!"

After a while, Thornton returned to his work. Every now and again, he saw Nicholas Higgins in the factory. For a brief moment, a twinge of anger overcame him.

If it were not for Higgins and the committee men who organized the strike, Thornton would not be in the situation that he was in now. The Mill would be running properly, he could provide for his mother, and he could rush to the South and propose to Margaret Hale, in person. All could have been arranged if it had not been for that strike!

Yet, in the next moment, Thornton suppressed his anger, seeing that there was no reason to be angry over the past, because it could not be changed. Also, if it had not been Nicholas Higgins, it would have been another rabble rouser who would have taken his place. Strikes were common. It was never a matter of who ran it, for there would always be another 'who'. It was merely a matter of when they would occur.

And as for Mrs. Thornton, she found herself in the state of restlessness. After all, she had changed her place of refusing to accept Miss Hale as a prospect for her son, to now telling him to hold off on retracting his proposal. It was painful to know that she had to change her mind.

Ah, the irony of it.

Chapter 17

The Place of Dreams

"Remarkable!" I cried when I beheld the Isle of Wight before us.

Standing on the ferry that transported us South, from the coast of London, the Isle of Wight was merely two hours away. Sailing along the wide-open Channel already had a cathartic feel to it, but now it felt as if we had been transported to exotic horizons. It did help that the sun was shining, and the weather was very congenial that day. Everything about it boasted of fair weather and pleasant experiences.

And when the Isle was in sight, all of us rushed to the railing, leaned forward, and beheld where we would spend our holiday.

"Yes," Mr. Darcy said, holding my hand, "may the skies be clear, and shores not be too crowded—as well as nothing but smooth sailing from thenceforth."

"Mr. Darcy," I said, "I think we might get our wish. After all, all roads seemed to be cleared up. All crises appear to be over. What do we have to fear? Nothing, I tell you. Nothing!" I laughed.

What a fool I was.

I wish someone had told me that, whenever someone said that it might as well be as if you had pointed your finger at the sky and invited a lightning bolt to come crashing down at you.

Oh well, in the future, I would learn.

The island's South was mostly cliff-bound. There were three rivers, the Eastern Yar. The Northern parts had more woodland areas.

It was beautiful.

"I can see the beaches," Jane said, laughing, "oh, we shall have a delightful time."

We arrived on shore, set ourselves up in the best hotel and spent the day unpacking, eating, and choosing what our itinerary would be.

The next day was merely us traveling along, enjoying the delights of the environment. Fortunately, Frederick Hale was a bit of a historian when it came to the Isle. It made sense, seeing as how he was once a sailor and would have a great deal of expertise on the matter.

"Human occupation has been traced on this island from the earliest of times," he informed us as we walked along. "Archaeologists are always discovering something from when humanity was just leaving caves. There are also Roman remains. Emperor Vespasian annexed the island in 43 CE. It was then annexed to Wessex in 661, bestowed on the King of Sussex. In 998, the Danes lived here, during their marauding era. In 1647-48, Charles I was imprisoned in Carisbrooke Castle, during the English Civil Wars. We'll see that area at the end of the week. And Osborne House, near Cowes, is Queen Victoria's residence."

"Do you think that we might visit the place?" Mr. Bingley asked.

"I hope that we can arrange that," Colonel Fitzwilliam insisted. "After all, being related to the honorable Lady Catherine de Bourgh has many favors in her gift, name and lineage." He turned to Kitty. "What do you think?"

"I should like to see it, but I have one problem," Kitty insisted.

"What would that be?"

"That ladies and gentlemen are not allowed to go sea-bathing together very much. It is not fair."

"Actually," Frederick Hale observed, "as to that, I have a secret."

"A secret?" Margaret asked him. "Frederick, what are you planning?"

"Well, being a sailor, one learns of the places to swim, where there is no impediment of being observed. No scandal, no prying eyes upon us."

"You know a part of the island where we can swim together?" Georgiana asked. "Oh, dear!"

"Miss Darcy, perhaps I am offering something that might be regarded as scandalous. But it's true, I do know a small beach along the South side, where the sand and the water are as congenial and picturesque as any other part of the Island. But that is only if we wish to do so."

"As much as I would like to pursue that avenue," Colonel Fitzwilliam said, "I think we should bathe at a proper resort before committing to any sort of scandal. And Darcy, Bingley and I can seek out this place and see if it is as you say, before we can take the ladies there."

"Perfectly reasonable. I hope that it is as I remembered it. Truly, I would be heartbroken if it were not so. Especially since I would like some more fond memories before I return to Spain."

"I am sorry that you have to leave so soon," Mrs. Hale said, "oh, my dear—nephew."

Frederick looked at his mother, fondly.

"Aunt, I shall miss you for all the world. I am glad that you recovered." Then he looked at his father, keeping up the pretense. "And you too, Uncle."

"Frederick," Mr. Hale assured him, "you will always be welcome into our lives, but I refuse to say farewell just yet. In the meantime, let us enjoy ourselves. Tell us more about the island since you are such an expert on the spot."

"Only if the company loves to hear lectures about history."

"We should not walk too far today," Dixon ordered us, pulling Mrs. Hale along in the invalid chair. "Mrs. Hale may be recovering, but she is still very delicate, and we must take all of that into consideration."

"We shall," I assured her. "Dixon, you shall not be contradicted."

"I hope that I will not," Dixon responded, "because that would be a very trying day for everyone."

"The Isle is one of the sunniest areas in Britain," Frederick continued to narrate. "Newport is one of the main towns here. It's the head of the Medina estuary. And Cowes is at Medina's mouth. You shall see some of the finest sailing boats there..."

As Dixon ordered, we did not walk too far that day, so not to exert Mrs. Hale's energy.

For all of that, what could not be denied was that, ever since Mrs. Hale had come, the sun and environment had done her a great deal of good.

"I don't care what anyone says," Margaret told me, "But there is something very mean about an ideal complexion for a woman being pale skin. Not all of us are born with skin white as snow. In fact, hardly anyone is. I think it is good that the sun makes us a little brown. In my opinion, it makes us look healthier."

When she said this, we looked at Mrs. Hale, and it was true. The tan that came from the sun did offer a glow to Mrs. Hale's cheek, her disposition seemed to be merrier, and she looked happy. Happier than I recalled ever seeing her at Milton.

The soonest opportunity that I could find of speaking with Margaret about this, the better. But of course, it had to be discussed alone and when in each other's confidence.

When we returned to the hotel, I went to Margaret's room. She was staying with Dixon, but we had the room to ourselves, since Dixon was tending to her mama. Before I would retire with Mr. Darcy, I found myself welcome, for Margaret wished to talk.

"Margaret," I whispered in reply. "We have a problem."

"What?" Margaret asked me, concerned.

"I do not think that your mother will ever want to return to the North. I genuinely think the air there does affect her. She's already a creature of sensibility. Her emotions affect her health. I do not think that she can weather a return to all that."

Margaret looked away from me, somber.

"I do not mean to speak so plainly," I said, trying to offer her some comfort. What was I doing, speaking so much about these situations when we were on holiday and so much away from it all? Truly, I will never understand the propensity of us, humankind, to dwell on the negative in such a happy moment.

"No," Margaret said, "you are right. I have been thinking of it for some time, as well. I want my mother to be happy and healthy, but father's life is in the North. And, despite all that I have ever realized, part of my life is there too. Meanwhile, at Milton the chimneys smoked, the ceaseless roar and mighty beat, and dizzying whirl of machinery, struggled and strove perpetually. Senseless and purposeless were wood and iron and steam in their endless labors; but the persistence of their monotonous work was rivaled in tireless endurance by the strong crowds, who, with sense and with purpose, were busy and restless in seeing after—stress and labor."

"What a painful irony that you have discovered, isn't it?"

"Yes. All that time, sad that I was leaving Helstone and the South, only to leave my heart in the North." Margaret chuckled sadly. "And now, here I am, in the very best of climates and society. I have a beautiful prospect before me, and I am thinking of Mr. Thornton, and the smoky prospect of Milton Common. Not only that, but I have been reminiscing."

"Reminiscing?"

"Yes, I have. I was thinking of the time when we first arrived at Milton. We both found the prospect of our lives to be so dreary, and bleak. We were determined to persevere. And we did. We thrived through it all. And we had to hold fast, for we would either sink or swim. And we were against the prospect of sinking. And now, looking back at it all, I realized too late..."

"What?"

"That I miss it. I miss every moment of it."

I smiled.

"Do you really?" I asked.

"Yes, I do. I miss when we met Little Molly. I miss when we would go around exploring. When I first visited you at Granger Hall. And we would see the mills and factories. And Bessy, Nicholas, Boucher."

"Even the strike?" I asked.

"Well, of course not that. But the fact of facing reality and being part of it all. Well, that alone is worth the risks of being thrust into life. All those moments of moments past. Things were simpler back then, even when we thought they were complicated."

"That's the beauty of single life and the main deficit to falling in love," I said, "when being single, you can order your life, and the strong always finds a way. But when falling in love, things become complicated. Paths separate, they deviate, and things are split. Perhaps, we can bring Mrs. Hale to Pemberley often. It is in the North, yes, but it is far enough away from the damp sort of air that hangs over Milton." Then I realized that anything I said still would not work. I could iron out the problem with all my powers of discerning, and there would still be something wanting. "Oh, what do I say? Life is never that simple anymore, is it?"

"No, it's not. And that's what frightens me."

She stood up and began to pace around the room, anxious.

"Father will want to return to Milton, and he will expect mother to go along with him. They are two people who are so much united. Father does not prefer to be away from her, and she does not prefer to be away from him. And I do not think that father can go back to being merely a clergyman. I think the energy of Milton is too much in his veins now. Even Pemberley might be too far away from the town. And if Mr. Thornton will have me..."

"Which he will."

"If he still wishes, then I will live in Milton as well."

She sat down on the bed.

"Oh, I have a headache."

I chuckled.

"Of course, you have a headache."

I kissed her forehead.

"Good luck trying to fall asleep."

When I returned to my room, Mr. Darcy was waiting for me.

We took one look at each other and knew what the other felt.

"Madam?" he asked.

"Yes, good sir?"

"You will take off all of your clothes."

"Oh, will I?" I challenged.

"Yes. Never mind, I shall do it for you."

Pulling me toward him, he ripped off my clothes and threw me on the bed. Falling into each other, I had to do my best to keep quiet as we enjoyed the intimacy of becoming one again.

When Mr. Darcy had reached his peak, he collapsed on top of me, his energy spent as I closed my arms around him, holding him in a protective embrace.

While doing so, he would occasionally rub his hands along my chest, caressing my breasts with his fingertips. As we remained there, happy in our own heaven, I told him about my conversation with Margaret. To my surprise, Mr. Darcy had an answer for our problems.

"Mr. Simpkins, my reverend at Kympton," Darcy said, "has recently written to me, considering retirement. He has inherited some money from a relative, in their will, and is considering staying with some family in Somerset. Since Pemberley is closer to Milton than Helstone, though still a distance away. He would not be too far from Margaret and Thornton."

"That would be a genius idea," I said, "and Darcy, that is a wonderful opportunity and offer to Mr. Hale. Mrs. Hale is accustomed to such a life, and she would feel the compliment of being connected to Pemberley. She could be outside in the fresher air more often. However, I wonder about Mr. Hale. He is so accustomed to being a tutor now, that I think that he cannot go back. He is a man of conscience and would never sacrifice his intellect to any sort of blind obedience."

"I am not the sort to have the archbishop have him swear to edicts that he does not approve of. Also, there are boys and men in the neighborhood who might want a clergyman who would also be their tutor. We could try it, Lizzy. Ask Mr. Hale what he thinks and then he can consider the matter."

"When will you ask him?"

"On the contrary, I think it would be better if you asked him. Or you and Margaret do it together."

"Why not you?"

"Who do you think that he would listen to more? His daughter and friend, or the Master of Pemberley. When it comes to the opposite sex, it is not as simple as you think. There are some things that women are better at confronting us men about. And some things that us men are better at confronting women over."

"Well now..."

"What?"

"That is a very intelligent deduction to make. Men and

men can connect on a level that women and women can do. But in other instances, both genders are of great meaning to the other, when it comes to most circumstances. Let it be said that both are vital to the others existence, in many more ways than just as daughter, mother and wife."

"And son, father and husband."

"Philosophy after lovemaking!"

"Aye," he chuckled. "We do it well."

He pressed his hands down my stomach, in between my legs and pressed his fingers deep within me. I bit my lip having to suppress my moans.

"Never fear, my dear," he whispered to me, "I will help you."

He covered my lips with his own, to help quiet me.

How I loved him.

Chapter 18

Chivalry

Sitting in the lounge at Granger Hall, Mr. Dennison was eating his midday meal. He had done so, specifically because he knew what to expect that day. For where he had sat, presented an excellent view of the road, and he was aware that Miss Maria Lucas was very good at always being on time. And she was.

The swish of her coat, the image of her bonnet, and her figure was as familiar to him as his own handwriting. Maria Lucas came down the street and Mr. Dennison jumped up from his seat, rushed to the window, to get a better view of her.

She is beautiful, Dennison thought to himself. *Just the sort of beauty that I like. The only one as beautiful as Miss Elizabeth. Except I am not afraid of her, as I was afraid of Miss Elizabeth. No. This is different. This is possible. I cannot have a woman that I fear. But I could have Maria. I could!*

He watched her as she met Charlotte Lucas at the front steps. Seeing Charlotte made him sneer. Like Elizabeth, she had a keen eye and a sharp wit. He always would have a resentment to women who could always get the best of him. Never would he know his insecurity arose from femininity being equally as powerful as the masculinity in himself. It was not in his nature to be so inflective about his own character.

Until what occurred in the next moment.

After he watched Maria disappear down the road with her sister, as they headed home, Mr. Dennison heard footsteps outside of the room. Hastily, he rushed back to the table, and he sat down, finishing his food.

Mr. Hunnicutt entered.

"Ah," Mr. Hunnicutt said, "just the man that I wanted to see."

"Me?" Mr. Dennison asked.

"Yes."

"Good God, whatever for?"

Mr. Hunnicutt did not even flinch. He was so accustomed to Dennison's comments.

"Is it so strange that someone would want to speak with you about something?"

"Hunnicutt, you never seek out my company."

"True, I do not. Therefore, you can very well imagine, that I come with an errand."

Dennison looked at him, coldly.

"I gather the sense that this is not going to be a congenial discussion."

"Do I look like I am about to chew you up and spit you out?"

"You always look happy. That's why I don't trust you."

"Of course, you don't. That is Victorian values for you; the concept of coldness. And my tendency to be a joyous person will always be strange to you."

Hunnicutt sat down casually opposite Dennison. There

was no malice in his look, and that's what unnerved Dennison. Hunnicutt was a man that could not be moved. It was a scary thing, in Dennison's eyes.

"What do you want of me?"

"I come about a woman," Hunnicutt responded. "That discussion that you never want to have but is always on your mind."

Dennison grunted.

"You don't know me at all."

"But I do. Men such as you, who despise women, are always secretly thinking of them. I know your sort, sir, and I am aware of what you are."

"And what am I?"

"A heartbroken man. It takes one to know one, so please don't pretend."

"There is no pretending. After all these years of us working together, you would know a bit of my history."

"Then let us go right to the heart of the matter. You are in love—or lust—with Miss Maria Lucas."

After such a declaration, Dennison was angry.

"I don't have to listen to this," Dennison spat, standing up and rushing to the door.

"It is not in your best interest to walk away from me," Hunnicutt responded casually.

"No?"

"No, because you know as well as I that I will pursue you, and publicly call you out for your affections, in the street. Now we can discuss it here, in private, or we can go outside and make a scene."

Dennison ground his teeth, but he did not move.

"Wise decision," Hunnicutt observed.

"What goes on in my heart is my business."

"It is, but when it concerns others, that is another matter. Miss Lucas is worried about your intentions for her sister. And Hanley and I have observed this."

"Miss Lucas ought to mind her own business."

"Her little sister is her business. And I will thank you not to argue with Miss Lucas about a discussion that I choose to have with you. I do this of my own accord, because I care for the Lucas sisters—almost as much as I cared for the Bennet girls."

Dennison looked at the floor.

"Are you ready to confess that you miss Elizabeth Bennet? Or Mrs. Darcy, as I ought to say."

Dennison rubbed his face.

"I don't understand," Dennison said, truly heartfelt and wistful. "Why do I miss her?"

"Because you are *you*. And you have been running from yourself for too long. Now your emotions have caught up with you, and they have come quickly. You barely know Maria, but it doesn't matter. You feel now, and it scares you. Doesn't it?"

Dennison did something that only Hunnicutt would have predicted: he almost began to weep.

"This is not fair," Dennison cried. "Why do I feel this way? Why now?"

"Because you have no choice."

"I cannot talk to her. But I want to talk to her. I try to avoid seeing her. But she's always in my mind. What do I play at? She will only hurt me the way others have."

"And that is why I will not let you near her," Hunnicutt insisted, "and nor will Miss Lucas or Hanley. Because you are not ready."

Dennison's eyes narrowed.

"You do not control me."

"But I can urge you," Hunnicutt persisted. "You are not ready to show your love, because you are too busy seeing the shadows of your pains in Maria's image. She is not that woman from your past. She is here, now, and you are harsh from your experiences. A man such as you need to learn softness, kindness, and what love really is. And how to walk away from rejected love, like a gentleman. You are still that frightened little boy who cannot overcome these things. Love is tenderness. Are you ready for that? You know that you are not. And until you are ready, you cannot address Miss Maria. You will hurt her. And Hanley and I will have to put a stop to it. Dennison, do not put us in that place."

"I don't know how to be any other way."

"Yes, you do. It is simple. You simply wake up one day, and say, today, I will be better. It's as simple as that. And until you do that, you will not be worthy of loving her or being loved by her."

Hunnicutt walked to the door and turned the knob.

"I know that you will follow my advice."

"And why would I do that?" Dennison asked.

"Because you are afraid of me."

"Afraid?"

Dennison scoffed.

"Laugh all that you wish," Hunnicutt continued, "but it's true. You are afraid of me, Dennison. Always have been."

"Yes," Dennison admitted, "I suppose that I am. I don't know why, but I am."

"I do know. It's because I am happy. And that frightens people like you. Your kind: rude, brash, emotionless, and an enemy of affection will always be afraid of those of us who are joyous, we smile, we laugh, we ran wild as children, and we even enjoyed the follies of our youth. You mask it all by calling us savage-like and unsophisticated, and insane. But you are afraid of us because we have something that you do not understand. We have a secret: we know how to be content with our lives, and it drives you lot mad. We spent our lives living, and you spent it waiting to die. What you cannot obtain naturally, Dennison, you can learn. Learn to be kind. And then you can speak more to Miss Maria. Never fear, mate. Despite all our history with you, we still believe in you."

Hunnicutt left Dennison there alone, to consider all his fears and what they meant.

As Hunnicutt walked through the halls, he passed Hanley's doorway. Stopping in, he saw Mr. Hanley packing away his books.

"Hunnicutt?" Hanley said. "How goes it?"

"That remains to be seen. I spoke with Dennison."

"About what?"

"A woman. The woman."

Hanley stopped what he was doing and looked at Hunnicutt.

"You did?"

"Yes, I did."

Hanley sat down.

"And what happened?"

"He will not go near her, until he has learned how to talk to her."

"Truly?"

"Yes. I threatened him—in my own sort of way."

"How do you manage it?"

"It's a gift. Now it's time for us to discuss your problem."

"My problem?"

"Yes. About your feelings for another lady. Another sister."

Sighing, Hanley raised his hand up, covering his face.

"You know?"

"Yes. I guessed."

"I don't understand what is wrong with me."

"Nothing is wrong with you. Your heart is alive, and so it beats, in hopes of loving something. Take comfort in the fact that both women you have loved were worthy of that love."

"But this hurts. I don't want to feel anymore."

"You have no choice. The second that you lose all feeling, that is truly when you ought to worry."

"I barely know Miss Lucas."

"I did not suggest that you ought to throw yourself in her way. I merely say that you ought to open yourself up to any prospect. One woman's heart was already secured before you had your chance. With Charlotte, it is another matter entirely. Her heart is open. She has no past loves to rival yours. Also, the only man to offer her a proposal of marriage did so out of revenge on his cousin. There was no real affection in the case."

"It is more than that."

"What else is there?"

"Sometimes, when a woman has been single for so long, without children, I have learned something. Often, they grow so accustomed to that style of living that it is all that they know. In fact, it seems to eventually be their preferred way of living. They have reached the point of preferring to be in situations where they do not have to think of having a husband to answer to, and they prefer getting their own way. Charlotte seems...free. In the manner that Elizabeth did, before the Derbyshire man had to come and remind her of moments past. Their history together won her over, but if they did not have that history...would he have won anything?"

"Ah, your mind has dwelled on what could have been. A familiar trap to fall into."

"You are about to tell me that you have never fallen into that trap?"

"Of course, I have. I am not stone, you know. But either you can focus on the 'what was', or you can concentrate on the 'what is'. And what is fact is that you have learned that your heart is strong enough to store two women in it. You have a second chance, Hanley. I think that you might grow to appreciate that."

"I wish that I could rally above this."

"You just have to feel what you feel. And the rest will fall in place. Tell Charlotte when you are ready."

"I do not think that I can suffer another disappointment."

"You can. It will just be another Milton story."

Mr. Hunnicutt prepared to leave.

"Hunnicutt?"

"Yes?"

How do you do it?"

"It's simple. I'm me." Hunnicutt smiled. "And there will never be another."

Chapter 19

Trouble in Paradise

The next day offered many possibilities for sunbathing. The main resort that we focused on was Yarmouth, and everything was promising about it, except for one prospect.

Today, we would reunite with three older acquaintances, and it did not seem like the most joyous of prospects.

"Brother and Mr. Darcy!" Miss Bingley declared, followed by the cries of Mrs. Hurst behind her, and Mr. Hurst who trailed behind, fully aware of the awkwardness of the situation.

Yes! Miss Bingley and the Hursts had fallen back into our lives.

When they had arrived, they registered into the hotel that we were staying in. Soon after, they sought us out and we met in the dining hall.

"Caroline and Louisa," Mr. Bingley greeted them, amiably, but hesitantly. After all, they were his sisters. They had not visited us sooner, because they had already made plans to stay with friends at that time of the year. Yet, it did not signify; Bingley was not blind to the fact that he had married a woman who was the last lady they wished their brother to pursue.

Mr. Darcy was not blind. He knew that Caroline Bingley had wanted to marry him.

I was not blind. I knew that Caroline Bingley hated the sight of me.

Jane was not blind. She knew that her previous friendship with both sisters was now flimsy and false at best, and that she was not what they wanted for a sister-in-law.

Margaret Hale was not blind. She knew the history between our families.

Kitty was not blind either. She knew that we were about to be showered with false praise, distributed by a family who were trying to find their way back into our good graces.

Only Colonel Fitzwilliam, Mr. and Mrs. Hale, Dixon, and Frederick were removed from the stain of prejudice.

After Bingley met his sisters warmly, they turned to the rest of us.

The first person that they greeted was Jane.

"So," Mrs. Hurst said, "we are sisters."

"Truly, we had known it," Caroline said, "when we first met you in Hertfordshire, we knew that you would be a constant part of joy in our lives. When we heard that you and Charles had married, Louisa and I looked at each other and declared: 'at last! Talk of a proper match'."

I rolled my eyes.

"Except for when they planned for Mr. Bingley to marry me," I heard Georgiana whisper to Kitty behind me.

I pricked my ears at this. They had spoken low, so no one else but me could overhear them.

"Truly?" Kitty asked. "You knew about that?"

"Oh, yes," Georgiana said. "I did. For that is why I

always was a little uncomfortable with the two sisters. I knew that their friendship with me was purely mercenary, for their brother's sake. Their affection for me was..."

"Forced?" Kitty guessed.

"Precisely."

"I have seen that before. Friendships not formed organically, so it does not feel real. And even though you cannot say it because you have no proof behind the superficiality, you feel it. So, it can never feel like you can establish anything on a level of nuance."

"That is what happened."

"That is the difficult business of friendships between us women: we prefer to form friendship, but instead we often form alliances."

"Yes. It's a self-defeating thing, isn't it? I do so wonder if men undergo the same problem of that."

"I hope so. I would prefer to think it more as a universal problem, and not a feminine one."

Georgiana smiled and then it was her turn to be put on display.

"Georgiana!" Miss Bingley declared, "oh, it has been too long since you and I had seen each other."

"Caroline and Louisa," Georgiana said, going forward and meeting the sisters casually. "You both are looking remarkably well and in the very best of looks."

"Ill health does not plague us," Mrs. Hurst said, "and we can see that you also have been enjoying the bloom of ideal youth. And we have been incomplete without your company. Haven't we been, Mr. Hurst?"

"Oh, what?" Mr. Hurst said, barely noticing the discussion. Mrs. Hurst was obviously ashamed of this and tried to cover it smoothly.

"Your sister was saying that she regretted the loss of my

sister's company, sir," Mr. Darcy refreshed his memory. "She was wondering if you agreed."

"Oh," Mr. Hurst said, and now it was his turn to feel ashamed. Darcy had a way of doing such. "Well, yes, my wife feels friendship closely. It is her skill, and I have yet to acquire it myself, but I am happy to see Mrs. Hurst's friend return to her."

"Thank you, Mr. Hurst," Georgiana said.

"And I suppose that I ought to congratulate you all on a triple wedding," Mr. Hurst said, trying to smooth things over even more, "it must have been a charming affair."

"It was," I said, "I can assure you, for I was there."

This forced the sisters to turn to me. Here came the moment of unwanted confrontation.

Here I was.

And there they were.

"Mrs. Hurst and Miss Bingley, and Mr. Hurst," I began, "you join us during a delightful time."

"We do," Mrs. Hurst said, "Miss Elizabeth, it is a delight to see you once more. Though our condolences are long overdue to you and your sisters, we are sorry for your loss. Losing both parents is difficult."

"Thank you. It was a trial."

"While our ladies suffered great misfortune," Mr. Darcy augmented, "the best compensation for it would be our affections."

"Precisely, and now there are more name changes," Colonel Fitzwilliam said, easily realizing that there was a silent tension under all of this. "Jane's last name has been changed to yours. Elizabeth is now Mrs. Darcy, and I can call my Kitty Mrs. Fitzwilliam, who will inevitably inherit the title of Lady Kitty Fitzwilliam when the time comes."

"Lady?" Caroline Bingley questioned.

"Oh, that is my oversight," Mr. Bingley said, "I forgot to include that in my letters. Do forgive me. I am so ill at letter-writing."

"Your humility, my dear," Jane said, "disarms reproof."

"Due to poor Miss Anne de Bourgh's passing away," Mr. Bingley explained, "Lady Catherine adopted Colonel Fitzwilliam as her heir to Rosings Park, making Mrs. Fitzwilliam as the new mistress."

Caroline and Louisa looked at Kitty in wonder and alarm. After all, now the sister who they did not consider was worth more than a few shillings of notice was higher in rank than them. Even in title.

"You are now in the level of peerage?" Caroline repeated.

"Often I do not think of it," Kitty said, "you can imagine that the revelation is very overpowering."

"I can imagine so," Caroline said, hiding her pain with a smile. "Well, Kitty, you and your sisters have quite the Rhodopis tale, do you not?"

"Cinderella is one of my favorites of the Grimm Fairy-tales. I did not know that you knew about the origins behind the story?"

"Oh," Caroline said, quietly upset that her superior intellect did not humiliate Kitty. "I didn't know that you learned about ancient Greek folktales."

"By a mere chance of good fortune," Kitty responded, "when I was in the North, a friend of mine, Raspberry Pitcher, was given a book about ancient Greek folktales in

7th century BC. That's when I learned about Rhodopis, the Greek slave girl who married an Egyptian King. And that was the first actual version of Cinderella."

"I thought that the first version was from the French," Mrs. Hale recalled, "oh, I feel quite ignorant."

"It is not your fault, my dear," Mr. Hale said, "with change of culture comes additions to stories, and then the person to take credit for it is the main one that we associate with the crowning achievement. Hence why most people associate Cinderella with being the creation of the Brothers Grimm. But even before the French adapted it, it was made into an Italian folktale."

"Yes," Kitty elaborated, "after its Greek origins, the Italian poet and fairytale collector, Giambattista Basille, published his version in the 1630s, and it was the first European version. But the story became popular when it was published by Charles Perreault, in French, in the 1690s. And then the Brothers Grimm published their version in 1812."

"It's a folktale with a long journey," Caroline said.

"Yes, it is," I said, "because it has a universal theme. The tale of a lady, who with no prospects and no hope of good fortune or a lovely fate, to have all tragedy overturn and be given the greatest life and love of all. It speaks to anyone, does it not?"

At last, Caroline looked at me in full.

"Yes, I suppose that it does."

"I remember once reciting a bit of Perrault's writing on the Cinderella theme," Georgiana said, as we walked onward. "Beautiful. Beautiful."

"Beautiful!" Dixon declared as we arrived at Yarmouth. The sight of the sand and the sea was enough to make her drop her maternal habit and marvel at the sight before her. Even though Mrs. Hale had been growing stronger by the day, Dixon still rolled her along in an invalid's chair. But when seeing it, Mrs. Hale rose out of it and stood along with the rest of us, marveling at the spectacle.

"At last," she cried, "I get to see the sand and waves again."

"If I had my way," Dixon issued, "we would stay here forever. I don't care what anyone says, the dirtiness of sand is worth wherever it gets to, provided that the sea air is there to always bring good health."

"What are humans?" I said to Mr. Darcy, "compared to the power of waves and the will of the winds? All nature is something to bow down to."

"We try to tame it with our machines," Darcy said, "but we will never get the better of her."

"Wisely put," Caroline had said next to us. This had made Darcy and I jump. We had no notion that she was standing that close to us. "In fact, I do not believe that I could have said it better myself."

She walked back to Mrs. Hurst, who had been speaking with Georgiana and Kitty.

"How long was she there?"

"No idea," Mr. Darcy said. "And it scares me."

"Me as well. I think she wanted to be close to you."

"No," Mr. Darcy responded, in denial, "surely, she..."

"Darcy, she fancied you a great deal. I still think, in her heart, that she has the impulse to be near you."

"Eliza?"

"Yes."

"I am terrified."

"Understandable. There is something very frightening about her. Don't worry. I will protect you."

"You will?"

"Of course," I said, amused. "I have been doing that for quite some time."

Mr. Darcy chuckled.

We walked along Yarmouth, admiring the scene before us with such quiet pleasure. The shore presented such a calming effect, that I do not believe that we all spoke very much. Rather, we were so mesmerized that we knew when all sort of conversation was not needed. This was as it should be, because with our three new arrivals, the scene had felt rather crowded. And there was no solution for what to do.

I had much to think on.

Afterwards, we did the traditional afternoon promenade, which was the focus for most ladies, and we also visited the sights of ancient architecture. Yarmouth was a picturesque sort of place that contained the Island's fascinating heritage.

The next day, we all planned to be of the unconventional sort.

Of course, with it being the times that they were, swimming in the ocean was not usually the object of visiting the coast. But there would always be a company like ours who preferred to use the bathing machines. Renting four of them: two for the men and two for the women, we had selected Ventnor. We all had purchased the lightweight clothes that sufficed for swimsuits.

When we all were dressed, we exited the machines, and we stepped into the sea.

Fortunately, the men were not too far away from us, therefore, we were able to see them at a short distance.

As the men and ladies beheld each other in our swimming clothes, we laughed. After all, they were not very flattering. But as we stepped into the water, we flinched at the coldness of it.

Soon, we adapted to the temperature, and all that was to be left was for Mrs. Hale to step down into the water herself. She was hesitant, having never gone into the sea before.

"I have seen it," Mrs. Hale said, "I have admired it, but now that I am here, I am afraid."

"Do not fear, Maria," Mr. Hale called out to her, going up to her, despite it not being proper decorum, "come in."

"Aunt," Frederick called, "it is delightful. I can promise that you will like it once you get in."

"Don't worry, ma'am," Dixon said, "I will be there with you, in every step of the way."

Encouraged by her family and Dixon, Mrs. Hale gently stepped into the water. Once she got in, she laughed.

"I cannot believe it," she cried. "It really is incredible. I am in the ocean."

When Frederick came up to her, he held her hand, while Mr. Hale held the other, and Dixon stood behind her, worried that she might fall backwards.

"See?"

"Oh, my dear boy," Mrs. Hale said, "is this what life is like for you, in Spain?"

"Yes, it is. And look what life it has given to me. It shall do the same with you."

"I do believe she will live," Margaret whispered to me, "yes, I do believe it. Or do I believe it because I must? I don't know."

I smiled and looked ahead as Colonel Fitzwilliam, Mr. Darcy and Mr. Bingley began to race along the water, to see who could outstrip the other.

Near me, I saw Miss Bingley, who also was watching them.

Deciding that there was nothing for it, I walked up to her, moving slowly through the water. I daresay that she did not see me as I waded along.

"They look handsome like that, don't they?" I asked her.

"Well," Caroline said, a little flustered, "they are amusing. Mrs. Darcy, I congratulate you. You have married one of the most illustrious persons in the land."

"Thank you, but would you believe that it is not the reason that I married him?"

"Faith, I did not even know that you preferred his company. In fact, from what I recalled, you seemed to prefer being at odds with him."

"I thought he hated me, so I thought it did well to return the compliment."

Caroline turned to me.

"That was what you thought?"

"Yes. He could not stand the sight of me when we first met."

"Well, I have the luxury of knowing something that you didn't."

"And what is that?"

"He did not prefer you when you first met. But it was a rash judgment that he soon did away with. He changed his mind, eagerly preferring your fine eyes to every other woman around him."

"Did that upset you?"

"What an impertinent question."

"I thought you wanted to talk about it. Or was I wrong?"

Caroline looked ahead, to avoid my gaze.

"Maybe you were. And maybe you were not." She took a sharp breath, running her hands over the surface of the water. "Yes, it did upset me. But do you know what was even more outrageous? Initially, he did not prefer you. And so, naturally, I adapted his mindset. Then he changed his mind, to prefer you, and that made me hate you all the more. I know that it is harsh to hear, but I find that perhaps I am upset. I cannot control what I say just now."

"Did you love him?" I asked as Mr. Darcy rose out of the water and Colonel Fitzwilliam shoved his shoulder, laughing since Darcy had been the victor.

"Now that is too bold."

"Very well. You don't have to answer it."

"But I do. Don't I? Because if I don't, you will always look at me in the same way that you do now." Caroline gave me a side glance. "And I don't want you to look at me that way."

"How do I look at you?"

"With pity, and a sense of resentment."

"Is it any worse than how you often looked at me?"

"No, perhaps it is not. But still, you have asked me a question, and I suppose that I ought to answer it. Sometimes I wonder if I was ever in love with him at all. Or maybe I was in love with the idea of him."

"When you look at him and I, how much does it hurt?"

"As if my soul has been ripped from out of my chest."

"Then you were in love with him. Perhaps it started out in more mercenary ways. Maybe you did like his life, what marriage to him represented, and the level of society that it would have placed you in. But along the way, you did fall in love with him."

Caroline's face distorted as she tried to refrain from crying.

"I understand why you loved him. It makes sense."

"Thank you," Caroline spoke quietly, only by way of a whisper, "I am dying inside. I know that it's not your fault. And time has taught me that I have been evil to you. And yet, I still feel as if I am the victim of something."

"You are suffering under a broken heart."

"I am. It's tearing me from the inside out, and I cannot bear it. I thought when I came here, I should do all in my power to ignore the cries of my heart and make sure to be accepted into your society. But I realize now that I am not ready. I need time away from you all. But I cannot run. After all, a young lady cannot ride off anywhere alone, for she is not her own master."

"Maybe you are. You have a townhouse."

"My sister has one. And my brother. I'm a single lady: what property do I have to run to? What story could I give for why I travel alone?"

"Speak to Mr. Bingley. Tell him, very gently, why you must leave. Ask him for his help, not by way of a cold stranger, but like a sister who needs her brother to care for her. He would do that for you."

"Perhaps I should. I don't want you all to see me like this."

"I understand. Time will help you. I cannot say that you will wake up one day, and your love for my husband will be over. Some loves remain with us."

"Especially when he was my first 'big' love, as it were. And I don't want to do anything or say anything to make you all hate me even more than some of you might do already."

"We do not hate you."

"Yes, you do. And I understand why you would. I wish you to be on the other side of the world. I'm sorry. You don't deserve that. But it just came out."

"I know. Like I said, you need time. Talk to Bingley. Tell him the truth and he will make every excuse that could be made. But I will tell you this. Even if the pain does not fully die, over time, the loss of Darcy will hurt less and less. Soon, it will not hurt at all."

"I want to believe you."

"Believe me. In this case, I am right."

She took a few steps away and then turned back to me.

"Forgive me for my negative feelings towards you. I see that you do not deserve it. However, I still feel it."

She moved away from me when Darcy swam near me, his body underwater.

When seeing his figure, I braved it, and I dove under the surface. When doing so, I dared to open my eyes, and there was Darcy's face, underwater.

Despite that he had little oxygen left, he kissed me. I placed my hands on his face, kissing him in return as a little bit of water fell into our mouths. My breath passed into his mouth, and we were able to remain like that, each exchanging affection under the cover of the waves.

When we stood up again, we heard laughter and clapping. We turned and it was Frederick Hale and Bingley who had done the laughing and cheering. My sisters and Georgiana cooed at me.

Mr. and Mrs. Hale, as well as Dixon, smiled warmly, but Mr. Hale looked away a bit, out of modesty.

Margaret blushed and looked down; wild laughter was not her habit.

Mr. Hurst did nothing.

And Mrs. Hurst looked at her sister, worried. Caroline Bingley looked away, in the other direction. From our view, she could simply do it out of modesty. However, I knew the truth.

She was crying.

We would never be friends. That was just the way life had worked out for both of us.

At dinner, Caroline was not present. Mr. Bingley conveyed her apologies to us, saying that she had been seized by a headache, and that she would be returning to London the next day.

She had received a letter from a friend who expressly wanted her company in town.

Everyone in the group accepted this explanation, except for myself.

"That is the real reason that she is leaving?" Mr. Darcy whispered to me as we lay in bed together, having just finished making love.

After we had been intimate, I told him about the conversation that Caroline Bingley and I had with each other.

"Yes," I answered, "that is the real reason. She will probably remain at her brother's townhouse. She might be alone there, but solitude sometimes is best at times like this. Dearest, was I wrong to tell you?"

"No. After all, you did not tell me anything that I had not known, in some form or another. I always told myself that her feelings for me were superficial at best, or mercenary at worst. I represented the elevation of station that she wanted, but now that I think of it, what else was she to want? After all, this is the way we raise our children to be."

"That is true. We are born into a world where we teach the advantages of marrying well. That is the chief lesson that ladies of our station are taught. There is nothing the world scoffs at as poverty, as well as the pursuit of wealth. When does prudence of economy end, and avarice begin? I am sure that I still do not know. Nor does the world. And what of her love for you? How does that make you feel?"

"Lizzy, I am about to say something strange."

"What?"

"Her love for me...well, it scares me."

"Does it?"

"Yes. I know that I ought to be flattered, but I am not. In fact, her love for me always frightened me a little. We men are not meant to fear those sorts of things, but we are."

"Well, we women are often scared when a man feels for us, and his affections are unwanted. We worry about how extreme his emotions flow, and will he commit to any extreme action if his sentiments go unrequited."

"Precisely. That is what I worry over now. Unrequited love is a frightening thing, when the person feeling those emotions can be volatile. Not all people know how to control it. Caroline would deliberately change her way of thinking to accommodate mine. She would base her character around mine. Initially, my vanity was swelled by this, for she reaffirmed my own prejudices and conceit. A weaker man would take pride in having a parrot. But my mind has grown, as has my character. I do not want that sort of adoration. Do you really believe that she will grow to recover?"

"I hope so. After all, she is now aware of what she is

about. Confrontation of one's mentality is the first step to recovery."

"And what about you," he asked me, "how did her confession make you feel?"

"In truth, there is no emotional change with me. I suppose it was merely because she was saying out loud something I have realized long ago. Her acknowledgement simply confirmed my theories. And she and I will never achieve any sort of bond. In fact, I know that we might end our lives always being silent enemies who exchange pleasantries because that is all that we can do. But, if she does take my advice, our adversarial relationship will be nothing more than inactive, at best. We will not do anything to hurt the other, but we will never wish to be in each other's company."

"Until you have to."

"Yes, until we have to. And we might often have to."

I ran my hands through Mr. Darcy's hair.

"I do not like that she covets you, in her heart. But I do understand why she fell in love with you. How could she not?"

"You flatter me."

"You like it."

"Yes, I do like it."

The next day witnessed the departure of Caroline Bingley from our company, but she was not alone. Fortunately, Mr. and Mrs. Hurst realized that it would be best to travel with her. We neither told them to stumble on their way out of the Isle when they left it, nor did we urge them to stay.

They were doing right by Caroline, and she was doing right by us.

Let departures fall where they would. We knew to let them do so.

"They came," I uttered to my sisters, "they spoke, and then they left. That was the best thing that they could have done."

"Yes," Jane said, "I do not want to speak ill of anyone, but their company with us presented an awkwardness that even I did not know how to fill up."

Chapter 20

Thunder In Paradise

When a woman makes the announcement that she wishes to shop, the men in the company wish to do either one of two things:

Attend as well, because he wishes to enjoy the spectacle of what they buy, or shop for himself as well.

Or run to the hills.

Our gentlemen did the latter.

Fortunately, they had an excuse. Frederick and the men in the company went to the unknown beach that tourists were unfamiliar with. If Frederick was correct, then we would go there tomorrow, with it being his last full day with us.

That gave us all the excuse in the world to go off on our own, enjoying the shops that Yarmouth had to offer.

Dixon rolled Mrs. Hale along, initially, but over time, we all took turns wielding the recovering lady around, and she enjoyed every minute of it.

If it could be said that our holiday had fully brought life back to Mrs. Hale, then it would be the ultimate thing to boast about. My only fear was that Frederick's departure the next day would lead to any sort of relapse on her health. There are few people who loss affects their health, but Mrs. Hale was that sort of person.

"In two days," Jane announced, "I had hopes of us going to Shanklin. I was told that it is a lovely sort of spot and was a quaint village."

"Well, I don't see why we could not," Dixon replied, "I do not see why the men would not want to go."

"And with us all amenable to the idea," I began, "everything about it has the chance of—"

I was cut off when I saw a gentleman walking in our direction. He came toward us, tipped his hat, and gave the familiar smile that haunted my memory.

How could it be?

No, not now!

"Ladies, we meet again."

"Mr. Wickham!" Kitty cried.

Yes, Mr. George Wickham had found his way back into our lives.

I could not believe it.

What could possess him to greet us in such a way? And truly, it was quite impossible for him to be here. And yet he was.

"Mr. Wickham," I said, unable to hide my astonishment, "what a surprise."

"Yes, I suppose that it is, and—" Mr. Wickham cut off when he saw Georgiana Darcy standing there. He blushed and did his best to recover. "And I have fallen into your lives very randomly, haven't I?" He turned to Georgiana. "Miss Darcy."

"Mr. Wickham."

"I—well, you are looking very well. However, I declare that you always have."

"Thank you, Mr. Wickham."

The horrid man.

He was the one who told me that Georgiana Darcy had grown up to be very proud and had slandered her character. And now here he was, caught in the very lie by seeing her again. He looked at me and read the disapproval in my eyes. By me being in her company, it was evident that I must have learned of her true character. And he knew that I was aware of his deception. But even more, he had to wonder what Miss Darcy was doing with us. After all, he knew nothing about all that had transpired since he had left Hertfordshire.

"Well," Mr. Wickham said, "this is quite a surprise. Miss Bennet, Miss Elizabeth, Miss Kitty, and is that Miss Hale?"

"Yes, it is," Margaret said next to him.

"Well, you are looking as lovely as the Bennet ladies here. In fact, if I had not known that you were from a different family, I would have declared you for being a Bennet lady yourself."

"Well," Margaret replied, her eyes like ice, "proof of my lineage is before you. Mr. Wickham, this is my mother, Mrs. Hale, and Dixon, our servant."

"Ah, Mrs. Hale, I should have known that you were Miss Hale's mother. She evidently gets her loveliness from you."

"You are too kind, sir," Mrs. Hale said.

"No, I can assure you that I am not. When it comes to ladies' beauty, I always speak the absolute truth."

Even when you spend the rest of your time speaking lies.

"Also," Mrs. Hale continued, "since Mrs. Bennet is not

here to speak for her daughters, I must correct you. They all no longer carry the name of Bennet. Jane is now Mrs. Bingley, Elizabeth is Mrs. Darcy and Kitty is Mrs. Fitzwilliam."

"Darcy and Fitzwilliam?" Mr. Wickham uttered, looking between us.

"Yes," I confirmed. "I am recently married to your old schoolfriend, Mr. Darcy of Pemberley."

"And I am wed to another acquaintance of yours," Kitty confirmed, "Colonel Fitzwilliam."

"Well," Mr. Wickham replied, astonished, "that is a great shock. I must offer you three my congratulations."

"Thank you," I replied coldly, "the fortune is entirely on our side. After all, we have had the good fortune to have united with three honest and principled men."

"You can confirm this," Georgiana asserted, "after all, you grew up with my brother, George."

"Yes, I did," Mr. Wickham replied, "always have I respected the Darcy family."

"Really?" Georgiana repeated. "I was unaware of that."

By Jove! Georgiana, that was fantastically said.

"Well," Mr. Wickham said, "I regret if I ever gave off any other impression."

"Also," I said, "forgive me, Mr. Wickham for my frankness, yet sometimes, one can hear of false reports. When last I heard of you, you had deserted from the army. And yet, here you are, as large as life."

"I heard of that as well," Dixon confirmed. "It was the talk of the regiment when they were stationed at Milton."

"Ah," Mr. Wickham responded. "Yes, I daresay that I fell into a quagmire of misfortune."

"Some would call it misfortune," Kitty said, "others might call it wickedness and dishonesty."

Mr. Wickham showed how alarmed he was by this declaration—especially since it had come from Kitty. For so long, she had favored him, even more than I had. Her feelings were not romantic as much as they were that of a person who merely preferred the attention Mr. Wickham bestowed on Lydia and herself. And now, to obviously have lost her blind affection for him... well, he evidently had not foreseen that.

"Well," Mr. Wickham said, "whatever my flaws, I can easily say that I have made a proper recompense for my history. Recently, I was able to redeem my post."

"You redeemed your post?" I asked. "How?"

"Let us just say, that much can be bought with money. Especially when it was due to financial situations that led to me abandoning my post to begin with. And now, here I am, free of any harmdoing, and able to walk about the Isle during a sunny day. We are in a golden age of speculation and land purchases."

"Speculation?" Margaret Hale repeated. "You invested in a money scheme."

"I never knew that you were involved in that level of the economy," I said.

"Well, that is the beauty of life right now," Mr. Wickham responded. "South America is a place of wonder to the British settler, and sometimes, landowners need a little assistance in selling it to colonists who want a better life for themselves."

I observed his clothes, and I saw that he was dressed very nicely. Too nicely to not be independent.

"You have become a salesman for land?" I asked.

"Yes, I have. I was able to gather enough respectability,

clout, and when I turned myself into the army, reporting my crimes, I was able to discharge of any wrongdoing and any other charges that had been laid down to my account."

Debts! That's why he defected. Wickham had incurred a lot of debt, and so he fled to avoid payment. In some manner or another, he must have found a way to pay them.

"But enough of my history," Wickham continued, turning to the Hales, "and speaking of desertion, I recall that your family has also had its share of interesting encounters with her majesty's navy. Didn't it have to do with your son, Mrs. Hale? Unless I am mistaken, was his name Frederick Hale?"

When hearing Wickham mention Frederick's name, most of us froze from shock. Yes, Frederick's actions did get into the papers, but since it had been so long ago, most people would not have remembered the situation.

Especially not Wickham, who had little acquaintance with the family.

"You are mistaken," Georgiana clarified, "Frederick Hale is not Mrs. Hale's son, but her nephew. And he is of no crime to be spoken of."

I closed my eyes, highly embarrassed. I also took one look at Margaret Hale, who also felt the humiliation. Wickham would know that it was not so. If he read the papers, and somehow committed it to memory, he would know of the reverse. Unless he was not wholly aware of the particulars.

Yet if that were the case, we had one thing to benefit us in this circumstance: Wickham was slightly unnerved by Georgiana. For here was the woman that he attempted to elope with, and when it was discovered that he was marrying her solely for her inheritance, then he would naturally waver in her presence. After all, despite that he was practically shameless, there are few people still alive who have some sort of affection on the apathetic: childhood friends who they have a strong connection with, no matter how much they do not wish to.

"If that be the case, then I apologize," Mr. Wickham said, hiding his apprehension behind a smile. For those of us who knew of him, we were not fooled. He was affected. Very much so. "Perhaps, all those years ago, I was mistaken. When I read the article in the Gazette, it specifically spoke of a mutiny that was led by a Lieutenant by the name of Frederick Hale."

"When it comes to names, young Wickham," Dixon affirmed, "It's common to find the same name throughout the course of an empire. You must have been reading about another Hale man in the paper. The Frederick Hale in this family is a nephew, and he lives in Spain."

"Dixon," Wickham said, "I stand corrected. The mutineer that I read of escaped the trappings of the law, and there is a reward on his head for whoever catches him. If he were caught, the captor would have quite the bounty on his hands."

"I guess you are mistaken, sir," Dixon said.

Then he looked at Margaret.

"And Miss Hale? We have not seen each other since I attended that dinner party, and it was all too brief of a meeting. Where your cousin met that captain? What was his name?"

"Captain Lennox," Margaret responded.

"Did the good captain manage to snatch him up such a fine conquest as your cousin?"

"He did not catch anything, but achieved his prize sincerely," Margaret replied, coldly, "that cannot be said for all men, can it?"

"No, I suppose that it cannot."

Immediately, Wickham knew that he could not win with Margaret Hale. She was determined not to like him, and that was that.

There was only one problem with this scenario: Mrs. Hale never learned how to look deceptive. In fact, the pain of the situation was written all over her face. And if we were not careful, Wickham would read that deception.

"And I see that you are still up to a charming sort of nonsense," Dixon said to him.

"Dear me, Dixon," Wickham replied, "you do me a disservice."

"Do I?" Dixon countered. "You grouped Mrs. Hale's nephew with a lawbreaker. Now if that's not nonsense, then I don't know what is."

"I can see that my presence aggravates you ladies," Mr. Wickham said, "and I do not want to be a blight upon your view any longer."

"Yes," Georgiana replied, "do that little thing."

Mr. Wickham smiled, insecure, tipped his hat to us and walked away.

Suddenly, he turned back to us.

"I shall be staying on the Isle, at a friend's villa house, called Sienna Orchards. The family's name is Reed. Perhaps you may have heard of them. They are a naval family."

Reed!

That was the name of Frederick's captain. It could be a coincidence, but I did not put much faith in coincidences these days. If that was the same family, which was likely, then the mysteries were unfolding too much for me to maintain a proper pace with them. How in the world did Mr. Wickham become friendly with the Reed family?

How did he *truly* honor his debts? Speculation only works when you have money to gamble.

How did he manage to escape punishment from being a deserter?

How did he manage to walk about the world with such liberty?

"We have not made their acquaintance," Margaret Hale uttered.

"You really ought to; they are such a lovely family."

Once more, he nodded to us and left, with us entirely at a loss.

Once we were out of earshot, we turned immediately and began to walk quicker.

"No," I demanded, "do not walk quicker. If you do, then he might turn around and know that something is wrong."

"We should—" Mrs. Hale began to speak, but Margaret cut her off.

"Not here," Margaret insisted, "we must not speak of anything until we are inside and free of anyone overhearing us."

We walked on. Despite myself, I could not help but look back. As did Georgiana next to me.

When I spied him, he gave me a charming smile, that at one time or another, I would have been enthralled by.

Yet, now, I saw the haunting and sardonic tone behind it. His charm was almost malicious. There was almost a hidden menace beneath it all.

And then he saw Georgiana looking at him. And here, his smile slackened, and something like a blush came across his face. Once more, I saw a quick glimmer of humiliation run over his expression before it was masked by complacency.

They locked gazes before he looked down and walked away.

Quickly, Georgiana looked away from him and focused ahead. In her eye was at first an overpowered expression, and then it was replaced by a subtle rage.

Instinctively, Kitty came alongside her and took her hand.

"Georgie," she whispered, "are you well?"

"The villain," Georgiana hissed under her breath. "The villain."

"Yes," Dixon repeated, rolling Mrs. Hale along. "Despicable creature wrapped in handsome dressing."

Dixon leaned into Mrs. Hale, who was looking more overwhelmed by the minute.

"Don't worry, missus," Dixon assured her, "that fool will not get the better of us. Don't vex yourself. It will not help your health."

Despite her assurances, Mrs. Hale's eyes lost their animation, and she grew pensive and somber.

I could not blame her. For now, the holiday that had begun so assuring, turned into a nightmare where her son could easily be discovered and dragged into a court martial that could lead to his death.

We returned to our hotel room, and sat with Mrs. Hale, to give her company. At first, we didn't speak very much, because we were so unnerved. Then we suddenly began to speak at once.

"The horrid man," Georgiana said, going to the fireplace, and staring into the flames. "Why must so much cold-hearted tendencies be dressed up in such beauty?"

"I don't understand," Mrs. Hale said, "from what I heard of Mr. Wickham, wasn't he considered a charming fellow?"

"Charm, sadly," I said, "can be very good at concealing for the evil character that lies beneath."

"Mrs. Hale, and Margaret," Jane offered her condolences, "I am sorry. I had no knowledge that he was aware of Frederick's history. Truly, he never spoke of it."

"Probably because he was unaware of it," I said, standing up and falling into contemplation. My deductive skills were awake, and I was in a mood to understand everything that had transpired. "Remember that he is now on holiday with the Reed family."

"And Frederick's captain was Captain Reed," Margaret said.

"Precisely," I said, "I am of every belief that Wickham would have easily learned of Frederick's situation through the Reed family, if they have any connection to that same captain. Which is more certain than not. After all, Wickham specifically mentioned that they were a naval family. The connection is too much not to be identical."

"And Wickham deserted the army," Jane added. "The only way that he could have possibly cleared himself of any criminal history was if he managed to have some connection that could have absolved his crime."

"I am also curious about the debts that he incurred, and what he did to compensate his debtors. I don't fully buy the story that he told us."

"We are forgetting something important," Kitty said, gesturing to Georgiana, "there is someone here that we owe an explanation to."

We all looked at Georgiana, and I felt the pain of having to burden her with the history that we tried to suppress.

Afterwards, I looked at Margaret, Mrs. Hale, and Dixon. They each looked at Georgiana.

"With your permission," I said, "I think Georgiana has a right to know what we speak of."

"I suppose it ought to be mentioned," Margaret acknowledged. "It is unfair to not take you into our confidence, Miss Darcy."

Georgiana did not look confused. On the contrary, she looked resigned. Turning to Kitty, she smiled, out of respect for Kitty considering her.

"Thank you, Kitty, for caring to bring me into your confidence. However, you all do not need to worry over my ignorance on the matter, or fear of me being aware of Frederick's history." Georgiana looked at the Hales and Dixon. "I am aware that Frederick Hale is really your son, Mrs. Hale, and Margaret's older brother. I am also aware that he stays here, risking his life, to see you in better health. Just as I also am aware that he is practically banished from Britain because he led a mutiny, under Captain Reed. And his actions are punishable by death."

"You know already?" Kitty asked.

"Darcy told you," I realized.

"Yes. Mind you, he did not do it to break confidence with anyone here. It is merely that I am his sister, and he trusted me with his secret—out of respect."

"I am glad that he told you," I said. "That was the right thing to do."

"Georgie," Kitty assured her. "We didn't conceal

anything from you out of any disrespect for you at all. You are the best sister we could have obtained. It is merely to protect you and the Hales."

"Precisely," I said, "the less you knew, the more you could not be incriminated at all. Ignorance was our way of protecting you."

"And Miss Darcy," Mrs. Hale said, tears almost swelling up in her eyes, "I so much wanted as little people to know as possible. You must understand."

"I understand," Georgiana said, completely at ease, "believe that I am not offended in the slightest. With a secret such as that, a family of course does not ever wish to reveal it at all. I know what it is like to not want to expose anyone to the pains of one's past. We are all human. We all have a secret."

"Thank you," Margaret said.

"See, madam?" Dixon assured Mrs. Hale, "we are not forlorn or abandoned. We have friends here. Keep a cheery eye. I don't want your emotions affecting your health. That is not what Master Frederick would want. Especially since he risked so much to remain here to keep you in good spirits. Don't make his risk count for nothing."

"True, mama," Margaret said, sitting down next to her and taking her hands. "Frederick was aware that he might get caught, he even misses his wife, but he would rather remain until he sees you restored to life. Gather courage from that."

Mrs. Hale steadied out her breathing and tapped Margaret's hand.

"Yes, my dear. You are quite right. I will rally. Yes, I will."

While Margaret comforted her mother, I drew near Georgiana, who had returned to the fireplace. The flames danced in her eyes as she stared into its hypnotic movements, letting her memories haunt her.

"Georgiana," I began.

"Yes?" she asked, still looking at the flames and not at myself.

"First, I thank you again for understanding all of this. But let us talk of matters that are harder to hear of. Wickham."

Georgiana closed her eyes, exasperated. "I can assume that you know the history between myself and him."

"Like you, your brother was kind towards me and availed me of the truth. But he did it out of necessity. Like you, I too was ensnared by Wickham's charms. Darcy told me the truth, to remove me from the willful blindness that I placed on myself."

"There was not as much willfulness of it as much as over-persuasion," Georgiana said. "Wickham has a habit of pulling a significant proverbial wool over a person's eyes. Forgive my turn of phrase or my sudden change of habit of frankness."

"Not at all. I understand precisely why you are this way. We ladies are not always supposed to say only pleasant things. Sometimes, we must be honest about the world around us."

"Precisely. And with Wickham, I will not mince words. He has a black heart. Not a criminal one—excepting desertion. But I truly do feel that he has no knowledge of remorse."

"I am not too certain of that."

"You are not?"

"With most people, I believe that you are right. But with you, I do believe that there is something in him that is a little unnerved."

"It is the look of a man who knows that he has committed a grave error and does not want the rest of the world to be aware of it. If anyone learned that he tried to convince a fifteen-year-old girl, who is Mr. Darcy's little sister, to elope, there would be no end to the gossip, and it would hurt his reputation. If there's one thing that Wickham cares about, it is establishing his character everywhere."

"I am not so certain. One thing that your brother told me was that Wickham was very good at making friends. But keeping them was not his skill. He always manages to display his true intentions eventually. Not all villains are good at keeping their mask up forever."

"But he will always land on his feet. That's just his way."

"Other than that, how about your feelings? What was it like to see him again?"

"It was pure agony," Georgiana said, "and that's what has led to me being harsh in my speech. I thought he was out of my life forever, but here he is. Like an unwanted ink spot on one's white linen that cannot get out. And to see him!"

Georgiana's face displayed all the subtle rage of a woman who faced her worst memory. Her cheeks reddened and I could tell that she was wrestling through the emotions of seeing someone who broke her heart.

"Georgie!" Kitty called. "Come here. We have much to speak about."

Georgiana smiled.

"My sister calls you Georgie?" I questioned.

"Yes. I've never had someone call me that before. And yet, there seems to be something oddly familiar about it all."

Georgiana left me, walked over to Kitty and they began to talk immediately. Whatever else Georgiana was feeling, Kitty would seek it out. She had the gift for delving to the truth of a person's heart and helping someone come to terms with it.

Margaret came up to me as Dixon began to pour some tea for Mrs. Hale.

"I have been making decisions," Margaret said.

"And what are they?"

"When Frederick returns, we must get him to leave. The first ferry out of the Isle, to London, and then he must leave England."

"True. The suddenness will alarm him, but we must get him back to his wife."

"If only I could meet her," Margaret said. "That will never be, will it?"

"Maybe, one day, you can go to Spain."

"You and I both know that our lives are not always our own."

There was a knock on the door, I went to it, and it was our servant girl, Hannah. She handed me a letter, and it was for Margaret Hale.

I thanked Hannah and could not help but read the name of the sender.

"Margaret," I said, handing it to her, "it's for you. It's from Marlborough Mills."

Margaret looked at the letter, her eyes raising slightly.

"Who am I to care for my heart at a moment like this," Margaret said, putting the letter down.

"I think now is as good a time as any," I said, "lovers have a way of alleviating woes. Read the letter."

Margaret obeyed, sat down by the window, unfolded the letter, and began to read.

As she did so, we heard some active footsteps approach the door, and there was a hearty knock against it.

"I'll get it," Jane said, going to the door. When she opened it, our men walked inside, each filled with masculine energy. They all had smiles on their faces, even Darcy.

"What a good time that we found you all so soon," Bingley said, kissing Jane on the cheek, "oh, I cannot wait to take you there."

"Good fortune has found us," Frederick Hale said as he and his father walked up to Mrs. Hale and Margaret. His eyes were alight with joy. "Oh, the spot was as delightful as I had remembered it. With the right amount of servants there, we all can partake at sea-bathing in one of the most remote spots on the Isle, that is lovely, and the waves are calm and there is very little undercurrent. You all will love it."

Mr. Darcy came up to me and took my hand. In his eyes was the same level of amusement.

"You are happy with this," I said, equally as animated. Sadly, I knew that *that* look of pure joy in his eyes was about to evaporate. What I would give to avoid that eventual expression. But there was nothing for it.

"Yes, I am. Eliza, you would not believe, but it is a beautiful spot. And due to its placement, I do believe that we ladies and gentlemen can swim together with no hint of scandal. Oh, would you believe? I do not even care. Let anyone talk. We are three married couples, a sister, and a family. I refuse to care of propriety that does not count in my estimation. I think...that I now understand what you Bennets always felt when you were filled with such gaiety on events."

Oh dear! Why did this have to happen now?

What I was feeling evidently was displayed in my eyes because Mr. Darcy's animated expression deflated.

"What's wrong?" he asked me.

"Darcy, would that I could keep this soft look in your eye, for I like it so. But yes, something has happened."

"What!" We heard Frederick shout on the other side of the room. I turned and I saw that him and Mr. Hale's faces were horrorstricken.

And now the penny falls...

"Something happened indeed," I uttered, "Darcy, it is too distressing. Wickham is back in our lives. And he knows about Frederick's history."

Once the news was completely unfolded, many decisions were made.

"We have to get Frederick aboard the soonest ferry tomorrow morning," Margaret said, "and get him to London where he can book passage to Spain."

"Yes," Mrs. Hale said, "but is there any ferries that are departing the Isle today?"

"If there are, they will already be booked up," Colonel Fitzwilliam said, "however, if you like, I can go and make inquiries at the docks."

"Oh, do please, Colonel," Mrs. Hale said.

"If I am unsuccessful," Colonel Fitzwilliam said,

putting his hat back on, "then I will arrange for Frederick to leave on the next ferry available."

"Thank you, Colonel," Frederick asserted. "Thank you all for your kindness."

"I'll come with you," Kitty said, "if you don't mind, Richard."

"You think I'm going to say no?" Colonel Fitzwilliam said, chuckling gently. "Go on, lonely one, and get your shawl and bonnet. Then let's fly to water."

"Like two crows or geese?" Kitty asked, rushing to grab her shawl, and put her bonnet on as Colonel Fitzwilliam tied the ribbons for her to get it right.

"Take your pick. Though, I am not averse to being compared to a falcon myself."

"You'll be a falcon, and I'll be a BluJay," Kitty said, opening the door.

"Now that is a match made in an odd sort of heaven," Colonel Fitzwilliam said, closing the door behind them, "and since I was born on an odd-numbered day, it makes a great deal of sense. Good thinking, Kitty."

"One thing is certain," Mr. Darcy said to Frederick, "our excursion must be cancelled. Frederick, we will take you to your room and you must remain in there for the whole of the day."

"Yes, of course."

Mr. Hale took Frederick's hand.

"Frederick, promise me that you will listen," Mr. Hale insisted. "Do not go anywhere until it's time to get you to safety and far away from this Wickham character. The Reeds are here."

"Of course," Frederick said. "But whoever this Wickham is...what is he to do with my business!"

"He is a man who cares for money," I said, "and there is

a bounty on your head. Mix that with being friend to the Reeds, and he has everything to feel himself invested in your business."

"And that's what makes me wonder," Darcy augmented, "I cannot help but be curious how he even fell in with the Reeds, and how he managed to escape any sort of punishment for his desertion."

"I have my theories that the Reeds *are* connected to any sort of absolution of his crimes," I said, and yet, my curiosity was not enough. I wanted to know the truth, and my rash side was not going to be satisfied until I offered the suggestion. "So why don't we find out?"

"How so?" Jane asked.

"It's simple. I can assume that it is not difficult, by any means to become aware of the Reeds residence."

"I know precisely where it is," Georgiana said, "Sienna Orchards is widely known in this Isle. I knew it belonged to the Reeds, but Reed is a common name. Therefore, I never made the connection."

"Then why not call upon them?" I asked. "After all, nothing could be so harmless to do so, and nothing more flattering on their side than to meet the Master of Pemberley, the Master and Mistress of Rosings Park and Netherfield Park. I daresay that we don't even need to send a card first."

"What would be the purpose of doing that?" Mrs. Hale asked.

"Perhaps," I said, "If Mr. Darcy, Georgiana, and I do go, we can speak to Mr. Wickham, and maybe even clarify anything that he might tell Captain Reed, if Captain Reed is there. No wonder what he might be telling the man."

"And if I go," Georgiana said, "if Wickham feels any sense of shame, hinting that he might have tried to elope with me, might scare him from telling the captain anything. Like I said, he cares for reputation."

"That is better than nothing," Darcy said, "and I confess, that the more we know, the better. After all, Wickham has much to gain by turning Frederick over. The best that we can hope is to make him wholly unaware of where Frederick even is."

"Then do it," Mr. Hale said, "thank you all. At a distressing time like this, it does well to have such loyal and steadfast friends."

I turned to Darcy.

"I will be but a moment. If I am to look like Mrs. Darcy, I had best do it in my best coat and to make myself look as impressive as ever."

"Much can be gained from that," Darcy said, "we'll be waiting."

I raced to my bedroom, and began to take the coat from the closet, when I found that I was followed by Margaret. When she entered, she closed the door behind her, with the letter still in her hand.

"Don't worry," I assured her, "all will be well."

"I hope so. I need some cheering now."

"Cheering?" I questioned. "You have a love letter from a man who is sincere. Use that to give you hope."

Margaret's eyes betrayed her. While her face was unmoving, I detected that there was a problem.

"Margaret?"

Pause.

"Like I said," Margaret replied slowly, "there is no point in caring for my heart, when there are other problems at hand."

"Margaret... what does the letter say?"

"Nothing."

"Margaret?"

Quietly, Margaret sat down on my bed. She laid the letter down for me to read if I wanted.

"Thornton writes back to me revoking his courtship to me as well as removing any future proposal of marriage."

I could have been knocked down with a breath upon my face. This could not be happening. After all was said and done, this could not be happening. After finally finding her feelings for him, did Thornton really lose it for her? What evil was blowing through England?

"What?" I gasped.

"Yes."

"That cannot be true."

"It is, but not out of him losing his good opinion of me. Elizabeth, the strike knocked him down and delivered a great blow to Marlborough Mills. He is too much in debt, and now he has lost his business."

"He has?" I asked, horrified.

"Yes. He has lost Marlborough Mills, and everything he fought for. So, out of the loss of his fortune, his source of income, he has retracted his offers towards me, unable to support a wife, and refusing to chain me down to a marriage of poverty. He releases me...to save me."

Finally, Margaret began to weep. Now she had learned to love.

Chapter 21

Lightning Strikes

In the carriage, Darcy, Georgiana, and I rode to Sienna Orchards, the Reed house. Despite that we had not sent a card first, we were eagerly granted entry and the whole family greeted us—excepting Captain Reed himself and Mr. Wickham. Both men were currently out, but Mrs. Reed expected him within the course of half an hour.

Since Mrs. Reed was aware of the Darcys of Pemberley, she felt the compliment of their presence, and my newly appointed honor of being the new Mrs. Darcy also raised me to that same distinction.

Mrs. Reed was not alone. She and Captain Reed had no children, but she was surrounded by a group of friends who accompanied her. They were a noisy sort, and I was not upset with this. Since I had been so eager to see Mr. Wickham and give him a piece of my brutal honesty, I was not in the mood to make idle chatter. But Mrs. Reed and her friends were. In another life, I would have been annoyed with the constant nonsense that they produced, but what else could they talk about? It was evident that they were not given the best of education, and when you are not allowed the proper lessons, you are going to reduce your conversation to gossip and talks of finery. That being said, sometimes gossip is merely news, with an embellished polish. If it is true news, then the gossip is another way of being aware of what goes on around you. When it is false, it is dreadful slander.

When Mrs. Reed managed to find time to have words with me alone, she asked me how my wedding went.

"Unorthodox," I said, "and I preferred it that way."

"Did you? What was unorthodox about it?"

"Everything. It was a triple wedding, for a start. And when we married, we raced to the church. We were as eager to marry, and we could not wait."

"How romantic. I recall when my husband was that way when I first met him. Then you spend a few years married and the change occurs."

"Change?" I asked, "to what are you referring to?"

Mrs. Reed laughed. "Oh, surely your mother and father underwent the same sort of change that I speak of."

"I still need clarity on the matter, if I am to answer correctly."

"After a while, when you marry, a person's character can alter. I refer to the change that occurs when you transition from courtship to actually living with a person. When you first meet someone, they are so determined to ensnare you by showing you the very best sides of themselves. And then...when the doors are closed, and you are attached to them, the veneer drops, and you see the person's true character." She looked ahead of me, as if seeing an invisible nightmare. "All sense of romance evaporates. No more are there sweet words. Those words become talks solely of practicality, and then words of coldness. That marriage soon turns into an alliance of casual acceptance and indifference.

We are all a little mad; that is what it means to be human, of course. But for some, they are not aware of their madness. They are as much a stranger to their own insanity as if they had never become acquainted with it."

I was enthralled by her narrative. Not because I believed that I would walk down that path—I knew that I would not. Darcy and I entered our marriage so much aware of each other's true character. There was no chance of deception entering my life. But such a confession did shed light on Mrs. Reed's life—and what sort of man that Captain Reed was. A person can only know of a nightmare if they already had it or lived it. Mrs. Reed clearly had lived it.

"Are you familiar with this sort of fate?" I asked her. My question drove her from her own self-absorption, and she blinked, returning to the reality of being placed beside me. "Do you know what it is like?"

"I beg your pardon?"

"I asked...are you familiar with that sort of situation?"

She breathed in heavily.

"Perhaps I am not. Or perhaps I am. You all wait for Captain Reed to come. I would advise against it. My husband is not the sort who understands how to be pleasant company to visitors. Even when he ought to esteem them."

"But he is friends with Mr. Wickham, who I made the acquaintance of when he was in Hertfordshire."

"Oh," Mrs. Reed said, with a raised eyebrow. "You knew him when he was in the militia?"

"Yes," I said. "That's the last we heard of him. If Captain Reed is as you say, I wonder that he should prefer Wickham's company. After all, Wickham is often considered to be a very talkative sort of man."

"Well, that is simple. Wickham saved his life."

I blinked.

"Saved his life?" I echoed.

"Yes."

"Ah," I said, "that would explain a great deal."

I turned to Darcy and Georgiana, who were sitting amongst Mrs. Reed's friends.

"My dear, and Georgiana," I said, "I have learned something of an older acquaintance of ours. Mr. Wickham."

Darcy and Georgiana perked up.

"Have you?" Mr. Darcy asked.

"Yes, and it seems like we are about to hear a unique story. Apparently, Captain Reed is bound to Mr. Wickham in a surprising way. Mrs. Reed has told me that Wickham saved the captain's life."

Darcy and Georgiana looked in quiet alarm.

"Saved his life?" Georgiana repeated.

"Yes," Mrs. Reed said, her chest swelling with pride. "Mr. Wickham is one of the most charming men that I have experienced. He is very good at calming my husband's ill temper."

All her friends confirmed this. It was evident that Wickham had worked his magic over their minds, and they were enraptured by his good looks and charming demeanor.

"Pray," Georgiana said, "I am starved by curiosity. How did Mr. Wickham perform this gallant deed?"

"Well," Mrs. Reed said, "you know how some men have their pleasures that they enjoy. My husband is a bit of a gambling man. Nothing serious, but just a mere diversion for him. Well, that is where he met Wickham. Both my husband and Mr. Wickham had been fortunate at these particular games, but there were some people there who did not enjoy their success. From what I understand, there was a conflict, the losing men attacked my husband, and

Wickham saved my husband from being brutally beaten by one of the ruffians."

"Ah," Mr. Darcy realized, "now much has been made evident."

"Evident?" Mrs. Reed asked.

"Yes," Mr. Darcy said. "There are some parts of my one-time friend's history that was a little unknown to me. Now it is all laid out."

"Wickham was a friend of yours?" Mrs. Reed asked.

"Yes. He was raised on my estate, Pemberley, and my father paid for his education. Did he never tell you all?"

"No, he did not. I wonder why he wouldn't."

"Fascinating."

Mrs. Reed became loathe to have us leave, therefore, she offered to give us a little tour of their grounds.

We accepted and we followed her outside.

Walking up to Darcy, he offered me his arm, and I took it. With Georgiana on the other side of his arms, we followed the group.

"What do you think?" I asked. "This is a new sort of story."

"Actually, I am not surprised," Darcy pointed out.

"You are not?" Georgiana asked.

"Not at all. Wickham saved the life of a naval officer. The same officer who could acquit him of his desertion. When Wickham chooses to do a good deed, he only does it if it concerns him. You save a captain's life; he can save yours in turn."

"You think so?"

"I know my old school friend. That is how his mind works."

"Faith," Georgiana said, "that makes a great deal of

sense. The more I think on it, the more I can see how it all underwent."

"Also, Wickham would never engage in a fight that he knew he would lose. Everything was probably entirely on his side. And—"

"Peggy!" came a thunderous voice. "Peggy, we are home!"

While I did not see the speaker, I could assume that it was Captain Reed. When turning to Mrs. Reed, I saw her look with such dismay at hearing her name cried out for in such a vulgar manner.

We looked at where the voice came from. Out of the back patio doors, a man emerged. He was obviously slightly in the cups. His manner was staggered, his waistcoat had some buttons open, and his eyes were a little glazed.

"Peggy!" Captain Reed cried. "What the devil be bringing you out here? You know that I was to come at this time. If you were a horse, I would whip you for not preparing the tea for us."

I was horrified.

Between his vulgar habit to his implied violence toward his wife, I saw an accurate portrait of Frederick's description of the man. Everything that he had said was now justified. I could very easily see a man like Captain Reed sailing out to sea and being the very worst sort of officer to rule over sailors. There was a viciousness to him. That was evident.

I turned to Mrs. Reed, empathetic. She was obviously so very much embarrassed, and her eyes were filled with a loathing for her husband.

"Coming, Captain Reed," Mrs. Reed responded, removing her fan, and fanning herself, aggravated. "Is Mr. Wickham with you?"

"Yes, he is. You all can talk with him all you like. Your chattering is all nonsense to me."

"We have guests," Mrs. Reed said, "Captain, we have Mr. and Mrs. Darcy, of Pemberley, Derbyshire. And their sister, Miss Darcy."

"Pemberley?" Captain Reed echoed. "Mr. Darcy?"

And just like that, Captain Reed's personality underwent as swift a transformation as a coin that went up heads once and then switched to tails. When seeing my husband, he straightened up, checked his hair, and started speaking more pleasantly.

Frederick Hale was righter than ever.

Captain Reed was a man of pretense when he sensed a greater authority. But when he did not, his true character was presented for the world to see.

We all went inside, and standing on the other side of the room, drinking some wine, was Mr. Wickham.

When seeing us, he froze.

Oh, that was perfect. Seeing the mask sliding off his face, and replaced by shock, even for a moment, was as good a prize as any.

Of course, it did not last long. All the ladies eagerly approached him, fawning over the rattle. Feeling their praises swelled his pride and the smug expression returned to his face.

After the ladies spoke, Mr. Wickham had no choice but to address us. He used all his powers of pleasing and bestowed them on us.

"We have heard tales of your heroics," Mr. Darcy said, with solemnity. His cutting tone was so sharp that it could have sliced butter.

"Yea," Captain Reed said, attempting to hide his inebriation, "saved my life, he did?"

"How gallant," Georgiana replied, dispassionate.

"Thank you, Miss Darcy," Mr. Wickham responded, "That is high praises coming from yourself."

Georgiana nodded gently but said no more.

Soon into our meeting, I saw Mr. Wickham go to the table to get more coffee. I was too curious, and this was my only chance. Approaching him, I sought out to discover as much as I could.

When seeing me approach him, he smiled.

"At last, you seek me out," Mr. Wickham said.

"At last, Mr. Wickham?"

"Yes. I have long been wishing to talk to you."

"Have you?"

"Yes, there is something that I must know. Mrs. Darcy, I believe that you are unaware that you might eventually store a fugitive."

"A fugitive?"

"Yes. You have been greatly put upon. Those Hales that you travel with. I have reason to believe that the nephew is not a nephew at all. In fact, I believe he is their son, who is a mutineer to Captain Reed. If you knew the crime he committed."

"First," I insisted, "you are mistaken. I can confirm that your viewpoint is mistaking identity. That is not Mr. Hale's son, but his nephew. It is a common mistake. And I would thank you not to slander a good man's name."

"Ah, is that what this is?"

"Wickham, please tell me that you have not told Captain Reed about this. For if you have, you have incriminated an innocent man, and you will drag the Hales' good name into unnecessary repute. That is what we have come to tell you. You allowed yourself to be misguided."

"Oh, I have?"

"Yes, you have. And even if the Hales did have a son who led a rebellion, I can understand any provocation on mutiny. From what I have seen of Captain Reed, every rumor that I have heard is true. In such a circumstance, I do not see how a mutineer is any worse than a soldier who deserted his rank, due to debts being unpaid. From all that I have heard, is that not what you have done? In the North, Colonel Forster's regiment was camped at Milton. I was informed of your tendencies."

"All of my debts of honor have been paid."

"No doubt through your friendship with the Captain. I know the truth now. There is more to your story."

"Were we not good friends once? Miss Elizabeth, what has happened? We used to be one mind in all things."

"That changed when I discovered that you lied to me. That you planned to elope with my new sister, who deserved better."

"Who told you such a thing?" Mr. Wickham asked.

"My brother," came a voice behind him, "and me."

His eyes turned cold when he turned, and Georgiana was standing behind him.

When hearing Georgiana's voice, Wickham's face froze over, his hands flexed, hearing every lie he ever told me leak out and be faced with.

"Mr. Wickham," Georgiana said, "What an interesting thing to hear you say."

"Miss Darcy," Mr. Wickham responded, "I was just..."

"Yes?"

Wickham cleared his throat. Evidently, he was stalling for time. When he was about to speak again, perhaps to offer some other lie, his throat seemed to lose all power as he beheld her eyes.

Georgiana's look was neither angry nor vengeful. It was wistful, heartbroken, and she was on the verge of tears.

"How could you?" she asked, her tone harsh and sincere. "It was terrible enough that you used me for your mercenary habits. That you didn't care about me at all. That you used me to compensate for your own terrible behavior. But then you slander me, you lie about everything, and you label me as the villain of the story. How could you?"

"I..."

"George! No more lies. Stop it. There is nowhere to run. No more evil to hide behind. Just tell me why you would be that malignant? We grew up together. Did our friendship mean nothing?"

"Not entirely so," he uttered.

"Not entirely so?"

"No, not entirely so."

"Then what is this to you? Tell me, for I am dying to know. What am I to you?"

"You must understand—"

"What?"

"Whatever my reasons for marrying you, I was not going to be vicious as a husband."

"I do not know that."

"Yes, you do. Yes, I have never been very good at managing finances and do confess to some extravagance. But would it have been so horrible to have been married to me?"

"Yes, it would have been. Because even now, you cannot give me an honest answer."

"What do you want me to say? That I am sorry?"

"Yes. I would like that."

Wickham breathed in heavily, and his skin had turned a pale white. It was as if all nerve and confidence drained from his face. All truth began to collide in him at once, and he finally had to confront his past.

"You have made a good effort at running away from your history, George. And it's here, before you, and you cannot run. Here it is. Face it and apologize."

Once more, Wickham was silent. If I had any deductive skills, I did not think he refused any apology because he did not believe in it. Rather, I think it was because he was incapable of apologizing. His voice could not fathom the words, even if his mind could fathom the thought.

"You cannot do it, can you?" Georgiana asked. "Because that would be too painful for you. That would mean that you will have to look yourself in the face every morning and see what you are. That would hurt too much, wouldn't it? To despise yourself. After all, you are all that *you* have left. A pity. If you had chosen to be a better man, you could have had more. But now you have nothing. This friendship with Captain Reed, you know that it will not last. They never do. Especially since you know what sort of man that he is. Very well. I wonder what Mrs. Reed and her friends will think about you and your true history."

Georgiana moved to leave his side, but he stood in her way. I took a step behind him, as a warning to him, but it was unnecessary. He only stood in her way to implore her.

"What do you want from me?" he asked. "Georgiana, please, tell me what you want."

"To hear you apologize."

"I can't."

"Why not?" she insisted.

"I don't know why. I just cannot."

"Even though you know that you hurt me, lied to all of Hertfordshire, defamed my brother's good name, and still cause more ruin. You cannot apologize for any of this?"

"Georgiana, please, I will do anything else, but do not ask me to apologize. I cannot do it."

The wretched man! The blind, self-deceptive, and horrible man.

He still could not face himself.

Georgiana was overcome, but she did her best to suppress her disappointment.

"You break my heart again, by not declaring your remorse."

"I am not saying that I do not feel remorse."

"Then what are you saying?"

"I just...ask me to do anything else. Just not to apologize."

"Very well, then I will stake my claim like a woman of spirit. My new sisters are on their honeymoon with my brother, cousin, and friend. The Hales are with them. I don't know what you have told Captain Reed. But I will not let you destroy the Hales life, like you almost destroyed mine. They have a nephew named Frederick. He lives in Spain. And yes, they do have a son who led a mutiny, and he fled to South America, and can never come back to England. He knows that he cannot. You will not mistake his cousin for him and thus drag the cousin into a whirlwind of injustice. Nor will you bring on this crisis to the Hales. You will forget what you have deduced today, and if you did tell Captain Reed that you believe that Frederick Hale is here, tell him that you were mistaken. This is not me forcing you to apologize. This is me telling you to look the other way. And if you don't, there will be consequences."

"Consequences?"

"Yes. Captain Reed may shield you now, but what happens if rumor reaches all of England that you were a deserter, who only was exonerated because you helped a drunken fool in a barfight. And that you are known for chasing after heiresses. You will not be welcome in any reputable house in Britain. Your name will spread over this kingdom with a fury."

"If you do that, then your name will be grouped with mine. You do not wish to do that."

"If that will lead to me putting an end to any evil rumors that you might spread, then I am willing to do that. And all you had to do was apologize. Now here we are. Think on my words. You think of yourself so very much. I give you the chance to save a life, and that life will be your own. That's all that you care about, isn't it?"

"Miss Darcy... Georgiana—"

"Good day, Mr. Wickham," Georgiana said, taking my hand, "Eliza, I am feeling a little overtired. Let's see if my brother will allow us to return back to the hotel."

"I am certain that he would, Georgie," I said, and we walked away. When Darcy saw us approaching him, he quickly began to make an excuse for us to depart, without his sister saying one word. I found this to be suspicious and was only satisfied when we were alone in the chaise.

Before that, the whole party saw us to the door, lined up as we got into the carriage and Captain Reed said something practically incoherent before we departed.

As our carriage drove down the lane, Mr. Wickham emerged from the house. Standing at the top of the steps to the villa, he watched us leave with a heavy expression on his face.

"What is he thinking now?" I wondered.

"If it's worthy to tell Captain Reed," Darcy theorized, "or if he loses more by trying to catch Frederick and collect the bounty on his head."

I looked at Darcy and Georgiana.

"I have the feeling that you both planned something together."

"We did," Darcy said, looking at his sister, "Georgiana, you can imagine that the whole time I let you and Wickham speak, I wanted to run over and throttle him."

"I know that you did, and I do appreciate that moment of intended vehemence," Georgiana responded, and then she turned to me. "I asked Fitzwilliam to give me the chance to speak with Mr. Wickham alone. I felt that, if I did not, I would not have the ability to say what needed to be said. I was hoping that he might feel any sort of remorse for how he abused myself. And, when I pulled that from out of him, I could appeal to his side that might not want to see a man incriminated so horribly. However, you saw it, Lizzy. He never apologized. He could not."

"It was very ugly of him."

"Yes, it was. As such, I did the best I could to improvise. All that could be done, therefore, was to casually imply all that he would lose if he would report Frederick Hale and throw him to the injustice of a court martial."

"Georgiana," I marveled, "I never would have known that you had so much..."

"Fire within me?"

"Well, yes. That is truly the wonder of it. You had so much courage then."

Georgiana blushed.

"Every now and again, I surprise myself. And it is so brilliant because I do like surprising people. Now, all that we can do is hope that Wickham makes the correct choice."

"Even if he does not, Georgiana, you are an event," Darcy complimented her.

"Oh, brother, stop! You are making me blush even more."

"Now, I want to hear every single aspect of your conversation. Sister, leave nothing out."

Georgiana retold everything twice. To her brother when we rode back to the hotel, and then to the others when we joined them.

Chapter 22

Tales of the Heart

In Milton, the ups and downs of industry and endeavors continued about their natural course.

While the bells sounding out the constant comings and goings of the laborers from the factories, the rise and fall of some were currently underway.

One angle of Milton life could be Maria, Little Molly, Cynthia, Roger, and Osborne Fitzpatrick playing in a nearby field that rested far away from the mills, where they were pulling flowers from a patch.

Another angle was Nicholas Higgins, and his daughter, Mary, toiling away on the last week that Marlborough Mills was to be open.

The next angle was of Rasby leaving the hotel, having collected her second to last set of wages. For in a fortnight, she would travel down to Rosings Park, where Kitty and Colonel Fitzwilliam would meet her, and there her fate would be decided.

As she walked along the street, there was another angle of Mr. Thornton walking in the other direction. Listless and with a storm cloud over his head as he contemplated where else to go with his life. He had lost his wealth, his home, his factory, and now he had lost Margaret Hale.

Where was he to turn? What was he to do?

Down many more streets, along many more pathways, the view switches angle to the interior of Granger Hall.

Charlotte Lucas was sitting in the back of the lecture hall, taking notes for Mr. Hunnicutt's class. When he finished, he escorted her out of the room, much to Charlotte's delight, for Hunnicutt was always of a very nice temperament and they got along tolerably well.

While she was copying notes in the library, Mr. Hanley entered. Both men looked at each other, and Mr. Hunnicutt was no longer in the mood to allow inaction to take hold of the situation. Excusing himself from their company, he walked up to Mr. Hanley and whispered into his ear.

"Remember, the worst that can occur is if she says no."

"That's what I am afraid of."

"Just don't forget. It's life and life only."

Giving him one more significant look, Hunnicutt left them alone.

"Mr. Hanley," Charlotte greeted him over her shoulder. "You are looking as if someone ate your favorite poem?"

Mr. Hanley chuckled wistfully.

"And that is a sad chuckle, if that has been known to exist," Charlotte lowered her pen. "Or am I reading things incorrectly?"

"I hardly know."

"And that is a strange answer. Pay me the compliment of thinking that I have learned to read your moods. Is something wrong?"

"Perhaps."

"Well, am I allowed to know what it is?"

"You ought not to, but you also ought to as well."

"Hanley, you are being mysterious. You must help me."

"I... oh, dear! This is so terribly painful."

He adjusted his spectacles and then he rubbed his hands.

"You are truly upset about something," Charlotte said, "you always rub your hands when you are intimidated by news."

"Do you know what hurts the most?" Mr. Hanley burst out, suddenly. "It's that you know me so well. It's that I cannot bear it."

"Cannot bear it?"

Charlotte was astonished. At this point in the conversation, she was unaware of where to proceed. As such, all she could do was sit there and let matters unfold.

"No, I cannot," Hanley declared. Now it came to the moment. The storm in his heart had become a full tempest and he could not refrain any longer. "I cannot bear how you walk in, and I feel instantly lighter. I cannot bear how much it hurts when you leave, and I feel alone. I cannot bear the agony of my heart being awake again. And—oh, my word! I am beginning this all wrong."

Charlotte may have been silent, but internally, every part of herself was tingling with alarm and amazement.

"Miss Lucas. Charlotte. Please, I understand that what you feel for me is no more than professional camaraderie. And I can understand if you do not return my affections. All that I ask is that you allow me to display the feelings that have developed within me. Charlotte, I have come to feel a passionate attachment to you, and it cannot be denied. My hope is to enter a courtship, but one word from you will determine it all. If you feel nothing for me now, then all I ask is for you to consider my request. Sometimes, affection takes some time to grow."

"I do not need more time," Charlotte professed.

"You do not?"

"No, I do not." Charlotte closed her eyes, folded her hands on her lap as she gathered her nerve. "Mr. Hanley, I thank you for the compliment of considering me, but I must tell you—I have been in this place before."

"Before?"

"Of being the woman who a man chose after he could not have Elizabeth. I am aware that you once felt very tenderly for her."

Mr. Hanley placed his hands in his pocket, to hide that he was flexing them.

"You do not need to be censorious of Lizzy," Charlotte continued, "I was aware of your affection for her when I first saw you together. Elizabeth always boasted that I was very good at deducing other people's affection for each other in a room. So, yes, I know that you once adored her."

"I confess, that I did."

"I do not blame you. Men are drawn to her, in the same way that I am drawn to her as a friend. I cannot blame you for that. But what I cannot undergo is being the woman chosen because you cannot have her."

"That is what you believe?"

"Yes. Because it has happened before. A man once offered her his affections. She refused him, and so he turned to me, throwing a proposal at me that was obviously done to recover from his bruised heart. That is not how I want to be loved. I have learned pride, Mr. Hanley. And I cannot unlearn it."

"But I am not that man," Mr. Hanley insisted. "Please, whoever he was, do not place me in the category of him. After I discovered that I could never marry Lizzy, I was against love. Rather, I was almost an enemy to it. I did not want to feel anything again. And then you entered my life. And my heartbeat didn't die. Rather, it quickened. I didn't fall in love with you to rebound from a lost affection. I fell in love with you, despite every plea inside of me to never fall in love again. So, this is real. And I will hold to it."

Charlotte Lucas was not a woman carved from stone, and she never would be. Despite her logical side still reasoning out the possibility that Mr. Hanley might not know himself fully, beauty still must have its attributes.

Mr. Hanley's profession of love was the most beautiful thing that she had ever witnessed.

Emotion swelled within her, and she knew that she must speak. But to say what? For she felt, in that moment, nothing she could have said was going to be the correct thing to say.

"You mean that?" she asked. "You really mean all that you say?"

"Yes, I do."

Charlotte bit her lip, growing sad.

"Are you certain? Because if you are not, and then your affection proves to be a flimsy one, then that would hurt me in ways that you cannot imagine."

What a sentence to hear! For Hanley, it was like that of a drowned man being thrown a lifeline and being pulled back to the surface.

"You really worry that I am being inconstant?"

"I cannot help but fear that."

"If you fear that, then that means that maybe, your heart beats alongside mine. Charlotte, you are too generous to trifle with me. Does this mean that you might feel even slightly for me?"

"I confess that I am not fully governess over every sensation that washes over me. Perhaps I never considered you because I never thought that you considered me. But now that you do, I do not find myself repulsed by the declaration. On the contrary, I think it beautiful. And I find great joy in hearing it."

Hanley was overcome. Rubbing his face, he looked away, placed his hand on the windowsill and steadied himself.

"Please," he replied, desperate, "speak plainly with me now. Can I request a courtship from you? If you find that you do not want me, then I shall leave the table of your adoration without saying a word. You can send me away at once. And I would still respect you. I merely ask this."

Charlotte felt all her nerves tingling within her arms, chest, and neck.

"Forgive my anxiety," she apologized, "this just feels so very different since the last time that I was proposed to. And so, my feelings are very different, and they are overpowering me. You offer me a courtship?"

"Yes, I do."

"If I say yes, do you promise to be kind to me? I find nothing more handsome than a kind man. And a constant one."

"Of that," he insisted strongly, "I promise you."

"Then yes."

"Yes?"

"Yes. I do welcome your courtship. And if we prove that we are a delight together, then you have your wife."

Wife!

Of all the words to hear.

Giving way to the weight of the moment, Hanley cried out her name, sat down beside her and offered her his hand to take. Amazed, Charlotte placed her hand in his and he kissed it.

"Charlotte," he continued to whisper, "may I endeavor to deserve you."

"Well now," Charlotte said, half-laughing, half-crying, "this is a delightful start, now, isn't it?"

"Yes, I daresay it is."

Ignorant that they had an observer, Charlotte and Mr. Hanley sat in the library, talking as lovers do. Meanwhile on the other side of the door, Dennison had approached it.

Overhearing everything, Dennison's heart felt hollow. It was a mixture of jealousy and self-reproach. Hanley had obtained his Lucas sister, and here he was, still alone, outside of a door, listening in on happier people.

Initially, Dennison was very angry. But the wrath was subdued when he had to confront the storm of conflicting views within him.

Of course, Maria would never have him. He had done nothing but give a bad first impression, a second, third, fourth and fifth. How could he have expected anything else? And yet, his volatile demeanor had served him well over the years. It made him strong and appear imposing to anyone who would cross him.

And yet, he drove so many away. Was he to always do the same with Maria Lucas?

He walked back to the lecture hall and sat at one of the seats that gave him a good view of the road.

Fully aware that this was one of the days that Maria was

bringing Little Molly and the Kirkpatrick children to visit Charlotte and Hanley, he decided to wait.

Could he change?

Could he, Dennison, rally into a pleasanter way of being?

At this stage in his life, his personality was too set in one direction. But that direction that he set himself along was not an organic one. He had hardened his heart, deliberately, when he suffered disappointment. For truly, he was not always like this.

When he was a younger man, he had ideals, dreams, and passions. There was once a generosity to his heart. Was there any chance of that part of himself being awake once more?

Was it too late for him to understand how to love, and be worthy of being loved in return?

He remained like this for quite some time, until he saw Maria Lucas coming down the road, with the four children holding hands with her.

It felt as if insects were crawling up his legs, for that was how nervous he was.

Jumping up, he walked briskly down the hall, came down the steps and stood in front of the building.

It was rendered impossible for Maria to not see him. When she did, her eyes did not become downcast but rather grew more animated. In a confrontational sort of manner.

"Ah," Maria called to him, "you come to greet me."

"I do."

"So, what is it to be this time?" she asked. "Will you curse me with threats of locusts, or that I get plagued with boils on me?"

"I've cursed you with threats about the seven deadly plagues of Egypt before?"

"You don't remember?"

"No, I don't."

"Well, I do. And I will say this now. Be mean to me all that you wish when we are alone. I have the courage to weather your foul mind. But do not do it in front of the children. Little ones are never given enough time to be young, because they grow up so quickly and life spoils them. Be kind to them. That's the only order that I place on you. Surely you can suffer a lady making that request."

"I have been very dour, haven't I?"

"Your words, Mr. Dennison. But I do agree with them. You still haven't promised."

"And I should. I will not do anything to offend."

Maria was surprised by this.

"How interesting. I didn't think that would work. Well, while I have you under my power, can I ask you to do me the honor of greeting the children?"

"Another favor?'"

"Another rule of conduct."

"Very well."

Dennison removed his hat, greeted Little Molly, Cynthia, Roger, and Osborne.

"You are being nice?" Little Molly said to Dennison.

"I suppose that I am."

"Are you ill?"

Maria suppressed a chuckle.

"You think that's funny?" Dennison asked her.

"Of course, I do. I was about to ask you the same question."

"Oh," Dennison chuckled.

"But truly, are you ill?"

"Of the mind, perhaps. But not of the body."

"Well, I must say, that if you are sick, then this is the best sort of disease to catch."

"I'll lead you inside to see your sister and Hanley."

"And you are escorting us?" Maria asked, as they walked up the steps. "Who are you and what have you done to Mr. Dennison?"

"I promise, I am real."

"Are you? After all, I have heard tales of the changeling. The only reason that I rule out that theory is because you are not a child, but a grown man."

"Can't a man wake up one day and decide to be kinder?"

"Some men, yes. Others, no. Is that what you have done? Wake up and decide to be kinder?"

"If I said yes, would you believe me?"

"If I did believe you, would you consider me wise for being that trusting?"

"No," he said, smiling a little, "I don't suppose that I would. In fact, I would call you very foolish."

"Precisely. Do not ask me to take leave of my senses."

They reached the library, and Charlotte and Mr. Hanley embraced Little Molly and the other children.

As they did so, Maria remained beside Mr. Dennison.

"So," Maria continued, "what brought on this change?"

"Perhaps I just decided to wake up this morning and decided to be a better man."

"A wise practice to adopt, but practice makes perfect. Will you continue this practice?"

"You are toying with me."

"I always toy with you. It's the only way to talk to you. Besides, are you about to tell me that you do not prefer it?"

"Well, I do take amusement in the liveliness of your mind."

"Thank you. Now tell me truly, Dennison, is this change something that you wish to practice doing often?"

"If I would say that I was, what would you say?"

"I would say that time has to be your friend, and you have to prove it."

"Why is this important to you? I am not against it at all, but I really wish to know why my alteration of character is significant to you?"

"Because I wonder why you do it."

"I do it—perhaps, because I would like for you to know me better."

"I know."

"You do?"

"Yes. I have known for quite some time."

Dennison looked at Charlotte as she picked up Cynthia and twirled her around.

"Ah, your sister."

"Do not seek revenge on her in any sort of way. She is my sister and has every right to tell me what to be wary of. How long, Dennison? How long have you favored me?"

"Perhaps you might not want to know."

"I do not fear men's affections for me. Never have. So go on and tell me."

"Since the day I first saw you."

"But you had not fully met me."

"I know. And it changes nothing. I felt a strong attachment to you, from the very first, and it took a great hold over me."

"And this change is to..."

"Make an attempt."

Maria Lucas sighed.

"Dennison, while I appreciate the gesture, I cannot

determine its permanence. Therefore, I know not what to tell you."

Taking what he could from this reflection, he did not groan and look away but turned more toward her.

"Are you implying that you are not against my feelings for you? It is merely that you are worried about my changeable state, and that it is a pretense."

"Precisely. What if I did grow to feel for you and you became vicious again?"

"If that is the case, then you could divorce me."

"The world frowns on the woman who divorces the man, even if she is right to do so."

"Divorces have happened quite often, and there is no point in fearing the world on that score. If I were to prove my constant attempts to be a better man, would you consider me?"

"First, you have to be a better man for the sake of establishing a friendship between us. No more and no less. And if that friendship proves true, then I will consider more. But that is all that I can say."

Dennison half-smiled.

"I can agree to that. Well, I'll be buggered."

Along the Milton streets, Thornton once more found himself riding on the omnibus to take him further out to the fields and countryside of Darkshire.

The more that he left Milton behind, for a moment he had hoped that he could remove his cares. The woes of his current predicament could be left behind, *for the moment*.

Until he recalled that this was the precise journey that

he took when Margaret Hale had rejected him. He had run here before, and he was doing so again.

When reaching the last stop on the bus, Thornton disembarked, and he walked along the green. Eventually, he came upon a church with an old, rundown cemetery beside it.

The headstones were long and thin, and they spoke of many deceased parishioners who were resting underneath.

Walking along it, he noted how many of them were buried either next to their spouse, or their children. Some even were married for rather long lives together.

Their stones mocked him, for it felt as if they had accomplished what he could not.

He would not have his wife, his fortune, his success, and his future. He was a man cast down. And the sun would never shine upon him again. For now, all would be dark, storm clouds would be placed above him. And he was hurled into the unknown that haunted any man who life decided to be very hard upon.

At last, he reached one particular headstone. It was a woman who rested next to her husband. She was a widow who outlived him by four years, but together they rested. On her stone was a quote, much to his surprise.

'Life threw me many an obstacle.
So, I decided to be difficult,
and throw obstacle back at it.
That's what love is.'

Thornton thought on that quote, and he felt the shadow rest even more on his shoulders. Even in her death, this woman knew more than he did. And perhaps obtained everything that her heart set forth to conquer.

Next to her, her husband rested, clearly being her first and last chief love. A way was found, and she looked on love like death: if she could face it, without fear and trepidation, she could conquer it, and fear would fade.

The sun would always shine on her grave, and the dead felt as if it lived more than he did as a living man.

Sitting down, he rested his head against her headstone, resting his body against it.

Where was Margaret now? Of her, he knew that there was nothing to fear. She was a strong woman, who could rally from anything, and not be knocked about by the ways of the heart.

But he hoped, in his heart, that she felt the same anguish.

The same loss.

And the same storm of heartache that clung to him.

However selfish it is for one to wish another to feel the same sorrow as they, it can be determined that he was not wrong to have such a wish.

And he was not alone. Margaret may have been enjoying the delights of the Isle, but her heart was torn, as his was.

Torn from the prospects of what could have been, and what should have been. They could have been married soon. They *should* have been married soon. Everything about it was correct, and now it would never be.

Miles apart, their hearts were unified, and both looked up at the sky above, wondering at the love that stretched over hill and mountain, till at last, they were connected, for a brief moment.

Margaret Hale saw Thornton, with her waking eyes.

Thornton saw her, in the depths of his soul.

Parted forever, but not fully parted at all.

Chapter 23

The Tempest

That night, on the Isle, storm clouds found their way over the resort.

Out of the window, we saw the elements threatening, and it matched the sentiments that we felt within.

All of us knew what was at stake. Tomorrow would bring either Frederick's escape to freedom, or he could be detected, and it would bring him to his death.

We knew this.

No matter what plea he made, no matter how obvious Captain Reed was not fit to lead anyone, justice would not prevail.

No matter how right Frederick behaved for protecting those under his power, life would not be fair.

Rain fell from the sky.

Would Wickham listen to Georgiana's plea that he say nothing to Reed, or declare that the Hales were here alone, and that Frederick was not with them at all.

For all that we knew, Reed could easily arrive at our hotel tomorrow morning, in hopes of getting revenge for the man who set him adrift on the open seas.

We heard the sound of thunder.

The matter was too serious for us to make light of anything.

The thunder grew louder across the night sky.

In the heat of the night, under the cast of darkness, we felt so bleak.

None of us could speak, for wonder of what tomorrow would bring.

Either it would present Frederick Hale with his great escape, leaving England, perhaps forever, and to a wife which none of us would see.

Or to the prospect of being discovered, dragged into a court martial where all judges would deem him guilty from the very beginning, and a noose would await him at the end.

The duty of the hangman.

Suddenly, in our bedrooms, we all jumped when seeing lightning strike against the black and thunder following behind it.

Was nature making its decision?

Was it foreshadowing things to come?

Or was it merely judging everyone now and giving way to a brighter day tomorrow?

If the sun were to shine as Frederick was taken away, what then? What a horribly taunting prospect for beauty to make its judgment, not with mercy, but with sorrow.

Would fortune forsake us?

First Thornton was penniless and had lost everything to a situation that was beyond his control.

Margaret lost the man that she finally found the ability to love.

And then to lose her brother afterwards?

How would she bear it?

How would any of us bear it?

The lightning struck across the sky again, followed by thunder.

Darcy sat next to me as we watched the tempest rage on around us.

Our eyes were watching the skies.

Our eyes were watching time.

Our eyes were watching heaven.

Our eyes were watching God.

The tempest raged on.

And the storm was beyond our control. As it knew it was.[1]

1. This segment is inspired by the title of the novel by Zora Neale Hurston, *Their Eyes Were Watching God.*

Chapter 24

Judgment Day

The next day, we all woke as solemn and with as much a sense of foreboding as we had experienced the day before. As we left the hotel, heading toward the harbor, where Frederick would meet his ship back to town, he would brook passage to Spain on The Asp.

We all looked at each other, and it was evident that none of us slept, for fear of what this day would bring.

One hill would turn, or the other would.

And the storm had done its duty by nature, for the next day, the sun shone as bright as ever.

Despite that it was not a cold morning, by any means, Frederick wore his hat lower than usual, and we got him into the chaise quicker than ever.

Our plan was simple. Once we arrived at the harbor, Frederick would not leave the carriage until they were fully prepared to set sail and were about to raise their anchor.

The ferry's name, The Kelly, was prepared and there were quite a few people who were assembling, to go on board.

"If we let Frederick go now," Margaret insisted to her

parents and us, "then he could mix with the crowd. His face would fade in with the others."

"Splendid idea," Mr. Hale said hastily, "Also, if we stand around him, many passersby will not get a clear image of him. We must protect him."

"Yes," Mrs. Hale said, "have him hold my arm in the group. When people see a young man helping an invalid older lady, they never focus on the man's face, but the lady who he helps."

"We must be quick about it," Colonel Fitzwilliam urged us, and we made fast work of it. We ushered Frederick out of the carriage, he took his mother's arm, and he crouched a little, his face near hers, his visage being blocked on the right side.

We surrounded him and made it appear as if we were happily conveying a friend to the walkway, missing his presence to the very last.

All seemed as if it was successful. We had reached the ramp for Frederick to walk, and he was just about to place his foot on the wood, when we heard a cry out.

"Darcys? And Hales?"

Not that voice. Anything, but that voice!

We all turned, and Mr. Wickham was standing a little distance from us.

He knew!

He had guessed.

The horrid man. Why did he have to be here?

I looked past him to expect Captain Reed to come lumbering from behind him. But there was no one. It was merely Wickham, by himself.

We all halted, even Frederick.

Wickham stared at all of us as he quietly walked forward.

"Now," he began, "I see the whole party at last. Old friends and casual ones."

"Wickham?" Darcy began.

"Yes?" he replied simply, but his tone was ambiguous. "I do believe there is someone here that I have not seen much of at all. Mrs. Hale, is this not Mr. Hale with you?"

Mrs. Hale did not respond but only looked horrified as Dixon held her shoulder.

Then Wickham's eyes fell upon Frederick.

"Ah, and this must be your nephew. Is that not so?"

"It is," Dixon confirmed. "This is Frederick, Mr. and Mrs. Hale's nephew. And Miss Hale's cousin."

"To be sure," Mr. Hale uttered, stepping forward protectively. "He came to pay his respects to our family."

"How proper." Wickham looked at him most acutely. "Mr. Frederick?"

"Mr. Wickham," Frederick said.

Both men locked gazes, each not tearing their eyes from the other. Mr. Wickham's greetings were redundant, as if we had not had this conversation before. What was he playing at?

"A fortunate man," Wickham said, "you look so much like your uncle."

"I do, indeed. The habit of family."

And this was the moment. What could be done? We were found out, and it was only a matter of minutes before Wickham would shout out Frederick's true identity.

I glared at Wickham.

Georgiana stared at him.

Darcy, Colonel Fitzwilliam, Bingley, and Mr. Hale's eyes were arrested.

Jane, Kitty, Mrs. Hale, Dixon, and Margaret were fearful.

Then, Wickham did something that I did not foresee. He looked away from Frederick and turned his attention toward each of us.

He looked on us individually, and each time, his eyes said something different. At last, he looked on Georgiana.

And looked more, and more.

Georgiana's eyes were a silent plea, but a strong one. It was neither feminine nor masculine, but otherworldly. It was as if the eyes of judgment were staring directly at him.

The storm of decision was staring on him, preparing herself for what he was about to do.

At last, he turned to Frederick Hale and spoke again.

"You leave the Isle?"

"Yes, I do."

Silence.

A heavy thing it was.

We prepared for the worst. We awaited the horror of everything that was not deserved. And for the unfairness of life.

Mr. Wickham opened his mouth and the silence ended.

"A pity to leave family," he said heavily. "I should not keep you. I hope the waters are smooth on your journey."

The astonishment of it all!

The shock of release.

All tension in us faded, our figures slackened from the

anxiety of knowing that we were about to witness a tragedy, and now it was the reverse.

Wickham was letting Frederick go?

The money that could be obtained from turning Frederick into the law, and Wickham was not going to do anything.

Frederick's expression transformed from bitterness to alleviation.

"Thank you, sir."

"You are very welcome. Good day."

"Good day."

Frederick Hale boarded the ship, at the final moments that *The Kelly* was prepared to disembark. The anchor was raised, the ship slowly took off, and we watched Frederick fade away from us. At last, he grew quite small, and our last waves of farewell were over and done.

Finally, we turned to Wickham.

"A thought just occurred to me," Darcy grunted over my shoulder. "And it's a horrible one."

He looked at Wickham with distrust.

"Wickham? Is anyone on that ship—"

"No," Wickham answered his question before he finished it. "There is no one on that ship who will arrest him, no one is aware of who he is, and no one is waiting for him back on the mainland."

We all were amazed.

Wickham had done a good deed. I never would have known.

"You did the right thing," Jane pointed out.

"Did I?" Mr. Wickham smiled sadly. "A strange feeling it is."

"But why?" Georgiana asked. "Why did you do it?"

"I... I cannot fathom why."

"Wickham, yes, you can."

"I don't..." He shrugged and walked away. After going a few steps, he turned back to us. Or rather, he turned to Georgiana. "I am sorry."

"You are?" Georgiana asked.

"Please, do not make me say it again. But I am. I swear, I am. Now enough. Enough for now."

"Very well," Georgiana said, "enough for now."

"You understand me now, I think?"

"No, but I will try."

"Thank you," he replied, grateful. "Thank you. I regret that we... I should never have hurt...never mind."

He put his hat back on, nodded to her, and departed.

All the storm clouds had quite gone away.

Chapter 25

An Interesting Walk

As he walked away from a company that he had successfully spent a portion of his life souring his reputation with, Wickham was a man divided.

Internally, many voices cried out within him.

He had let a criminal escape.

A mutineer.

But he knew Captain Reed and could easily believe that such a man would abuse his sailors, without any sense of shame.

But there was a price, a bounty, on Frederick Hale's head.

Wickham needed that money.

And what was Frederick Hale to him?

Nothing. He cared not if this man lived or died.

Yet, he spared him. He looked into the man's eyes and spared him.

Why?

But Georgiana was there. And he found that he could not do it. He could not destroy this man.

When he tried to elope with her, he did it without any

care or consideration for her happiness. It was plain and mercenary. He had no guilt at the time, nor any sense of shame.

But now he was.

Never before had he dwelled on the evil side of his character. Rather, he justified it, submitting it down to a natural habit that he had every right to possess. Indeed, he found justification in his behavior, and since the whole world lied about things, what made him eviler for doing the same? After all, even good people could be dishonest. They did it on a daily basis.

And yet, something awoke in him. It was a sensation that he was not accustomed to, and it shot through him like a bullet through the heart: regret.

Remorse of past offenses flashed across his mind, like the lightning of the night before. He felt the hurt that he had committed. He felt the evil of all those lies. And they stood up to him, like hooded figures of judgment who faced him, delivering their verdict.

Not all character alterations occur when life throws a dramatic lesson.

Sometimes, all it takes is a look.

A waking up one day and a change of outlook occurs.

Sometimes, just maybe, it is a matter of growing older, and wisdom creeps in, like mist that clarifies rather than confuses.

And so, a storm of confusion swelled within Wickham, as he walked aimlessly through the streets, back to Sienna Orchards: it was the actions of an ignorant villain, who did something heroic, for a moment. It was enough to confound all.

As he walked, he wondered what this change would do to him. If it would do anything at all. It is easy to presume that he either reformed in that moment, but that would not be the case. Sometimes, a selfish and inconsiderately deceptive creature cannot reform fully, but have more paths to walk down before the transformation is complete.

But what can be said of Wickham is that, as he walked, the world began to look different. And he did not reject the storm that clouded his previous ways but only wondered at it. And while his mouth did not smile, his eyes did.

Chapter 26

The Balance of Life

We all still stood there, amazed and unsettled.

Wickham had done the right thing?

It was almost too overwhelming a concept, too startling an idea.

None of us moved, as if a spell had been placed on us, until Kitty approached Georgiana from the back and held her shoulders.

"Well done, Georgie."

"I do not understand what has occurred now."

"I think you do. Whatever his past crimes, for a brief moment, you awoke guilt in him, and this might have been the only way that he could apologize."

Suddenly, Georgiana burst into tears.

"I know. But I cannot bear it. He should have discovered it sooner. I cannot bear it."

Mr. and Mrs. Hale raced to Georgiana, equally holding her.

"Let us get her back to the hotel," I urged, going to her as well.

"Of course," Darcy said, moving amidst our group and holding Georgiana up as he escorted her into the carriage.

She wept the entire way back and sought solitude in her room.

However, despite the agonies that she must have been undergoing, there was one revelation that I could not ignore.

"The universe really does understand balance," I said to the rest of our party, "years ago, Wickham hurt Georgiana terribly, only for his action to awake a remorse in him at the precise moment that a life needed to be spared."

"How very true," Mr. Hale said, contemplating, "now is that not an amazing thought? The poor girl had to undergo something dreadful, only for the penance to come years later, in a way that it saved my son. Elizabeth, you have stumbled on something extraordinary. As if one action leads to an equal and opposite reaction on another part of one's life has always been contemplated, but never before has there been such solid proof of things occurring in such philosophic correlation."

"It is so alarming that our son's life was bought on the waves of her past disappointment," Mrs. Hale said, "but it is such a wonder, and we owe her that."

"Yes, we do," I said, "and Georgiana's action does display the heroism of everyday life. And everyday struggle to endure what ought to be endured."

"That is the heroism that there will never be books about or will never make history," Mr. Bingley said, "because it is the deeds of ordinary folk. Much must be said for that."

Deciding to leave Georgiana alone, we decided to go for a walk. As we all met downstairs, the front desk had a letter for Mr. Hale.

"Never fear," Mr. Hale said, "I have a wonderful skill of

reading when I am walking. Let us go." As we left, Mr. Hale looked optimistic. "It is from Oxford. Oh, that is good, it must be from Mr. Bell. At last. I have not heard from him since we left Rosings Park."

As we walked, he unfolded the letter and began to read it. Since Frederick was safe, and Wickham was probably going to remain away from us, there was no need to worry over. If it were not for Thornton's sudden change of fortune, we would all be happy. But even that was not to be worried over, because Darcy had a plan.

"Margaret," Mr. Darcy spoke to her, "I understand that Thornton has told you of his situation."

"Yes?" Margaret said, heavily. "I have been considering writing to him, telling him that I will remain his friend, until he is ready."

"That is very good of you. But you shall not have to worry. I have decided to write to him, offering him a loan, so that he can run Marlborough Mills until he can maintain the business on his own."

When hearing this, Margaret's eyes lifted.

"You would do that?"

"Of course. He is my friend."

Eagerly, Margaret smiled and took his hand.

"Thank you, Mr. Darcy. I know that his plans might still not include me until he has achieved a level of stability, but that is a great kindness on your part. He deserves someone to be there for him."

"And he will. Never fear, Margaret. There is hope."

Her eyes lit up, in a way that was not customary. Knowing that more good fortune had found her, her demeanor lightened even more, only for us to be interrupted by a sharp gasp.

We turned to where we heard the cry.

It belonged to Mr. Hale.

"Mr. Hale?" Colonel Fitzwilliam uttered. "What's wrong?"

"My dear?" Mrs. Hale asked, reaching toward him from her invalid chair.

Mr. Hale's face was horrorstricken. He had stopped in his tracks, clearly disturbed by the letter.

"What news from Oxford?" Kitty asked.

Mr. Hale looked up from the letter, his eyes filled with shock and grief.

Oxford.

I knew. Even without him saying it, I knew. It could not be anything else. But dear lord! Did it have to be this?

"Dead," he uttered, beside himself. "Dead."

"Who is dead?" Margaret asked.

"My friend, Margaret. Mr. Bell. He is dead."

The storm had returned.

Chapter 27

When a Light Goes Out

Five days ago...

In Oxford's chief library, Mr. Bell was sorting through his books, when one of his students approached him.

"Professor Bell?" the student, Franklyn, called.

"Franklyn?" Mr. Bell said, closing one of his books. "Very good, I was hoping to see you."

"Thank you, sir. I confess, I was worried about approaching you, in this manner. Well, considering my last paper, of course."

"Ah," Bell deduced, kindly, "you are talking of your low marks."

"Yes, professor," Franklyn replied, ashamed, "I—um..."

"You were worried about approaching me after it, eh?"

"I confess that I was."

"And I confess to being surprised, myself. When it comes to your discussions of Aristotle's Poetics and his Cosmos, I thought you would have excelled."

"Thank you, sir. I confess, things have been weighing on my mind of late."

"Ah, and it has distracted you from your studies?"

"Yes, I confess that it has. I know that is a terrible excuse."

"Understandable. We older folk were once your age, you know. And we are aware that sometimes, outside influences can affect one's academic performance. Is the matter to do with family?"

"No, sir."

"Your thoughts of your future vocation?"

"No, sir, it's...well, it's complicated."

"Does it have to do with a woman?"

Franklyn blushed.

"Ah," Mr. Bell finalized, amused, "well, I daresay that I hit the metaphoric nail on the head. Haven't I?"

"Professor, I know that it's foolish."

"I may not be a married man, Franklyn, but I still am a man. I have been in your predicament before. And no worries. One bad mark does not a ruin make. Come to my office. I'll make us some tea, and we can draw up a means to have you redeem yourself."

Franklyn smiled.

"Thank you, sir. I should like that."

"Good."

Mr. Bell placed a book on the table, and suddenly, he felt a sharp pain shoot through his right hand. He halted, grunting as he flexed it.

"Professor?" Franklyn asked, concerned. "Are you ill?"

"No. Well, yes. I am sure that it is no more than a sudden cramp. These things have been known to happen."

The cramp disappeared as quickly as it had come.

"There, see?" Mr. Bell assured him. "It's just the habit of our body to remind us that it is working."

Both men left the library and began to walk through Oxford's halls.

"Now, as for this woman, I trust that she is a single lady. Or does another man secure her affections?"

"She is single, and unfettered, thank goodness. However, I feel as if she is too good for me, and I do not know how to talk to her."

"Ah," Mr. Bell responded, laughing, "I recall those days. You feel as if your words get caught in your throat and you lose your breath?"

"Yes! That is precisely it. And I have written some poetry."

"Do not write poetry," Mr. Bell advised. "Only write poetry when you have secured the woman's heart. Right now, she needs to feel invited to love you. That is both easy and difficult. But the chief way of doing that is making the lady at ease with you. The only way that I can advise is—"

His words were cut off immediately when the sharp pain returned to his hand, then it shot up in his arm and struck into his chest.

Mr. Bell stopped walking, clutching where his heart was, and his whole face distorted.

"Professor?" Franklyn uttered, seeing the look of horror on Bell's face.

"I—Franklyn!"

The pain struck his whole body, Mr. Bell spasmed and began to collapse onto the floor as Franklyn held him, trying to lift him up again.

"Professor Bell!"

Franklyn cried around him.

"Someone, help me! Please, God, someone help me!"

Hearing the cries, many rushed to his aid, only to find

Mr. Bell lying on the floor, held by his student as his face distorted with pain.

As for Mr. Bell himself, the agonies of dying were too much for him to consider what was around him.

'No,' he cried, 'this cannot be the end. I cannot go now. I have so much to—my friends, my students. I am so alone! I am terrified!'

With one last breath, Mr. Bell grasped at the very last bit of life that he had in him, before his heart suddenly gave out.

His eyes closed, with many crowded around him, crying to return him back to life.

His final breath escaped him, and Mr. Bell, the man who brought much light to every encounter he attempted to do so, had faded into the path that all must inevitably take.

Mr. Bell was gone.

Chapter 28

The Turning of the Page

A dark day.

We had started it with so much hope, so much joy of knowing that God had tempered judgment with mercy, and not death, and we were wrong.

Our walk slowed down, our hearts were heavy, and we felt the loss of something so utterly without meaning.

Yes, Mr. Bell was not young. But I never saw him as so very old either.

Eventually, we returned to the hotel, because we did not want the world to see our sorrow. And there was much for it.

At first, I spent much time talking of Mr. Bell's virtues to Mr. Darcy, but I wanted to speak to Margaret alone about it. After all, it was not just us Bennets and Mr. Hale that Mr. Bell was important to. He was also Margaret's godfather.

When I saw her alone, she was standing by the window, staring out, still as a statue. Even when I entered, she did not move.

"I had a feeling that you would come," she said, still looking away from me.

"You know me well," I replied, sitting down on a chair by the fire. Looking into the flames, I was imagining seeing that same illumination in Mr. Bell's eyes. There was so much animation to the man.

"My father is crying terribly," Margaret explained. "Mama is comforting him. Bell was very important to him and a true friend."

"Because he was a true man. He did not let the world puff him about with its pride or prejudices. He was a man of independent mind and thoughts."

"The letter said that he died quickly. I know that he was not young..."

"But you never thought of him as being very old either."

"Precisely."

"Neither did I. I suppose, we all know that death is inevitable, but there are some people that you tell yourself that they will never die. That was the way it was with Mr. Bell. I miss him, Margaret."

"So do I. And I cannot help but consider the balance of life again. This morning, we were cheering at knowing that Frederick was saved. And now we learned that Mr. Bell is dead. One lived and the other one died."

"Yes, I saw the parallel to that as well," I acknowledged. "It was as if nature was calling to us again, reminding us that where there is the sun, there is also the rain. Where there is life, death comes at the same time. One exchange for another. Of course, I know that is not the way of nature. Life and death come at random. But we are human, and so we are forced to see the patterns in life, even if they are not true."

"We see it because it is the only way that we can make

sense of our lives. It's the closest that we can come to feeling as if our lives have any sort of meaning."

Margaret's body shook, so I went up to her and held her.

"I don't want you to see me like this," she cried.

"I wish he were still alive too, Margaret," I replied, equally as sad, "I wish it so much. It is not fair!"

"No, it's not. He should still be here!"

I held her for a little bit longer, before she asked me to leave her alone, to keep her grief to herself. Granting her wish, I left her room, but I stood in the hallway.

At first, I thought to go to my room, but I found that I could not. Passing the servant, Hannah, on the landing, I told her to report to Mr. Darcy, to tell him that I had gone for a walk, and that I would return soon.

As quickly as I could, I escaped the hotel. For some reason, I felt confined in its walls.

I just needed to get out. To the open air, where I did not have to suffer the stuffiness of curtains and drapery closing in all around me.

Through the streets, I passed people.

Couples walking aimlessly.

Workers coming to or from work.

Chimney sweeps who tipped their hats to me.

The wind whipped around me, and I felt the burst of life.

The same freshness that Mr. Bell would no longer have and no longer need where he was going. But now, his soul was released, and his earthly cares were over.

But Mr. Bell loved life.

He clung to it, with every fiber of his being. While many

others looked on life as a dull and drear thing—an episode of drudgery that had to be endured until they would undergo the great release—Mr. Bell was different. He knew life to be the best thing to undergo. He seized upon it and did not let it overwhelm him, but grabbed ahold of it, took it for all it was worth, and did all according to the whims of his heart and head.

With him, logic and sentiment went hand in hand. One was not meant to suppress or overwhelm the other. But they stood together, as complements to each other. Mr. Bell understood balance in a way that most of us did not grasp until life had taught us a painful lesson first.

But it was more than that.

Mr. Bell was the one who assisted the Hales in setting up at Milton.

If it were not for him, Mr. Hale would not have been given a chance to change his life.

Margaret never would have met Mr. Thornton and become so much a part of the world as she had wished to.

When our parents died, Mr. Bell arranged for us to get work and find a house for us on Frances Street. He arranged for us to meet with the bank and set up our accounts.

Through him, I met Mr. Darcy again and it led to us falling in love. It led to Kitty and the Colonel walking down the same path together. It led to Jane and Mr. Bingley reconciling, and we became a love of three happy marriages.

The man, without knowing it, had given us our futures. And now his life was over.

As I turned a corner, a gust of wind swept past me, and I felt the burst of vigor.

Mr. Bell, wherever you are, do you feel this new life brushing past us?

Can you sense it? I hope that you do.

To my left, I saw activity.

Sitting on some steps, was a lady who was offering some breadcrumbs for people to feed some birds who crowded the street. It was only a couple pennies.

For reasons that I could not explain, I felt compelled to do so. Walking up to her, I gave her two pennies, she smiled at me and handed me a bag.

I swept some crumbs on the ground and the birds rushed towards me, eating the bits. Laughing sadly, I threw some more to my left, and more birds swarmed. Laughing a little more, until my chuckles turned to weeping, I threw some more until my bag was emptied.

The birds swiveled around, looking for every morsel that they could find. As they moved around me, I watched their hustle and bustle.

So full of life, happy to be given something. Happy to thrive and knowing what life had to give them.

Until they would lose in the end, as we all were meant to do. What is it all about if you are to always be defeated? If you are to always lose eventually?

Or maybe that is what it is all about. Maybe, we are not supposed to win, since the Great Reversal is meant to occur. And because of such, the eventuality of us losing is definite, so that it makes those brief moments, where we do win, all the more enjoyable.

But who knows?

When one bird finished, it flew off, into the skyway.

I watched its progression as its black wings were augmented by the blue sky. Go to the heavens, it did. Soar among the clouds. Just maybe, it would find Mr. Bell's soul in its journey. And it would tell him that we were still here. And we will never forget all that he did.

When I was finished, I returned to the hotel, where Mr. Darcy was waiting for me.

"Where were you?" He asked. "I was worried."

"Good," I said, "I want you to be worried." Not caring who saw, I wrapped my arms around his waist and collapsed against him. Instinctively he held me. "I always want you to be worried when I move too far away from you."

"Don't worry," he assured me, "I always will be."

Chapter 29

One Last Gift

Determined to return to London, we cut our holiday short. After all, we might not have arrived in time to attend Mr. Bell's funeral, but we at least could visit his grave.

When we returned to London, the Hales stayed with us Darcys at Mr. Darcy's townhouse. For the first time, I would be attending a home I could call my own. It was a lovely place, and I marveled at its grandeur.

The Colonel and Kitty arrived at Lady Catherine's townhouse, which we were to dine at the next day, and Jane would see her new residence, for Mr. Bingley's home was no more than a couple streets from where Darcy and I lived.

Now that I was in a sensitive state, I asked Darcy if I could visit my relatives, the Gardiners, before doing anything else. He agreed to this, and my eyes widened in relief as I cast an eye on a familiar place: Gracechurch Street.

The warmth of familiarity felt as if it was folding its arms around me. I did not have to worry over the Hale joining us, because the Hales and the Gardiners always got along very well.

When we arrived, the joys of family were immense!

My aunt and uncle Gardiner greeted us with so much gentility and affection that it calmed the sadness of Bell's departure from my mind.

"Elizabeth!" Aunt Gardiner cried. "You are returned to us."

"And with a new name and old friends," Uncle Gardiner said, "nothing is more remarkable. Mr. and Mrs. Hale and Miss Hale, it is a delight to see you again."

"It is a delight to see you as well," Mr. Hale said, shaking Uncle Gardiner's hand. "Edward, you and your generous wife are a sight for this old tutor's memory."

"And Mr. Darcy," Aunt Gardiner said, "welcome to our humble abode."

"Thank you, ma'am," Mr. Darcy said, "your home is delightful."

"You are too kind. I am aware that our domicile must appear shabby in your eyes."

"Not at all, I assure you."

We all sat down to dinner, and we were quite a merry party.

"Mr. and Mrs. Gardiner," Margaret asked, "I have been starved with curiosity. How has Boucher been getting on in your establishment?"

"Oh," Uncle Gardiner answered, "very well actually."

"He has, indeed?"

"Oh yes. He may not be a man of strong conviction or cleverness, but he is a dedicated, loyal, and steady worker. I prefer those sorts, for they make model employees."

We all laughed.

"He loves his lodgings as well," Aunt Gardiner added, "when he and his family saw their new residence, the animation was apparent."

"In Milton," I answered, "they lived in a house that was quite like a hovel. Wherever you placed them must have felt like a step forward."

"And they feel it most keenly," Uncle Gardiner continued, "Poor Boucher has six children and none of them are old enough for factory work, but he tells me that he earns more wages with me than he did in the North, and food is better here than it was at the butcher's shops in Milton. And the more that I learn of the man, the more I am convinced that he was not meant for Northern factory work. People like him are more adaptable to our slower southern habits. Either way, he is prospering. All of your actions were honorable and led to great fruition."

"Thank you."

"And what of Longbourn?" Aunt Gardiner asked, shifting the discussion back to family. "What news of Mary and Mr. Collins?"

"They are well," I said, "Mr. Collins and his child are in good health. Longbourn looks as it always did. Hertfordshire still feels consistent with the memory of it. Uncle Philips is still doing his best to recover from losing our aunt. And Mr. Collins proposed marriage to Mary."

All the Gardiners reacted precisely as I wished. In surprise and quite the uproar. It made me smile.

After dinner, we ladies separated from the gentlemen for a time, so the men could enjoy Uncle Gardiner's good port.

While doing so, Aunt Gardiner approached me while I looked at the new books she had on display.

"So," Aunt Gardiner said, "Margaret told me that you all are planning to go to St. John's cemetery. Mr. Bell is gone?"

"Yes," I answered, looking downcast once more, "he is. We may not have been there to see his funeral, but we can be there to say farewell."

"From what you always told me, he was a good man."

"Yes, he was. But more than that, he was special."

"Of course, he was. But in what manner was he, by your description?"

"I cannot fully explain it. He simply had a magic to him that was beyond any other. His happiness was genuine, but he also helped us in many ways. And with all things considered, he reminds me of you both."

"Us both?"

"Yes. You and Uncle Gardiner. When our parents passed, you were there for us. When the Hales needed help, Mr. Bell did not abandon them but was of assistance. I cannot tell you, but like you and uncle, he had a way of entering a room, and you knew that you no longer were alone."

"A good man then."

"He even understood linen."

Aunt Gardiner chuckled.

"Then I am sorry for you. But now, his soul is free."

"That's what we tell ourselves to soften the blow, but that is the problem: his soul was already free."

She tapped my hand and soon the gentlemen joined us again.

"Well," Uncle Gardiner said as the men entered, "I am curious of this new acquaintance in your midst."

"Midst?" I asked, turning to Mr. Darcy. "Well, Mr. Darcy, what have you unfolded without me?"

"Do not worry," Mr. Darcy assured me, "there are no secrets being displayed. I merely told him about how Raspberry arrives at King's Cross tomorrow and that we are going to meet her."

"Kitty!" Rasby cried.

Her train had arrived at the station, and we all had formed to meet her. A new arrival of a dear friend always does raise a certain level of cheer to a party and seeing Rasby safely finding her way back to us was a joy. As she emerged from the train, all us ladies rushed to her on the platform and embraced her, much to the shock of others around us.

"You found me," Kitty cried.

"Of course, I did," Rasby said, "and I'm in London. I cannot believe I was brave enough to do it. Lizzy, Jane, Margaret, Mr. Bingley and Mr. Darcy and Colonel!"

"You will love our home, Rasby," Colonel Fitzwilliam said, "we will stay at our townhouse for the duration and then comes the trial."

"Trial? Oh." Rasby rolled her eyes. "Am I of the understanding that I shall have to endeavor to convince Lady Catherine that I am worthy of gracing any hall in Kent?"

"Never fear," Kitty assured her, "the Colonel and I have a plan. It deals with a tinge of shrewdness, some higher examples being used, and an ounce of trickery."

"My wife is a unique sort of cook," Colonel Fitzwilliam supported.

"Delightful," Rasby said, holding Kitty's hand, "I confess, I am nervous."

"I would say that you have no reason to be," Kitty smoothed over, "but I would be lying. Never fear, all will be right in the end. Miss Darcy, this is my dear friend, Raspberry Pitcher. Rasby, this is Miss Georgiana Darcy. Georgie, you will soon call her Rasby, like the rest of us."

Georgiana was a little surprised when seeing Rasby, but I was of the impression that it was more surprise that this new arrival was Kitty's closest friend, and not a common acquaintance with us all equally.

"Well," Rasby said, "as for the Great Lady Catherine, I promise, Kitty and Colonel, I will do everything in my power to be as genteel as I can be. But how long do I have to prepare?"

"We will remain here till the end of the week," Colonel Fitzwilliam said, "and forgive the morbid introduction to London, but today we are to go to Saint John's cemetery."

"Cemetery? Who has passed away?"

We all looked at each other. How did we forget that Rasby still did not know?

And now she would hear it, and we would have to undergo distributing trying news once more.

When seeing us all look unsettled, she was even more curious.

"Who has died?" she asked us, looking around. We all looked uncertain as well as somber. It was as if our voices evaded us, and we did not have the courage. Rasby loved Mr. Bell. Growing even more serious when she saw how depressed we all were, her tone became more intense.

"Who has died?" Rasby asked again. Looking at us all, she made a very important deduction. "Kitty? Where is Mr. Bell?"

Kitty looked at the Colonel, then she looked at the ground. Rasby looked at us all, imploringly.

When saying our names each, she looked at us all individually.

"Lizzy? Margaret? Jane? Colonel, Mr. Darcy, and Mr. Bingley? Mr. and Mrs. Hale? Dixon? Where is Mr. Bell?"

Kitty grabbed her hand and looked at Rasby. The truth was written in Kitty's eyes.

"No," Rasby said, "please, no."

No one contradicted her.

Rasby collapsed into Kitty.

All of us stood in front of Mr. Bell's headstone.

"I wish that we could have gone to the service," Mr. Hale announced."

"I know, dear," Mrs. Hale said, holding his arm, "he was such a loyal friend to you."

"I never thought that I would lose him. In truth, I always thought that I would be the one to depart from this earth first."

Next to us, Rasby was resting her head on Kitty's shoulder, morose.

"I never got the chance to say goodbye to him properly," Rasby uttered.

"None of us did," Kitty responded, "and a part of us has been lamenting that fact ever since."

"Did he die alone?"

"No," Dixon responded, "but at Oxford, with one of his students rushing to help him."

"Very well. He deserved to die with someone around him."

Crouching down, Mr. Bingley read the words on Mr. Bell's headstone:

To the Last, I Lived

"That he did," Mr. Hale said, placing his hands together, in prayer, "that he did. Bell, to the very last breath you had in you, you seized life by the reins, and you chased after it. It never outran you, but you ran with it. There was a light in you, friend, and it warmed all those around you. To this prayer, I offer to you. Even in death, keep living. Even while your soul has been placed back in the ground, keep living. When all other lights go out, keep living. And you will find your place, in the kingdom of heaven."

He placed his hand on the ground, patting the earth.

"Rest, my fellow scholar. And we will see each other again."

Taking Mr. Darcy's hand, I led us all away, back to his townhouse, where we could enjoy each other's company at the dinner he had arranged.

The next day, we had a surprising visitor.

"Mr. Lennox," I said, when he entered. Mr. Henry Lennox, Captain Lennox's brother and Edith's brother-in-law, had come to pay us a visit.

"Mrs. Darcy," Mr. Lennox said, and then he looked at Margaret, "And Miss Hale?"

When he had arrived, Margaret and I were sitting in the parlor. I was going over curtain choices and Margaret was composing a letter to Mr. Thornton, urging him to not abandon any chance of them marrying just yet. We received him there, and the surprise was immense.

"Nice to see you once more, Mr. Lennox," I said. "You come upon us at a studious time. It is a pleasure to see you."

"It is a pleasure to see you once more. Imagine my surprise when I learned that our old friend, Miss Elizabeth Bennet of Longbourn was now the present Mrs. Darcy of Pemberley, Derbyshire."

"I was just as surprised as you were, it seemed."

At last, he turned his attention back to Margaret.

"Miss Hale?"

"How do you do, Henry?"

"I am well. You are looking very well if you do not mind me speaking thus."

"Thank you," Margaret replied, looking down at the floor.

He looked blatantly at her, and it was an obvious look of affection and subtle desire. Despite her rejection, he still evidently felt for her.

After this clearly unnerved Margaret, I cleared my throat, to force Mr. Lennox to shift his attention back to more presentable behavior. He took the cue, and he remembered his purpose.

"Well, as much as I take great pleasure in seeing old friends," Mr. Lennox said, "you know that I am quite economical with my visits. I prefer to have some news to distribute."

"Oh," I replied, charmingly, "you have news? We always love news, don't we, Margaret?"

"Yes, we do," Margaret answered simply.

"Well," Mr. Lennox said, "Miss Hale, I come on your behalf."

"My behalf?"

"Yes. My practice puts me in the way of the late Mr. Bell's estate, property, and I am attached to the firm that oversees his last will and testament."

He removed a set of documents from his suitcase.

"I have brought copies of his will and yours to inherit."

"Inherit?" Margaret repeated.

"Yes. After all, you are his legal goddaughter."

"Yes, but we never talked of any inheritance before."

"Perhaps because he did not foresee any need to tell you it so soon. He did appear to be in the perfect picture of health when I last saw him."

Mr. Lennox laid out the documents.

"Mr. Bell left me part of his estate?"

"He left you everything."

Margaret and I looked at each other, astounded.

"Everything?" I repeated.

"Yes. All his assets and property."

"Even in the North?" Margaret asked.

"Yes."

She sat down and began to read over the documents.

"That includes Marlborough Mills and Mr. Thornton's home."

"Thornton?"

"He is a manufacturer and magistrate in Milton."

"Then yes, you are its new owner."

Shedding all propriety, Margaret turned to Mr. Lennox, passionately.

"Henry, please tell me honestly. How much, economically, do I stand to inherit?"

"Mr. Bell was a very prudent man. In the bank, you have almost nineteen thousand pounds."

I covered my mouth, astonished.

Margaret's face was just as amazed as I was.

"Nineteen thousand pounds," she repeated, breathy.

"Yes."

Standing back, she gasped out in wonder.

"Mr. Bell left me all that?"

"Yes."

Sense has its virtues, but we humans are creatures of sensibility. Even Margaret, in this moment, could not suppress the reversal of so much. She let out a cry and grabbed Mr. Lennox's hand.

"Henry, do you mean this?"

Mr. Lennox did not speak, for he was too busy looking at her hands holding his.

"Henry!" she repeated.

"Yes," he answered, "you are an heiress to property and roughly nineteen thousand pounds."

Margaret collapsed on the sofa, half-laughing, half-crying.

"My dear Mr. Bell," she uttered, then she turned to me. "Elizabeth, please, get my parents and bring them down here. I have a journey up North to make."

"Of course," I replied merrily.

With alacrity, I left the room. But before I went to the music room, where the Hales and Dixon were listening to Georgiana play, I went to Mr. Darcy's study. At first, I knocked on the door, but I rushed in before he could tell me to enter.

When seeing me look excited, he lowered his letters of business as I raced up to him, sat on his lap, and kissed him passionately.

With no time to react any other way, he returned the kiss until I had removed my lips from his.

"Lizzy, what brings on this cheerful mood? Not that I am complaining."

"You had better not be," I laughed. "Go to the parlor. We have a visitor, and would you believe—it's a whole new world. Mr. Bell is still saving us, even from the grave."

"Is he?"

"Yes. I shall get Georgiana and the Hales, so we can rejoice at this news together."

I went to the music room and retrieved them all, bringing them to the parlor. When I was there, I turned to see Mr. Darcy's eyes alight, as mine must have been.

"You see the new world that I speak of?" I asked him.

"Yes, I do. I very much do."

When seeing her parents, Margaret rushed toward them and took their hands.

"Mother and Father," she extoled, "life is returned to us."

"Margaret?" Mrs. Hale asked. "What are you talking of?"

"I'm talking of a reversal of chance and journeys that must be taken. I am going to the North. And I am going to save my husband."

When a person decides to be a hero, patience is not their chief virtue. When Margaret told her parents and Dixon about her inheritance, they both were amazed.

"I knew that my dear friend provided for you," Mr. Hale said, astonished, "but he never told me the amount or how substantial it would be."

"My daughter is an heiress?" Mrs. Hale cried. "Who would have believed it! Oh, I shall grow distracted."

All were happy, except for Mr. Lennox. When hearing Margaret mention a husband, his eyes betrayed him. Once the news was distributed, he left as soon as it was respectful to do so.

Margaret was adamant. She did not want to write to Mr. Thornton herself, but rather wanted to tell him the news in person. I understood why. We all did.

Her parents agreed to return to Milton with her, but there was much to gain by us going along. After all, since Pemberley also was a brief distance from Milton, we could always go there afterwards, to confirm that all transitioned smoothly.

Mr. Darcy agreed to this, for he was eager for me to see the home that I would spend most of my life in.

We made our farewells to our friends and family in London, and once more, we found ourselves riding up North, on the train.

To Darkshire, we arrived, and soon we saw Milton Common ahead.

Once our train rolled along the platform, Dixon immediately hailed a cab for us, and we were riding to Marlborough Mills.

Through the familiar streets that Margaret and I used to go down during many an adventure, there was something beautiful about the familiarity of it.

It was well, for now Margaret Hale would spend the rest of her life there.

"Look," I announced, "there is Nicholas Higgins with Mary."

Margaret followed my gaze and there were our old friends. Nicholas and Mary were walking down the street. Mr. Darcy tapped the coach to stop, opened the door and gestured for us to greet our friends.

"Nicholas and Mary!" I cried. They turned to where their names were called, and their eyes lit up when seeing us.

"Miss Bennet and Miss Hale!" Nicholas cried out. "You came back to us?"

"We do, Nicholas," Margaret responded. "I heard that Marlborough Mills has closed."

"Yea, Miss. It has."

"Chin up. Soon you will be back to work by the end of the week."

He looked quizzically at us as we closed the door again, waved to him and rode off. As we did, he smiled at us and waved.

"Do you know what this means?" I asked her.

"What?"

"You will now have to live in Milton."

Margaret smiled.

"It is not places that matter. But people. And these people are real. Their love is real. I now know, that's what I wanted all along."

"Oh, Margaret," Mr. Hale uttered. "Never would I have known."

"It is not your fault, Papa. I have very often been too good at hiding."

We rode on, and eventually we arrived at Marlborough Mills.

Empty.

That was the first thing that we saw when we arrived at the Mill and in front of Thornton's one time home. Due to Mr. Bell's passing as well as Margaret never taking the time to inform Thornton that she was his new landlord, there was no need to worry of Thornton and his mother not being anywhere else.

The courtyard was empty and there was a desolation to the place. There was no sound from the factory, no wagon drawing back and forth. The entire mill had been deserted. And it was a dreadful thing to see.

"A place that was once so busy," Margaret said to me, "so teething with life, and now look at it."

"It feels dead," I uttered. "It feels dreadful."

"Come," Darcy said, taking my hand and offering Margaret his arm, "we have a friend to save."

"Yes, we do."

As we stood before the front steps, looking for any signs of life from within, the door opened and we expected a doorman to greet us, but there was no servant.

It was Mr. Thornton.

When he saw us, his necktie was undone, his top button on his waistcoat was unfastened, and he was in his shirt-sleeves. It was obvious that he slept very little.

"I saw you," he said to us, "from the window."

"Yes, John," Mr. Darcy said, "we are here now."

"You are not alone," Mr. Hale assured him. "We would not have you so."

"Thank you." He looked at Margaret. "Margaret."

"Hello Mr. Thornton," she said, her voice breathy, filled with emotion.

"You came back."

"I came home."

When hearing her use that word to describe Milton, and Marlborough Mills, in particular, Thornton's eyes shifted gently.

"Home?" he repeated.

"Yes."

Slowly, he walked down the steps and took her hand in his.

"This will not be my home any longer but come in while you can."

"It will be your home for many a year," Margaret said, "I promise you."

"You saved me once. I cannot be saved now."

"Sometimes good things come in twos."

"Yes, they do."

Heedless of our existence, Thornton guided Margaret up the steps, and Darcy and I gave each other a look.

Offering me his arm, we followed the Hales up the steps.

When we entered, we were led to the sitting room.

"Forgive my mother for not being here," Thornton said, "she is out, giving her farewells to our neighbors, as a take-leave."

"The poor woman," Margaret said, "for she will do a double labor. To go there, giving farewells, only to go again and tell them all that she is not leaving at all."

Thornton looked at her, and then he turned to Darcy and me, sadly resigned.

"Is this where you save me again, Darcy?" Thornton asked. "A loan of some sorts?"

"I had every intention of being there to catch you when

you fell, Thornton," Mr. Darcy said, "but this time, your savior, once more, protects you from the crowd."

Thornton looked at Margaret.

"Margaret?"

"As you must have heard," Margaret explained, "Mr. Bell has passed away."

"Yes, I did. I was sorry for it. And sorry for you."

"Thank you. I miss him every day. What's more, he thought of me, in ways that I never foresaw. After all, I was his goddaughter, and to my surprise, he left me all his estates and his assets."

"He did?"

"Yes. Mr. Thornton, I am your new landlord."

Mr. Thornton was astounded, then he guffawed gently.

"You are my landlord?"

"Yes. And as landlord, you and your mother are going nowhere, and Marlborough Mills will never be silent again. Mr. Thornton, I have some nineteen thousand pounds lying just at this moment unused in the bank, which at present is merely bringing me in only two and a half percent. If you were to take this and use it to run Marlborough Mills, you would give me a much better rate of interest and will be doing me as much of service as yourself. You can make it into one of the finest mills in the country. I know you would. I believe in you."

And now it was Thornton's time to speak. And he answered it by being speechless. For what was he to say? Once more, Margaret had saved his life a second time. But not only that, he had her love, and she gave him the next day, and the day after that. And the day after that.

He walked up to her and took her face in his hands. Giving into the comfort of her cheeks being held by the man that she loved, Margaret kissed his fingers.

Closing the distance between them, he kissed her passionately. Willing herself to be as close to him as could be, he grabbed her waist and held her to him tightly. Accepting the thirst of his affections, Margaret wrapped her hands on his shoulders, claiming him as her own as much as he claimed her.

"Come away, dearest," I whispered to Mr. Darcy, "come away."

Obeying, Mr. Darcy and I left the house, leaving Thornton and the Hales time to themselves. We walked along the mills, until we saw a door open. Since there was no one to censor or despise us, we walked into the factory and began to move along the rooms.

As we did so, we saw the machinery as it lay quiet.

"When I first came here," I said, "Margaret and I were both alarmed at all the noise but also enthralled by the bustle and activity of it all. Now, to see it all so quiet, it feels almost as if we were watching so much fade."

"It was here, in the mill, that Boucher told me more about you and your sisters, and about the Hales," Mr. Darcy clarified.

"Really?" I asked, surprised.

"Yes, it was."

I laughed.

"Poor and fortunate Boucher. Now he is free of the mistakes that haunted him. Everyone has the right to begin again when they deserve to."

"Yes," Darcy said, looking at me fondly, "second chances."

"They can be a beautiful thing, can't they?"

"When last I looked, they have been known to happen in both the South and the North. Lizzy, thank you."

"For what, tall one?"

"For giving me a second chance."

"Always," I assured him, "always. And thank you, for never releasing me from your heart. And I think that I am right—that you want to kiss me now."

"On this, my dear, we always agree."

Mr. Darcy leaned down and kissed me. There among the machinery, the Master and Mistress of Pemberley were locked together, in a fond embrace.

When we released, Mr. Darcy chuckled, to my surprise.

"You laugh, sir."

"I do. Because I have done something interesting."

"Such as?"

"I have stumbled on an idea."

"Should I be frightened or not?"

"I think you will like it."

Chapter 30

Ever After

A joy of a day it now was.

As I stood in Kympton, the church on Pemberley's grounds, in my bridesmaid's gown, Mr. Darcy's arm was linked in mine, for he was groomsman to the Milton manufacturer and magistrate.

"Yes, Mr. Darcy," I assured him, "this was the greatest idea you have ever had."

"Mrs. Darcy, I would like to think so."

For in the course of two months, not before it was too soon, or before it was too late, many arrangements had been made. After Thornton and Margaret finally gave into the whole and wonderful truth of them being perfect for each other, and that a union ought to be obtained, Darcy had proposed that they marry in Pemberley's grounds, at the church.

Feeling the gratitude of friendship and affection for all the company, Thornton and Margaret accepted, and my coming to Pemberley, my new home that I now was to see, I would soon be hostess to a large family, honored guests and arrange a wedding.

With eagerness, I applied myself to being mistress to one of the grandest homes that I had ever seen.

And now, here we were, on the wedding day of two of the most important people in our lives. To see them on the path that they were on and remembering all the paths they had to walk down to get there, Darcy and I were at ease. For we had seen it all as well, experienced it all, and felt all the memories inside of us.

The music struck up, and Mr. Darcy and I linked arms.

"First I was a bride," I said, "and now I am a bridesmaid. I like how backwards that is."

"And I was a groom. Now I am a groomsman. Let us see if I can endure it."

"Mr. Darcy, you are like the Rocks of Stonehenge; nothing will knock you down. Not even a wedding march."

We walked down the aisle, and as such, I looked over all who had come as they stood among the pews.

When seeing them all, I did not just see their faces, but the stories that each face told.

Jane and Mr. Bingley were there, showing the joys of two people who were so well-suited from the very beginning.

Next was our sister, Mary, and Mr. Collins. While it can be determined that Mary would always be too good for our cousin, sometimes uneven matches do have the ability to suit well. Being unable to support the idea of Mr. Collins waiting for another woman to love his child the way that she did, Mary accepted the idea of allowing a courtship between them, that I foresaw would lead to marriage eventually. If she did not love Mr. Collins now, a few more years of him adoring her, referring to her good judgment for everything, and she would grow to have the same feelings for him.

In another pew Kitty, Colonel Fitzwilliam, and Raspberry was there, with Plato seated next to her as well.

Their bond, as it is with so much, was not maintained lightly. When Rasby did arrive at Rosings Park, Lady Catherine, as could be expected, was not delighted. However, with a few remembrances that British royalty was so much desirous to emerge from the Dark Age of its past, that it was adopting such people into their circles, Lady Catherine was made to see the fashionable side of such an arrangement. Rasby now was Kitty's companion and found herself raised to a level of life that she never would have dreamed. Her mother would have felt that all her efforts had come true.

Able to get time to take his leave, Plato was able to join us and was able to witness his sister raised to such a distinction. Despite it all, I could tell that many of the parishioners' eyes were on him, out of either wonder or alarm. Plato stood there, smiling, and completely unnerved by all around him. He would spend the rest of his life that way.

Georgiana stood on Kitty's other side, aware that she was forever friends with us, but wondering if she would ever be on the same level of intimacy with Kitty as Rasby had obtained. Over time, Kitty would grow to develop a friendship between them all, until Georgiana found a suitable man for herself, and then she would have to walk down the same path that the bride behind me was about to do. However, she already had no choice but to accept that Mr. Wickham was her first chief love, and that, despite how long it took him to repent his ill-treatment of her, she would never choose a man who did not possess the same levels of gallant tones and charm.

Lydia and Denny stood in the next pew, and I wondered at my sister's nerve. She was quite late into her pregnancy and would hear nothing of us telling her to remain where she was. Determined to believe that her child could endure anything, she insisted on coming to Pemberley, to witness the happy event—and also because she knew that we would force her to remain in Pemberley for her laying in. And that was precisely what she would have wanted. Lydia would always be transparent—maybe that was her charm after all.

In another pew was Mr. Hanley, with Charlotte Lucas and Maria. Now that would be a story that I would be told of again, and again, but I wished I was there to witness. To my surprise, Mr. Hanley's heart had fully recovered, and his affections took a little turn to the lady who deserved it and eventually welcomed it: Charlotte. Now at last, she would be given her prize for choosing to reject Mr. Collins, out of compassion for myself. She found a better match to a more steadfast man.

Maria Lucas—now, what path could I have imagined for her? Sometimes, reality will always be stranger than fiction. For who would have thought that Dennison would have developed a passionate attachment to her, that she was wise enough not to rush into just yet? However, as she herself described it: 'he is terribly good at attempting to win me over, and I am just as interested to see if he wins'. No present confirmation was given yet, but in time, if Dennison proved to be the better man that he promised he would be, then Maria would have to face the dilemma of choosing such a complex sort of character. I could not determine her fate and so I leave it up to the whims of whoever might conjecture for how it would be.

In another pew was Mrs. Thornton, along with Fanny and Mr. Slickson.

As I walked down the aisle, my arm linked in Darcy's, I

saw Fanny look resigned, but not with contempt towards me. It would always be impossible for her to fully relinquish her affection for my husband, but she still had that ability to have undergone the wonderful transformation of believing in second attachments.

With Mrs. Thornton, she would have no choice but to accept that the last woman she wanted for her son, was the first woman that her son needed. While a part of her mind would always look at Margaret and think 'oh, that woman!', another part of her mind could overcome the first with feeling that she had been right all along, that Margaret had always intended to catch her son.

At the front pews was Mrs. Hale with Dixon. Mrs. Hale's health would never fully be perfect, but for the moment, it was maintaining, and Dixon would have her mistress longer in her life. Especially now that her husband had returned to what he originally set out to do, while maintaining what he eventually became. Mr. Hale had accepted Mr. Darcy's offer of being both the vicar at Kympton, as well as being a tutor to many young men and sons in the area. Thus, he was returned to the level of society that he once maintained, while never sacrificing his intellect.

And what of Darcy and me? Well, I should have thought it was evident: we were destined to be the happiest of couples in the world.

But presently, there was another couple who had every right to be happier, for this was their day. And theirs alone.

Mr. Darcy and I stood at the end of the aisle, next to Edith Lennox, who had come to be Margaret's other bridesmaid. As Darcy stood next to Thornton's left, Darcy wished Thornton well, as Margaret Hale appeared, dressed in a beautiful white wedding gown, with white roses in her hand. And to walk her down the aisle...was our Uncle Philips.

When seeing her, Thornton smiled.

After all that he had endured, that he overcame, and to receive the greatest gift of all.

Margaret did not pay any attention to those around her but only had eyes for her future husband as she walked down the aisle, with the sunlight shining upon her from the church windows.

The beauty that comes from being in love added another glow to her fair cheek. She reached the end of the aisle and stood next to Thornton.

And there they stood, in front of our newly appointed vicar, Mr. Hale!

Yes, father of the bride was now serving as the clergyman to give his daughter away to the first true friend that he had met in Milton.

In his eyes was the joys of a father who would thus deliver his daughter to a worthy man.

He began the service.

As he spoke, I looked at Darcy. Our eyes met, and we felt the renewal of our vows.

Behind him, I saw the light from the window. On a nearby tree branch, I saw a bird perch along a set of leaves, watching the scene within...

...Mr. Bell, yes, I know that you see what goes on here. You would have laughed and perhaps even declared that you knew how it would all have ended eventually. But one thing is certain: your soul will always be felt along the winds of Derbyshire, for by bringing us all to Milton, you had been the means of uniting us.

Mr. Hale finished his service, pronounced Thornton

and his daughter to be husband and wife, and now the husband could kiss the bride.

Leaning into each other, Thornton and Margaret solidified the constancy of their perfect pairing, and they kissed before us all, as the wishes, hopes, the confidence, the predictions of the small band of true friends who witnessed this ceremony, were fully answered in the perfect happiness of the union.

Looking into Darcy's eyes, we knew. More than anything we knew and felt the pride of seeing that here, in Pemberley, came the perfect alignment of the North and the South.

The End[1]

1. For all of you, who saw this series to the very end, thank you so much. I hope this was worthy of you. Good day.

THANK YOU FOR READING

Did you enjoy this book?

We invite you to leave a review at your favorite book site, such as Goodreads, Amazon, Barnes & Noble, etc.

DID YOU KNOW THAT LEAVING A REVIEW...

- Helps other readers find books they may enjoy.
- Gives you a chance to let your voice be heard.
- Gives authors recognition for their hard work.
- Doesn't have to be long. A sentence or two about why you liked the book will do.

About the Author

Ney Mitch has been a long-standing Jane Austen enthusiast, having written forty novels that were inspired by her various works. Since stumbling on Miss Austen's books after graduating from college, she has always dabbled in Austen inspired literature, ranging from writing works for teens to adults. Originally, her desire was to adapt Jane Austen's writing in a way to help young adults connect with her, however over time, she has spread her aims to other genres and styles. Having received her BA Degree at Desales University, she is a writer, both literary and dramatic, as well as being a Historic Reenactor.

 facebook.com/courtney.mitchell.589

 x.com/CMMitchelPsyche

 pinterest.com/shebaanna

Also by Ney Mitch
with Satin Romance

Austen Gaskell Series

Curiosities & Contemplation

Resolved & Resigned

Triumph & Tragedy

Woes & Worries

Love & Labors Won

Economy & Ever After

The Memory Series

Moments of Moments Past

Moments of Moments Present

Moments of Moments Future

Moments of Moments Infinite

Pride & Prejudice Reimaginings

Rapture & Rebellion

Fortune & Misfortune

Desire & Destiny

Pride & Peace

Resolve & Revelations

Hope & Hopelessness

Faith & Family

Kitty Bennet Adventure Series

Vanities and Vexations

Forms & Fashions

Romance & Recklessness

Nuance & Novelty

Doubts & Difficulties

Follies & Forgiveness

Joys & Judgements

Happenstance & Holidays

Exploration & Endeavors (Coming soon!)

Romance & Revolution Saga

The First Impression

The Second Impression (Coming Summer 2026!)

Chances Series

Chances Are

Chances Come

Chances Fade

Chances End

Novels

The Tale of Mr. & Mrs. Bennet: A Pride & Prejudice Christmas Tale

The Wonderful Time of the Year

www.ingramcontent.com/pod-product-compliance
Lightning Source LLC
La Vergne TN
LVHW100516110826
845146LV00002B/662

* 9 7 9 8 8 8 6 5 3 4 4 7 4 *